≈ ≈ ≈

You heard about the girl? The words of the old man with the rotting teeth rang in my head. *Era l'età della vostra figlia.* I didn't speak Italian, but I was around it enough to be able to piece together what was being said. The old man had said something about age—your daughter's age. *It would be a shame.* A shiver washed over me. Did the late night phone call that sent mom flying into my bedroom have some connection to the old man?

≈ ≈ ≈

Painting
The
Invisible Man

❧ ❧ ❧ ❧ ❧ ❧ ❧

Rita Schiano

reed edwards company

Painting The Invisible Man stands somewhere between a contemporary historical novel and a roman a clef. Although the story is based on a known event, it must be understood that the thoughts and emotions shown through the characters have emerged from the author; and that the author, having direct knowledge of the known event, has merged memory with imagination to create and re-create some of the scenes. It should be made clear that *Painting The Invisible Man* is not an effort to reproduce or solve the known event. The author of the book has attempted merely to tell a dramatic story.

For information regarding permission, please write to: Permissions Department, The Reed Edwards Company, P.O. Box 0562, Wilbraham, MA 01095-0562

First Printing September, 2007
10 9 8 7 6 5 4 3 2 1

Printed in The United States of America

Cover Art: David Jarratt

Published by:
The Reed Edwards Company
P.O. Box 562
Wilbraham, MA 01095-0562

Schiano, Rita.
        Painting the invisible man / Rita Schiano. −1st ed.
                p.   cm.
        LCCN 2007926115
        ISBN 978-0-9795347-0-6

        1. Fiction. 2. Italian heritage--Fiction. 3. Mafia and organized crime
        --Fiction. 4. Crime--Fiction.   I. Title.

ISBN: 978-0-9795347-0-6
Library of Congress Catalog Number: 2007926115

Quoted text from *The Hundred Secrets Senses* reprinted with permission from Penguin Group (USA) Inc. *The Hundred Secret Senses*, by Amy Tan, © 1995, first edition, published by G.P. Putnam's Sons, New York.

For my parents…
…with all my love

and

for Michelle…
…who never stops believing

Special Thanks

Terri and Jim
Don
Paul
Jenna
MaryAnn
David
Justin
Sarah (Salli)
and
Maggie

Chapter One

It's said there are no coincidences; everything happens for a reason. I don't know about that. I've never been one to bandy about pithy nuggets of wisdom. Life's experiences are far too complex to be whittled down to nine words. I prefer to think that what happened on the morning of October 20, 2004 was a keying error, a simple mistake; that the telephone call was synchronal, possibly even serendipitous, rather than some sort of causal determinism.

That morning I was energized, focused, and ready to work. My laptop was open and booted up. I had gathered my writing talismans: Webster's Encyclopedic Unabridged Dictionary, Roget's International Thesaurus, a freshly brewed Thermos of Starbucks' Caffé Verona blend, my *Sex and the City* cappuccino mug, and my hardcover edition of *The Hundred Secret Senses* complete with jacket featuring a stunning black-and-white photograph of the author. The items were in their assigned spots. Webster and Roget to my left; the Thermos stationed atop the buffet behind me. The filled mug of coffee sat at arm's length to the right of my computer, and my Muse, Amy Tan, watched over me from the back cover of her book placed strategically alongside the steaming mug.

Every creative person needs a Muse. Amy Tan is mine. I don't know her, mind you. Never even met her. And until last month I had not even read any of her books. I was having lunch with my client Rose Nash, a grade-school teacher-turned-children's author who was about to start the first leg of a three-month long book-signing tour. We had just finished eating our Veggie Delight mixed greens salads accompanied by Pellegrino with lemon. While in the midst of sharing a thick slab of chocolate mousse cake, Rose reached into her ever-present Fendi tote and pulled out a worn copy of *The Opposite of Fate: Memories of a Writing Life* by Amy Tan.

"Have you read this book?"

"I'm embarrassed to admit I haven't read any of her books," I responded as I scanned the page of praise. *An examined life recalled with wisdom and grace,* wrote Kirkus Reviews.

"Although I did see *The Joy Luck Club* and I do own a first edition of *The Hundred Secret Senses.* Mint condition. Does that count for anything?"

"Not a thing."

We both laughed.

"All the while I was reading this book, Anna, I kept thinking about you. There are so many similarities between..." Rose's voice faded into the background as I locked on the back cover copy.

> ...shares the story of how she escaped the curses of her
> past to make a future of her own...

Rose's voice faded in. "The way she reflects on the world reminds me of you; the way you express yourself. It's no wonder you are a writer."

I was touched—a business client who thought of me as a writer. I hadn't thought of myself as a writer for quite some time. For the past seven years I'd been pecking away at a novel. Writing furiously for days, weeks, and then writing nothing for several months at a time. But I would not abandon the story. I loved the characters too much. And every time I got back to them, I fell deeper in love. But love was not enough to keep me regularly engaged in their unfolding.

I attempted to hand the book back to Rose, but she threw her hands high into the air as if I was brandishing a gun.

"No. I want you to keep the book. And I insist you read it. Don't make me demand a book report!"

I laughed heartily. "Okay, Teach. I'll read it. I promise."

Later that night while reading Amy's musings, I felt I had found the eastern counterpart to my western soul. I identified with her personal struggles: Both our lives had been touched by a tragic family history, and by a brutal murder. Both our lives were dominated by our ethnic heritage. Both of us sang in bands.

2

PAINTING THE INVISIBLE MAN

Our greatest difference? She wrote about it; I danced around it. Amy heard the echoes of her family history and resonated with them. I chose to cover my ears until the knelling ceased. It was no wonder that so many years had produced so few pages.

Halfway through *The Opposite of Fate* I decided to read *The Hundred Secret Senses*. The book had been collecting dust in my office for several years. I plucked the book from the shelf. The hardcover creaked as I turned it over for the first time. The crisp front pages seemed to yield gratefully as I ran my fingertips down along the spine's edge pressing them flat—a technique learned in grammar school. I skimmed the acknowledgements, pressed two more leaves. Chapter One.

> My sister Kwan believes she has yin eyes. She
> sees those who have died and now dwell in the World
> of Yin, ghosts who leave the mists just to visit her kitchen...

I carried the book into my bedroom and snuggled under the comforter. I read for hours and hours, fighting fatigue as dusk melded into night and night into dawn. Just as the sun rose above the horizon I drifted off and entered the world of my dreams....

I am walking deliberately down the cobblestone path that leads to the Ponte della Paglia. The early morning light reflecting off the oil slicks tainting the waters of the Grand Canal dances prismatic colors. The *lap, lap, lap* of the water is a subtle percussive accompaniment to the low hum of a lone *vaporetto*. I'm eager to reach the Straw Bridge, which spans the Rio di Palazzo connecting San Marco and the Castello districts of Venice, before it is teeming with tourists. The Ponte della Paglia offers unimpeded views of San Giorgio Maggiore across the lagoon and the Ponte di Sospiri—the Bridge of Sighs—behind it.

As I approach the bridge I notice a lone figure leaning over the railing peering into the water below. I proceed cautiously. In the dim light of dawn I see the figure of a woman, perhaps of Asian descent. She is pulling hand over hand on a thick rope attempting to retrieve something from the lagoon. I watch curiously from a distance as an earthen jar attached to the end of the rope rises from the muddy water. She grasps it gingerly, and crouching, places the jar carefully on the bridge. The chords in her neck bulge as she struggles to remove the lid. A guttural "Uh!" escapes her lips as the lid gives way.

Even from a distance a putrid sulfuric odor assails my senses. My gagging, choking cough causes the woman to bolt upright.

"You like thousand-year-old eggs?"

Now I thought it was gross enough that this Chinese delicacy was buried in the ground for several weeks, but to eat eggs that have been submerged in a Venetian lagoon? My stomach lurches.

Her small hand disappears momentarily into the jar. It emerges, dripping a blood-red viscous liquid that congeals quickly as it comes into contact with the morning air. She walks towards me with a deliberate gait, stopping just inside the comfort zone of my personal space. I step back with a forced nonchalance she doesn't buy. The woman takes two steps closer, all the while staring intensely into my eyes. I try stepping back again, but feel the bridge railing at my back.

She extends her hand. "Here." Her fingers spread open revealing a translucent, black egg. "Eat." She forces the egg into my mouth. It dissolves slowly like rancid custard. My gag reflex kicks into rapid motion sending ripples of nausea coursing through me. I spin around and begin vomiting violently into the water below. The retching slowly subsides, giving way to fierce, dry heaves that send spasms of pain deep into my gut.

The woman closes in. She reaches around me placing her small, cool hand on my forehead. It is a soothing, comforting touch—a mother's touch—a touch I hadn't felt in many, many years. Thick tears stream down my cheeks.

"You feel bad now, but you be much better later." She smiles broadly, knowingly.

With both hands I wipe the tears from my cheeks. As my hands pull away from my face I see they are covered with thick, congealing blood. I scream in horror.

4

I awoke with a start. "Who's there!"

In the distance was a voice—lilting, female, ethereal. Although I was in that odd state of consciousness that resides between sleep and wakefulness, I tried to focus. I was certain the voice was real. I listened intently. Nothing.

My heart beat furiously in my chest. I took long, deep breaths trying to slow the rapid palpitation. Within moments the beat surrendered to its natural rhythm.

I snuggled back under the covers and pulled the comforter up under my chin. The book, which had slipped from my hand and onto the bed as I drifted off to sleep hours before, fell to the floor with a *thud*. I leaned over and picked it up. Amy Tan seemed to be staring raptly at me from the book's back cover. I studied her face. She was not the face in my dreams, but her eyes, the intensity in her eyes, was familiar.

Time to write.

It was the voice. Only this time it wasn't in the distance. It was close at hand; it was coming from the book in my hands.

Time to write, Amy Tan spoke again.

I shook my head in that ridiculous way people do when they feel groggy, as though it were possible to jar oneself into a full conscious state. I looked at the clock on my nightstand. It was 1:07. I had slept away the morning. I yawned deeply, trying to force a cleansing breath into my body.

"Actually, Amy, it's time to work." I yawned again as I placed the book on the nightstand. I started to walk away, but the book drew me back. I looked down at it resting front cover up on my nightstand. It simply didn't feel right. I turned the book over. Amy smiled at me gratefully.

After a quick shower, I checked my e-mail, wrote a press release for one client, researched the health effects of ozone generators sold as air cleaners for another client, and ate a Fluffernutter sandwich while watching CNN news.

The Opposite of Fate lay on the coffee table next to my plate. The subtitle, *Memories of a Writing Life,* drew my focus. I tried to remember what it felt like to be a writer. My last novel came out in 1997. Sure, I had published a few short stories since then, but brochures, press releases, and newsletters became the bulk of my portfolio.

Business writing. The opposite of writing.

I thought about my story. *Newmanuscript.doc.* God! Was I so disengaged that I hadn't even given the story a title? Seven years, and no title? Titling a story is like naming a child. In the Jewish tradition the naming of a child is a most profound spiritual moment. The chosen name is a statement of character, indicative of the child's path in life. Most writers agonize over their book's title. The title defines the story's essence.

Newmanuscript.doc .

I headed down the hallway to my bedroom. Maybe by reading more of Amy, Anna would be more inspired to write. In some ways Tan's Libby-ah was like my Carmen. Both women sought a meaningful life, both tackled issues of loyalty, connectedness, and family secrets.

I reached for the book.

No more reading. Time to write.

"What?"

It's been said that a picture is worth a thousand words and this picture certainly had a lot to say. Amy's intense eyes snared mine. *No more reading. Time to write.* Her penetrating stare bore into me like a hammer drill trying to grind away my malaise. *Time to write. Write for you.*

I looked at Amy's smiling face. "I don't have time to write for me today, Amy." Great! Now I'm talking to a picture.

Time to write. Write for you.

"Easy for you to say, Amy. You get advance money to write. My business clients pay me to write for them. That's how I pay my bills, Amy."

Write for you.

"Yeah, yeah, yeah. Whatever."

I laid on my bed and tried to block out Amy's nagging by focusing on her writing. I opened the book to the dog-eared page.

> As it turns out, Kwan was right about the sounds in
> the house. There *was* someone in the walls, under the
> floors, and he was full of anger and electricity.

PAINTING THE INVISIBLE MAN

No more reading. Time to write. The voice intruded again. *Write for you first.*

The sound in my house was not in the walls or under the floors. And the sound in my house was clearly a voice. Amy's voice. Her tone was not full of anger, but it was full of electricity. And suddenly I was charged to write. With Amy Tan as my Muse I began a disciplined routine of writing first thing each morning; writing for me. And by that morning, October 20, 2004, *Newmanuscript.doc* had grown to forty-one pages. Forty-one good pages.

Chapter Two

Opening the file labeled *Newmanuscript.doc*, I scroll through looking for the yellow highlighted text that signals my starting point. I read through yesterday's words and begin editing the draft, honing every turn of phrase. Before long I am lost in the lives of my characters. Every now and then I drink my coffee, growing more lukewarm with every sip, and look over at Amy watching over me from the back of her book jacket. It's a good writing day.

And then the telephone rings.

Not wanting to disrupt my flow I wait for the caller I.D. to come up. Wireless caller. I recognize the number as that of Rose Nash. We had been playing telephone tag for three days. I have to answer the call.

"Anna, I was beginning to think I would never hear your voice again." Her cheery voice makes me smile.

"How's the tour going?" I ask.

"I'll be glad to get home, although Robert is thinking…" Our connection starts to fade out.

"Rose…Rose…You're breaking up…Rose!" Ah, cellular technology! If I were the ad agency for Verizon's competitor, I'd spoof their "Can you hear me now?" commercial with a guy on the other end screaming, "No! Dammit! I can't! Try moving a few steps!"

Rose's voice breaks through. "Can you hear me now?"

"I can hear you," I chuckle.

"What?"

"Nothing. You were saying?"

"I've had good press coverage on this tour. So would you please scan the papers and add the clippings to my web site?"

"Will do."

"Thanks, Anna. How's the book coming?"

Rose is one of the few people with whom I talk about my writing. If Amy is my Muse, then Rose is my taskmaster. As an added incentive, Rose had promised to ask her agent, Robert Bellini, to look at the manuscript when I was done.

"Good. I've been very disciplined…"

"What? What did you say?"

"I said I've been very disciplined." I shout, like people talking to the deaf tend to do.

"You're breaking up, my friend. I'll call you this weekend when I'm home." We lose our connection before I can say goodbye.

I look at the clock. 8:43. If I start now I should be able to knock off Rose's work by noon. I glance at Amy. Her eyes bore into mine. *Write for you.*

The phone rings again. It is Rose. "I forgot to tell you. Robert is e-mailing you the list of cities where we had press coverage. You should have it by nine. If possible, could you post all the stories by noontime?"

"No problem." My decision is made for me. I look at Amy as I place the telephone back in its cradle. "Sorry Amy. But, I promise to work again tonight. I'll even take you to Starbucks with me."

Saving my work, I shut down the iBook and refill my coffee mug before heading down the hallway to my office. I press the power button on my iMac and wait. Another voice intrudes.

"I don't fucking get it. You take over the guest room for your office, and now your shit's all over the dining room table," Edie screamed, throwing the Domino's Pizza on the kitchen countertop. "I go through the trouble of getting us dinner and you think you could've at least set the table?"

"I'm sorry, I lost track of time," I scrambled to remove my index cards, notepads, and other writing necessities. "I'll have this cleaned up in a minute."

" 'In a minute' dinner will be cold."

"Just heat it in the oven. It'll be fine." Christ! You'd think she had spent five hours preparing a gourmet dinner instead of five minutes picking

up a cheese pizza.

The oven door slammed. "I don't understand why you don't use your office."

"I do use my office. But my office is where I work; the dining room is where I write. It's a different energy in there."

"Next thing you'll be taking over half the house with your index cards and fifteen-thousand pens and Post-its and little scraps of paper."

I smile. Shortly afterwards, I took over the whole house.

I log onto the Internet and check the e-mail. The list from Robert is waiting for me. Rose's personal appearances had taken her to twenty-three cities and towns. Of the twenty-three, eleven had generated articles and reviews. I fortify myself with a long sip of coffee and begin culling the articles from the various newspapers, importing them to Notepad to be posted to her web site.

I login at *The Providence Journal*. The familiar banner elicits a small smile. Having grown up in Cranston, Rhode Island the newspaper was daily reading in our household. I click on archives, type in Rose Nash. The screen reads:

Results **1 of 1** of about **1** for **Rose Nash.**
September 6, 2004 — BORDERS WELCOMES AUTHOR-ILLUSTRATOR ROSE NASH

I click the link.

For stories more than fourteen days old use pay-per-click.

My account with ProJo is already established so I key my choice. Within moments the order is processed.

Your order for 10 Articles - $12.95 is confirmed.

"Shit!" I hit the wrong tab! Now my credit card was being charged $12.95. "Damn it!" I yell at the computer.

10

I click on My Account and begin the process of canceling my order. As I am about to hit SEND, the computer freezes. "Son of a bitch!"

Searching through the myriad pens and pencils that fill an old, worn Dutch Masters cigar box on my desk, I find my rebooting tool: a straightened paper clip. Inserting it into that secret little pinhole most Mac users eventually discover, my computer comes immediately back to life with a musical *ding.*

Within minutes I am back at Projo.com. But before I can click again on My Account, the telephone rings and the message *Your session has been interrupted. You are no longer connected to America Online* pops up. "Son of a bitch!" Goddamn dial up. I tried getting DSL Internet service, but the operating system on my five-year old computer is now too old. Frigging planned obsolescence. It pisses me off.

I grab the receiver. "Hello," I say with a mix of impatience and anger.

"Is Mrs. Matteo at home?" the voice asks, mispronouncing my last name *Matt*-ee-o instead of Mah-*tay*-o.

"No, I'm not," I answer and hang up.

I log back onto Projo and start the correction to my account, then change my mind. To hell with it. What's ten bucks? After I retrieve the article on Rose, I decide to make the most of my error. I still knew people in the Providence area. Might as well see what folks were up to. "Okay Nick, you're first."

I type Nicholas Fragola—my high school sweetheart. Last I had heard he'd become a cardiologist and was still quite the eligible bachelor. Rose was single again. Maybe I would play matchmaker.

> Results **1 of 2** of about **2** for **Nicholas Fragola.**
> March 2, 1992— FRAGOLA JOINS PROVIDENCE HOSPITAL CARDIAC UNIT
> May 24, 1994 — FRAGOLA, MCCREARY WED

Forget that. I type in my own name.

> Results **1 of 1** of about **1** for **Anna Matteo**.
> August 3, 2001 — BOOKSTORE CELEBRATES 10 YEARS WITH GALA EVENT

I scan down to my name.

> ...and former Cranston native, writer **Anna Matteo**, brought the crowd to its feet with a hilarious and heartfelt reading of her short story, *Pillow Talk*.

That's a keeper. Click. Print. "Now who?" I think a moment. And then it was as if my fingertips were resting on a Ouiji; the letters P-A-U-L M-A-T-T-E-O appear suddenly on screen. I stare at the name—Paul Matteo—and try to recall the last time I'd typed, or written for that matter, my father's name. I couldn't remember. My hand moves again, as if guided by a supernatural power. *Click.* Within moments the screen reads:

> Results **1 of 6** of about **37** for **Paul Matteo**.

I skim through the first set of headlines.

> November 10, 1995 - MOB ENFORCER GETS JAIL TERM
> October 4, 1995 - JUDGE ORDERS ARSONIST KEPT IN JAIL
> September 17, 1995 - LAWYER FOR ACCUSED MOB ENFORCER SAYS CLIENT NOT DANGEROUS
> September 13, 1995 – FBI TAPES SHOW HE'S DANGEROUS
> June 26, 1993 - FEDS FILE ILLEGAL GAMBLING CHARGES
> April 30, 1992 - LAWYER SNARLED IN MURDER PLOT

"What the fuck?" This can't be right. All thirty-seven articles are from the 1990s, nearly twenty years after his death. Why would my father's name be in the news again, *thirty-seven times* after all those years? I click on the first listing.

> The Providence Journal (RI)
> November 10, 1995
> **MOB ENFORCER GETS JAIL TERM**
> Angelo Capraro, who prosecutors allege was a mob enforcer, was sentenced Tuesday to three-and-a-half years in prison. Capraro admitted to conspiracy charges after a two-year FBI investigation into construction fraud and illegal bookmaking in the Cranston

area. Assistant U.S. Attorney Matthew Frye said Capraro boasted of killing Cranston gambler **Paul Matteo** and "getting away with murder."

"Jesus." I click open the next article.

The Providence Journal (RI)
September 17, 1995
LAWYER FOR ACCUSED MOB ENFORCER SAYS CLIENT NOT DANGEROUS
In the Cranston office of Ricci Construction, Angelo Capraro and his co-workers talked about more than construction. They bragged of 20-year-old murders, meetings with mobsters, suspected informants, and silencers. And the FBI caught it all on audio- and videotape.
A federal prosecutor played excerpts of the tapes Thursday afternoon, hoping to convince a judge that Capraro is too dangerous to be released from custody.

I skim down to my father's name highlighted in boldface type.

Capraro, who has a long record of felony convictions including robbery, assault, and arson, was acquitted in December 1979 of the December 1976 murder of Cranston gambler and produce dealer **Paul Matteo**. Former defense attorney Gregory Haynes was not available for comment.

Former defense attorney Gregory Haynes? I wonder when Greg stop representing Capraro? Was it before or after he met Sophie?

On the tape, Capraro griped that **Matteo** refused to give him $5,000 in the 1970s when Capraro was serving time for arson. He said **Matteo** "owed him" because he never told police **Matteo** was involved in the robbery.

13

Referring to a conversation with his wife, Capraro is heard on one tape saying: "I ask for help, and he turns me down ice-cold. Paulie **Matteo**. Ice cold. I tell Connie, 'Listen Connie, talk to him again. You tell Paulie I got lots on him. His hands are as dirty as mine. You tell him, if he don't help, when I come home, I'm gonna give him what he got coming.'"

When he got out of prison, Capraro said he confronted **Matteo** and demanded half of the weekly take from a poker game **Matteo** ran. **Matteo** threatened to tell the FBI. "Coupla months later, he was dead," Capraro said, laughing.

Capraro's words swirl in my mind like a swift tidal current. *You tell Paulie I got lots on him. His hands are as dirty as mine. You tell him, if he don't help, when I come home, I'm gonna give him what he got coming.*

I awoke early the morning of December 21, 1976. I'd been home on Christmas break for three days and was finally caught up on my sleep. The end of the semester had been harried since I was taking six courses instead of the usual four. I had accelerated my senior year so I could finish college in January. My best friend, Lisa, and I wanted to go to New Orleans for Mardi Gras in February. It would be our last hurrah before her marriage to Matthew later that spring.

I knew Mom would be awaking soon. She had to play a funeral mass at St. Stephen's where she was the organist and choir director. I went downstairs and retrieved the newspaper, which, thankfully, the delivery boy had placed between the doors rather than toss onto the snowy front steps. "Whoa!" I said, the bold headline catching my attention.

CHICAGO MOURNS MAYOR DALEY

I scanned the news story as I headed towards the kitchen. Tossing the newspaper on the counter, I began my favorite morning ritual: making coffee. I filled the percolator with cold tap water and measured the coffee grounds with exactitude, placing each spoonful carefully and evenly into the percolator's basket. With the basket firmly on the stem, I lowered it into the coffee pot and placed the pot on the front burner. With the turn of the knob a blue flame popped beneath. While I waited for the gurgling water to make its way up the stem and spew forth like a geyser, I went into the living room to admire the Christmas tree Ma and I had decorated the night before. It was filled with memories of Christmases past. For as far back as I could remember, "Santa" would leave a wrapped ornament for me under the tree. A prominent bough would be left bare awaiting its new adornment.

My reverie was interrupted by the slow percussive beat and the tantalizing aroma coming from the kitchen. I breathed in the heavenly scent of roasted coffee beans as I adjusted the flame with the precision of a maestro conducting the beat to a steady rhythm. While the coffee was brewing, I filled the creamer and took two cups and saucers from the cupboard. Ma was still formal in her thinking. Mugs were for *cafones*. I filled my cup and settled at the kitchen table with the newspaper. I leafed through to the entertainment section. Maybe Ma and I could catch a movie tonight.

I heard her come down the stairs and open the front door. "I've already got the paper," I called out. Ma came into the kitchen dressed in her nightgown and robe. "Morning Ma. I made coffee."

She filled the cup I left for her on the counter and took a quick sip. "What a treat! I've gotten so lazy. Sometimes I just mix the instant with tap water."

"Gross!"

She joined me at the table. "Let me have the front section." She scanned the headline. "Mayor Daley died!"

"I saw. The last of the big city bosses."

"The end of an era."

I waited until Ma finished reading the article. "I was thinking maybe we'd catch a late show tonight. *Silver Streak* is playing at the Loews."

"Who's in that?" Ma asked as she perused the obituaries, noting if any of the deceased would be holding services at St. Stephen's.

15

"Gene Wilder, Jill Clayburgh, and…" I drew a blank. "What's his name?" I tapped my head, trying to stimulate the short-circuiting synapse in my brain. Snap, crackle, pop. "Pryor. Richard Pryor."

"I like that Jill Clayburgh," Ma said as she skimmed her horoscope. "Jeannie and I saw her in that movie about Clark Gable and Carole Lombard. Of course, she's not as pretty as Carole Lombard. She's odd looking. Different. And that actor that played Gable? What's his name?"

I shrugged my shoulders and chuckled. "Aren't we a pair!"

Ma laughed heartily, her considerable bosom jiggling.

"Brolin, I think."

Ma nodded. "That's right. James Brolin. He was pretty good. Really captured that raised eyebrow expression Gable had." She tries to imitate Gable's signature affect and fails desperately.

I loved my mother. She could always make me laugh. I went over and kissed her cheek. "It's good to be home." She returned the kiss. "You want a warm up?"

"I'm all set."

I refilled my cup and grabbed a biscotti from the jar. "Ma, you want one?" "God, another murder," she spoke as she read. "Listen to this. You'd think they were describing your father. 'The body of a middle-aged man was found shot to death last night on a desolate road in western Providence County. The victim, described as a well-dressed, white male somewhere around 50 years old had been shot several times in the head and body,'" she read aloud. She looked up from the paper as I sat back at the table. Concern crossed her face. "Have you talked to your father since you've been home?"

"Actually, no. I've been leaving messages with Gloria for the past three days. Gotta say, it's not like him. But I think he's mad at me because I didn't spend much time with him when I came home for Thanksgiving. We had a quick breakfast the day after and then I headed right back to school. He seemed miffed I wasn't staying the whole weekend." I sipped my coffee. "Did he say anything to you?"

Ma gave me a look that said 'Oh, please! Like he would talk to me about anything?' She focused back on the news article and then, with a quick shake of her head, dismissed whatever thoughts were brewing in her

16

mind.

"Well, if this was your father, at least he'd be happy they described him as well dressed!" We shared a laugh.

Ma jumped up suddenly from her chair. "Oh, look at the time! I've got to get to church." She grabbed the biscotti from my plate, dipped it into her cup, took a small bite, and smiled mischievously as she placed it back half eaten. She washed her cup and saucer at the sink. We had a dishwasher, but Ma rarely used it.

"What time do you start teaching today?"

"Not until two-thirty, so I thought I'd do a little more Christmas shopping after church." Ma loved Christmas and relished showering her children and grandchildren, siblings, nieces and nephews, and friends with gifts. "Guess who my two-thirty is?" I gestured with my hands that I had no clue. "Do you remember Mary Guinta? She took piano lessons maybe ten, twelve years ago. She was older. Maybe six, seven years older than Anthony." I shook my head, no recollection. "Well, it doesn't matter. I'm teaching piano to her son now. William. Not Will, Bill, Billy, or Willy. He insists on being called *William!*" She rolled her eyes. "God! I feel so old! I'm teaching my students' children!"

"Well, Ma, you *are* old," I kidded her. "You forget you're a grandmother."

"I don't feel like a grandmother," she intoned. "You'll understand one day when you're my age."

In truth, Ma adored being a grandmother. Tony's children were the lights of her life and she doted on them endlessly. The day we found out Virginia was expecting their first child Ma couldn't contain her excitement.

"My Tony and Ginny are expecting! I'm going to be a grandmother!" she announced to the butcher, the store manager, all the cashiers—anyone and everyone within earshot in Dicksen's Market that day had to share in her joy.

"*Buon fortuna!*" Mr. Pirro, the butcher, wished her. "But how can that be, Theresa? You are much too young to be a grandmother!"

"Oh, Joe!" Ma squealed with modest flirtation.

Later that evening I spied Ma in the bathroom staring into the mirror, her fingers gently lifting and pulling back the skin alongside her distinctive cheekbones. Then her hand slid along her throat, smoothing the skin that had begun to fight gravity. "A grandmother," she said to her reflection. The following morning Ma's outfit was accessorized with a scarf tied artfully around her neck. "I decided I'm too young to be a grandmother." She pronounced the word as if it was a death sentence. "I want the baby to call me Nana," she announced.

From the staircase, Ma called out to me. "Anna. Do me a favor, would you? Shovel a path to the studio door."

"Will do, Ma." I took another biscotti from the jar since Ma had made quite a dent in the first one. As I sat back down I reached for the front section of the newspaper, to the page Ma had been reading.

BODY FOUND ON DESOLATE ROAD

The body of a middle-aged man was found shot to death last night on a desolate road in western Providence County. The victim, described as a well-dressed, white male somewhere around 50 years old had been shot several times in the head and body, according to Providence County sheriffs deputies.

The man was face down at the side of the Albion Road in Cumberland. The body was discovered just before 10:30 p.m. by a passing motorist. Investigators said the victim was fully clothed and had no wallet or identification.

I went to the phone and dialed Dad's apartment. No answer. I felt momentary panic rise in me. "No, that's a good thing," I reassured myself. "They're probably out having breakfast." I grabbed the coffeepot from the stove and refilled my cup. "Yeah, they're out to breakfast," I tell myself again.

Ma stopped by the kitchen before she left. "What time is that movie you want to see?"

"Nine-thirty. Wanna eat at Dino's first?"

"Sounds good." She kissed me lightly on the lips. "Save me the crossword."

18

I rinsed out my cup and saucer and washed the percolator before heading upstairs to change into a sweat suit. Might as well get the shoveling done before I shower. I wasn't halfway up the staircase when the doorbell rang. I jogged back down and peered out the window. A cop car was parked in front of the house. "Now what," I muttered as I opened the door.

"Is Anthony Matteo at home?"

"Anthony doesn't live here."

I grew up distrustful of the police. Having cops or FBI Agents pound on the door, especially in the middle of the night, was not uncommon. They were always looking to bust my dad for something. And now, it seems, it was my brother's turn.

"May I come in?" he asked a little too politely.

I hesitated. "May I see some identification?"

He reached into his back pocket for his wallet and flipped it open for my inspection. Officer Michael Burns, the ID card number matched his shield. I stepped aside. Burns entered, respectfully wiping his snow-covered boots on the doormat.

"Your name please, Miss?"

"Anna. Anna Matteo."

"Is Anthony Matteo your brother?"

I nodded.

"Do you know where he is? We went by his home, but no one answered."

I knew Virginia would be at work by now, and the kids were most likely with her sister, Emma. She always watched the kids on the days Ginny worked. But I truly had no clue as to Tony's whereabouts.

"What did he do? My brother."

"It's not that at all. I just need to talk to him." Then he paused inordinately long. "There's been an accident."

"Wait a minute," I said, confused. "Tony was in an accident?"

"No, Miss Matteo. Your father was."

I swear my heart stopped beating. "My father was in an accident?" I asked slowly as a chill rushed over me. I could barely get the next words out. "Is he all right?"

19

"No, Miss, I'm sorry. He's dead."

I swayed and would have fallen had he not reached out and grabbed my arm. I pushed him away. "You're lying." At first the words were inaudible. And then I screamed at him. "You're fucking lying!" I pummeled his chest with my fists. "You'd say anything to get me to help you find my brother!"

He grabbed my flailing hands and held them securely. He wasn't at all rough. He was, in fact, very gentle. And I knew by his manner that he was telling me the truth.

"Miss Matteo, if you want you can call the station and talk with my lieutenant. He'll confirm what I've told you."

There was no need to. I shook my head. "Where was the car accident?"

Officer Burns looked at me with a mix of dread and sadness. "I'm afraid you misunderstood. A man was found shot dead last night..." His voice faded and Ma's drifted in. *Listen to this. You'd think they were describing your father.* "There was no wallet or identification on the body. All that was found on the body was an electric bill addressed to Vincent Funaro Construction. Do you know Vincent Funaro?"

I nodded, even though I was struggling to comprehend. I was hanging in that suspended state of disbelief, where you know what you are hearing is the truth, yet the emotional mind can't wrap itself around the reality of the message.

"I went to the Funaro residence earlier this morning," the officer continued. "Mr. Funaro wasn't home, but his daughter said she had just had breakfast with him. When I showed her the bill, she informed me it was for an apartment that her father rented to a Paul Matteo."

I nodded again. It was true. Dad lived in one of Vincent's many apartment complexes.

"We're looking for your brother because we'd like him to identify the body. I specifically waited for your mother to leave. I think it would be too painful for her to see the body—"

"—Would you please stop saying the body?" I could no longer fight back the tears. He reached into his pocket and handed me a neatly pressed and folded white handkerchief.

20

"Yes, of course." He seemed genuinely contrite. "As I was explaining, I think it would be too painful for your mother to view your father's body the way we found him."

I wiped the tears from my face and eyes. "I could...I could go," I stammered. "I should go and do it."

"Actually, Miss, Mr. Funaro already came to the morgue and identified the... your father. Really, it would be best if your brother came down. You don't want to remember your father like that."

Usually in a crisis my rudder is steady, my course of action clear and direct. But I was completely at a loss as to what to do. "I did tell you the truth, Officer. I really don't know where Tony is. I just came home from college three days ago. I haven't seen him, or even talked to him, since I've been home."

And then the true reason behind his search for Anthony hit me. Fear washed over me. "You're not looking for my brother because you need an identification. You just said Vincent Funaro identified my father. You're thinking something may have happened to Tony, too."

Officer Burns's voice was filled with compassion. "We honestly don't know. So any information you could give me would be helpful."

I thought of mentioning where Ginny worked, but changed my mind. If the news was bad I didn't want her finding out this way. I would call her after he left, see what I could get out of her without rousing suspicion. "You went by the produce company?" I asked.

He nodded. "No one's seen him."

"What about the club? My father owns..." I caught myself. Nothing from this point on would ever be the same. Nothing. Even minutia like the tense of speech. "My father owned a club over on Reservoir. The Cranston Businessman's Club. I don't know the exact address, but you could try looking for Tony there."

Officer Burns made a notation on a small, pocket-sized notepad. "Anna, is there someone you can call? Someone who can be with you?"

I nodded. "I'm going to call my uncle."

"Would you like me to stay with you until he gets here?"

"No, thank you." I shook his hand. "I'm sorry, sir. I didn't mean to hit

21

you before." The tears poured down my face. I held my breath hoping that if I stopped breathing the pain exploding inside me would stop too.

He placed his hand tenderly on my shoulder. "It's okay, under the circumstances and all." He started to leave and then stopped. "Anna, now that an identification has been made the media will be all over this. You should tell your mother as soon as you can."

Oh my God, Ma! What if she hears this on the radio while she's driving? She'll lose it for sure. "You can't hold off? She was going Christmas shopping after the funeral mass." The funeral mass...*Oh, God, Daddy*. I started to cry again, but tried fighting it with every fiber of my being.

"It's out of my control, Miss."

No sooner did I close the door behind Officer Burns, my knees buckled. I clutched the staircase railing and lowered myself onto the steps. "Oh, Daddy...Daddy...." I wailed ferociously. Spasms of pain rippled through my gut as if someone was kicking me relentlessly. My stomach heaved and I vomited coffee and biscotti onto the floor. I'd never felt so alone. I wished Ma was here to hold me, comfort me. Clutch me to her bosom. My tears stopped abruptly. Ma. I had to find Ma.

I went into the kitchen and looked at the clock. Nine-thirty. Funeral masses are short, it would be over by now. I called Uncle Peter and relayed everything Officer Burns had said.

"Anna, I'll be right over. Meantime, call Virginia. See if you can get a sense as to where your brother is without tipping her off. That was smart of you not to send the police to her."

"Okay," I sniffled.

"Also, tell her to keep a look out for your mother."

"I will. She said she was gonna do some shopping. It's a good chance Ma will head to the mall after the funeral." There was that word again. I began to cry.

"Anna, I'll be right over. Call Ginny now."

I found the clothing store's number in the telephone book. The wait for the phone to be answered was interminable.

"Merry Christmas. Thank you for calling Preston's"

22

"May I please speak with Virginia Matteo? It's her sister-in-law calling."

It seemed an eternity before Ginny came to the phone. "Hi, darlin'!" she said cheerfully.

"Ginny..." my voice wavered and suddenly I could not speak.

Her tone was immediately serious. "Anna, what happened? Is Ma okay?"

I told her about Dad. Ginny dropped the telephone from shock. I could hear her crying. "Ginny...Ginny..." I called to her.

She came back on the line. "Oh, Anna," she choked through her tears.

"Ginny, do you know where Tony is?"

"No. Oh my God! Do they think...?"

"No, no," I lied. "The police just want Tony to confirm the identification."

"He didn't come home last night. He doesn't..." She couldn't admit what we all knew anyway. Tony had a *comare*. It was one of those things that wives of Italian men had to learn to accept.

"I know, Ginny. You don't have to explain. And I'm sure Tony's fine," I tried to convince myself as well. "Right now, though, we've got to find Ma. If she hears this on the radio..."

Ginny pulled herself together. "Oh God! Anna, it'll kill her. I'll get everyone here looking for her. Don't worry. We'll find her."

"Let's keep checking in with each other," I told Ginny before hanging up the phone.

The ringing telephone snaps me back to the present. I check the caller I.D. Private caller. Instinctively, I know who is on the line.

"Hi Sophie," I answer.

"How'd you know it was me?"

"I know things."

"Yeah? Well, you've been nonstop in my thoughts, so I had to call. Is there something I should know about?"

My eyes well with tears. "You are good, Soph. Actually yes. Something is up. And you're the one person I can probably talk to about it. Are you going to be around this weekend? I'll come to Providence."

"Oh, not this weekend. We'll be in New York. But I'm coming to Boston tonight. That's another reason I called. Do you want to meet me for dinner? I'm staying at the Charles Hotel. We could meet there. They have a really good restaurant."

"Sounds great. What time?"

"Let's make it seven-thirty. I'm doing some image enhancement for one of your 'mature' news anchors. I have to be at the studio through the evening broadcast."

"Seven-thirty it is. So, you gonna tell me who's aging anchor ass you're trying to save?"

"No way!" She laughs, then stops abruptly. "Anna, are you ill?"

I nearly laugh. "I'm fine. It's not cancer or anything like that. We'll talk tonight."

I hang up. Dear Cousin Sophia. God love her. We've had this connection—like twins do—since we were children. Maybe it came from spending so much time together when we were young. Sophie's mom, Jeannie, and my mom were first cousins, which makes Sophie my second cousin, or my second cousin twice removed. I never did quite understand how that all worked. Regardless, we thought of each other as cousins and our respective parents as aunts and uncles.

In our parents' generation families lived close by. In fact, four of the seven houses on Caldwell Street were owned and occupied by the family— my grandparents had the corner house, Aunt Rosalie and Uncle Peter the house next door, two doors down from them were my great-grandparents, and next to them was Aunt Jeannie's family.

Jeannie was an only child. Ma, seven years older, was the big sister Jeanie never had. And Ma doted on her. It was an easier relationship, not fraught with sibling rivalry. Even in adulthood Jeannie looked up to my mother, turning to her for advice, for comfort. We spent a lot of time at Aunt Jeannie's house when she was going through her divorce. That's when Sophia and I became inseparable.

24

I pour myself a glass of jug Chianti. Carlo Rossi. It's good drinking wine. It's cheap. It's what I've been drinking most of my life. Seems once an Italian kid moves to coffee—at around age ten—a little wine automatically follows (as well as a little Anisette). I prepare a plate of Asiago and Gorgonzola cheese, a few pieces of the roasted garlic and rosemary bread I baked last night, and a dipping bowl of herbed olive oil. I head out onto the porch and allow my mind to drift back to the day my father died.

Uncle Peter arrived just as I hung up with Ginny. He embraced me and I wanted to stay in his arms and cry for hours, but there was no time. We had to find Ma and I had to start making calls. I needed to coordinate cousins and friends, some to get out there and find Ma and some to find Tony, and I needed to call all her students and cancel lessons for at least the next week.

"Jeannie's on her way," Uncle Peter said. "As soon as she gets here I'm going down to the morgue. Someone from the family should make this identification, not some stranger."

"Vinnie Funaro's no stranger to my father, Uncle Peter. And they wouldn't have released the name to the press unless they were sure."

"I don't care if the Pope himself made the identification. Someone from the family needs to do it."

Uncle Peter was right. What if it wasn't Daddy? What if this was some kind of ruse so he could go into hiding or something. *Go into hiding? For God's sake. Do you hear yourself, Anna? This isn't one of your secret agent television shows.*

By noontime, the "well-dressed, white male somewhere around 50 years old" had a name, and every radio and television news broadcast had breaking news. Virginia had salespeople on the lookout in every store, my aunts and cousins were scouring the city, and I had called all of Ma's music students scheduled for the upcoming week and canceled their lessons due to "a death in the family."

25

When Uncle Peter came back from the morgue I overheard him in the kitchen talking to Aunt Jeannie. "His face is partly gone. But I recognized the scar on his chest from the open-heart surgery." I ran upstairs and into the bathroom. I tried to steady myself, using the doorknob and the wall as supports, but I couldn't stay on my feet. I collapsed to the floor and dragged myself to the commode just as the vomit spewed forth. *His face is partly gone.* I couldn't get Uncle Peter's words out of my head. I vomited again and again until my stomach ached, wracked by dry heaves. I laid on the cool tile floor for several minutes, my breath shallow, panting.

"Anna?" I heard Aunt Jeannie calling to me from the stairwell. "Anna? Are you all right?"

All right? I wanted to scream. *You expect me to be all right, knowing my father's face had been ripped apart? That he had been left to die in the street like road kill? Yeah, Aunt Jeannie, I'm peachy.* "I'll be right down," I managed to choke out.

I grabbed onto the toilet bowl and pulled myself to my feet. I wobbled over to the sink and splashed handfuls of cool water onto my face. As I patted my skin dry I looked into the mirror and studied my face. I had his Roman nose, his quick and easy smile, his deep brown eyes edged with blue. I stared hard at the features I had inherited from my father. I had to try and remember his face, to erase the shattered image that now pervaded my mind. I couldn't. And the tears flowed once more.

Shortly after two o'clock my ears pricked as I heard the crunch of gravel in the driveway. We all had been praying Ma would make it home without hearing the news, and now we all were dreading her arrival. Through the front window I watched Ma grab several shopping bags from the back seat of her car. I studied her face. It was bursting with glee and the proprietary knowledge of the contents of those brimming bags. I watched as she closed the car door and looked up at the brilliant winter blue sky, smiling serenely.

"She doesn't know," I said as I fought back tears. It would be the last tranquil moment Ma would know for quite some time.

Uncle Peter, Aunt Jeannie and I waited for her in the front hallway. As Ma fumbled with her keys, Uncle Peter opened the door for her.

"Peter!" Joy in seeing her youngest brother beamed from her eyes. "What are you doing here?"

And then she saw Jeannie, and then she saw me. Her facial expressions cycled rapidly like one of those flipbooks I had as a child—from bewilderment, surprise and joy, to shock, confusion and fear. The bags bursting with Yuletide bounty fell to the floor as she clutched at her heart. "Anthony. No! Oh, God, no! Something happened to my Anthony!"

Uncle Peter took her arm. "Anthony's fine, Theresa. Come sit down." But Ma wouldn't move, or perhaps couldn't move. She looked me straight in the eyes.

"Uncle Pete's telling the truth, Ma. Tony's fine." My mouth went dry as I spoke. "It's Daddy. He's dead."

Her anguished wail came from the depths of her soul. Had Peter not been holding her arm she would have collapsed to the floor. We guided her unsteadily to the sofa. Aunt Jeannie held out a glass of anisette. "Theresa, drink this."

"No!" Ma cried as she pushed away Jeannie's hand. The Venetian aperitif glass slid from her hand, smashing on the marble coffee table.

Jeannie pulled a handkerchief from her sweater pocket, catching the licorice-smelling rivulets before they made their way to the rug. She knelt down and sopped the puddle filled with tiny shards of burgundy and gold glass.

I held my mother's head to my breast and cradled her in my arms. She sobbed uncontrollably, crying "Paulie...Paulie ...Paulie" with every gasping breath.

A cool autumn breeze flits across my skin sending goose bumps up and down my flesh. I pour a second glass of wine and wipe the tears that had been flowing down my cheeks. I hadn't allowed myself to think about that day in many, many years. The raw emotion that stirred surprised me. But I knew myself well enough to know that I would not be able to stuff it back down. Something was brewing deep within my being and was about to rear up and break lose, and there would be no running from it.

I shake my head, perplexed. Whatever made me type my father's name today? Why now, after all these years? I'm hopeful Sophia can shed some light on this. I chuckle with incredulity. Cousin Sophia...Sophia Franconi Haynes.

The autumn air was crisp that day, September 13, 1986. The deep blue sky was cloudless; a picture perfect day for a wedding. I pulled my ivory pants suit from the closet rung, and tore open the dry cleaner's plastic wrapping. My new sling-back pumps were a perfect color-match and my slacks broke at just the right length.

Despite the dozens of cars outside St. Agnes Church I managed to find a parking spot within half a block. I scurried up the steps to the church vestibule, nodding my regards to smiling strangers lining the way. The usher approached and extended a gentlemanly crooked arm. "Are you with the bride or the groom?"

"Yes," I answered with a nod and hurried past the bewildered groomsman. I slid gingerly into the last pew on the bride's side of the church. Within moments the organ blared *dum, da-da-dum, da-da-dum-dum..* Everyone stood as the bridal party made its way down the aisle.

Here Comes the Bride... "Look how beautiful she is," whispered a woman straining her neck two pews down. And she was beautiful in her gown of silk organza and Chantilly lace. A matching headpiece held her illusion veil. She carried a bouquet of white roses, orchids, and stephanotis. She caught my eye as she glided by. Her smile was a mix of joy and bewilderment as she tried to place my face. I nodded my congratulations to the bride, then closed my eyes fighting tears.

As the stranger bride reached the altar, the groom stepped up and by her side. "I'm so sorry, Sophia," I whispered, and then discreetly exited the church.

I waited until midnight before returning home. I was certain that my telephone had rung every fifteen minutes since the reception ended. I could hear the phantom echo when I walked in, as if the walls had absorbed the persistent ringing. I hoped by now she would have given up.

I was wrong. *RING! RING!! RIINNGG!!!* The bell's tone seemed to take on the fury of the messenger.

"Hello?" I said timidly.

"Where were you?" Ma screamed.

"Didn't you get my message?"

"Everyone was there. Everyone was asking, 'Where's Anna? Where's Anna?' Especially Sophia. How could you not show at your cousin's wedding?"

"Ma, I don't want to talk about this tonight. I'll call you tomorrow. I promise. I'll call Aunt Jeannie, too, and apologize. And Sophie, when she gets back from her honeymoon."

"And apologize to him, too. He's her husband now. He's part of our family."

I chuckled to myself. Him. Her husband. He. Even she couldn't bring herself to speak his name.

"I know. I will." A heavy silence hung between us. "I'm sorry, Ma. I just couldn't do it." I wanted to tell her that I was there, vicariously. And that the bride I saw today was surely as beautiful as was Sophia. Now in retrospect, my avoidance act seemed even more disrespectful.

"Well, sometimes we have to do things we don't want to do, Anna. This isn't like deciding to not floss your teeth. This was your cousin's wedding."

To not floss my teeth? Where does she get her analogies? I tried not to laugh. "I know, Ma. I have to make peace with this."

"Yes, you do. Sophia loves him very, very much. And he adores her. We need to be happy for her and accept this. I've spent time with them. You need to do that, too. Get to know him. Greg is a good man."

She spoke his name.

After graduating from college Sophia parlayed her journalism degree into a job as a local news reporter for WPRI-TV. The Providence courthouse was her beat. CNN was in its infancy and the news was still reported and controlled by skilled journalists, and not media personalities, pundits, and celebrity hosts. Already a savvy businesswoman, Sophia knew that the advent of the 24/7-news cycle would burgeon, and that the mainstream news media would have to reinvent itself. The need to fill all that airtime would mean more on-camera exposure for attorneys. What was once a fifteen-second, on-air clip might now last two minutes. Sophia noticed, too, that many attorneys were not skilled in dealing with the media, and so began her career as a media consultant.

Within a year SAF Media Group was brimming with clients. When Sophie invested her earnings in a condo I reluctantly agreed to help her move. Being adept at hooking up electronics, I took on the task of setting up the entertainment center. After connecting the television to the cable feed, I routed her new Bose speakers through the cable box, creating surround-sound.

"Hey, Soph! Come listen!"

A press of a button and her living room was like a movie theater with sound coming at you from all sides.

"Anna, you're amazing!" she kissed my cheek.

I clicked over to the local news channel. Greg Haynes' image filled the screen.

"It's nothing more than courtroom rhetoric," Haynes was saying. "I urge the Magistrate not to detain my client based upon the ramblings of old men who talk big to puff themselves up."

"He's certainly found his stride in front of the camera," I said offhandedly to Sophie who was busily unpacking a carton of books, stacking them onto built-in bookshelves. "Remember how he used to fumble through news interviews during my father's trial? If only he had sounded that incoherent in the courtroom. Maybe, then, Capraro would not have been..." my voice faded as the realization hit. Sophie was not looking at me as I talked. She was purposefully distracting herself.

"You're working with him," I stated, dumbfounded. I grabbed her by the shoulders, forcing her to face me. "Sophia, tell me you're *not* working with him. With *him?*" Shock and anger battled for first place inside me. Sophie would not look me in the eye, and I could not stop staring at her turned cheek. I backed away, not trusting the fury that was roiling within.

PAINTING THE INVISIBLE MAN

Defense attorney Greg Haynes was high profile, especially after his two successful defenses of Angelo Capraro, my father's murderer. Excuse me, alleged murderer. Although brilliant in the courtroom, Haynes was lackluster in front of the camera: the perfect client for SAF Media Group. And he would be good for business. His reputation extended throughout New England.

"I don't believe it!" I said with incredulity. "I can't believe you'd do that to me." I picked up the remote control and hurled it across the room, smashing it against the wall.

Sophie started towards me, but wisely stopped. "Anna, listen to me. I turned him down several times. Told him Paul Matteo was my family; my Uncle Paulie. But he was so persistent. And the more I got to know him, the more I could separate the man from the job. Greg's a good man."

There was gentleness in the way she spoke his name, and I knew immediately what had transpired. "Oh, God. You're dating him, aren't you? He's not just a client; you're involved with him. You're involved with Greg Haynes." I felt sick to my stomach and light-headed. My eyes were like binocular lenses trying to bring a distant vision into focus.

She nodded her head almost imperceptibly. "I'm in love with him, Anna. And I didn't know how to tell you; how to tell Aunt Theresa."

I crumpled onto Sophie's mahogany desk. She came and sat beside me. We sat in silence for what seemed an eternity.

Chapter Three

Exiting the Mass Pike, I head towards Cambridge. Minutes later I am pulling into the garage under the Charles Hotel. Parking garages make me tremendously uneasy and I am relieved to find a spot close to the elevator.

The elevator deposits me in the lobby of the hotel. I spy Sophia standing by the front desk, talking animatedly on her cell phone. It always amazed me how she managed to control those lively hands when she was on the air.

She sees me, waves. I raise a hand indicating I'll wait here until she's done with her call. Within seconds, Sophie snaps the phone shut and rushes over. I'm ensnared in a bear hug before I know it.

"You look great! I love your hair this shorter length, frames your face. Did you color it too? Here, I brought you a present. I'm famished. Let's get a table."

"I'm glad you like my hair. Yes, I colored it. Thank you for the gift; you shouldn't have. And I'm famished too. Let's eat." We giggle and hug each other again. Sophie's energy has always been boundless.

We settle at the table and peruse the menu. While Sophia is deciding aloud between the "salmon or chicken Florentine," I peek inside the gift bag. "It's Starbucks' new blend," she tells me. "Komodo Dragon. Have you tried it? It's awesome. There's a mug in there too. Lord knows you need *another* mug!"

"A girl's gotta collect something! Thanks, Soph." I kiss her cheek.

The waiter takes our order. As soon as he is out of earshot Sophie blasts, "So, what do you have to tell me? What happened? I've been a nervous wreck all day. Were you telling me the truth? Are you sick?"

"Slow down, cowgirl. Let's drink a little wine and then I'll tell you everything."

By the time I finish telling her the details of my on-line discovery we need to order a second bottle of Sterling Vintner's Collection Merlot. "I mean, Jesus, Soph, I always knew my Dad was heavily into gambling, but robbery? They referred to Capraro as a mob enforcer. And I'm reading this and I realize I don't have a clue as to who my father really was."

"I don't remember him much...Uncle Paulie. I remember one Christmas, at your mom's house, we were downstairs in her music studio, banging out *A Little Bit of Soul* on the piano. Remember that song? Da-da-da-duh, Da-da-da-duh..."

I chime in. "Da-da-da-duh-duh-duh-duh, da-da-da-duh!" We laugh hard, falling into one another.

Sophie continues, wiping tears of laughter from her eyes. "All of a sudden this figure appears next to the piano. It was Uncle Paulie. He ruffles my hair, says 'Merry Christmas' then, poof! he's gone. No sound of a door creaking open or slamming shut, heck, that little poodle of yours–Chopin was it?" I nod. "Yeah, Chopin never even barked. Then we'd go upstairs and there he'd be again, in the kitchen, holding court, pouring Galliano from a bottle that was so obscenely huge it came with its own pouring stand!"

I start laughing, not really sure which is funnier, the memory of that humongous bottle of Galliano or Sophia's comedic delivery.

"Yup," she continues, "that's my memory of Uncle Paulie. Kind of like the Invisible Man. One minute you see him, then you don't."

I stop laughing. The Invisible Man. The phrase rang true. And the one person who had the most complete picture of Paulie Matteo's life and death was not at this dinner table. "Remember those painting kits we did as kids? You know which ones I mean? The Last Supper. The Face of Jesus."

"Paint by Numbers?" Sophie says.

"Yeah. Paint by Numbers. That's what I feel I need right now. A Paint by Numbers kit—so I can paint the portrait of my father and see the Invisible Man."

The waiter arrives with our dinner. A second waiter refills our water glasses. "Another bottle of wine, ladies?"

"You don't think two were enough?" I respond.

33

The waiter looks perplexed. "She has a very dry sense of humor," Sophia explains. "We're fine for now. Thank you."

I cut into my grilled swordfish with the edge of the fork. A heavy silence settles over us; the ambient sound in the dining room is muffled by the pounding of my heart echoing in my ears. I put down my fork and look at Sophie. We both know the question that is hanging in that silence. The question I'm apprehensive to ask. The question Sophie is dreading I'll ask.

"Soph, did you ever ask Greg if Capraro really did it?"

Sophia's words are measured. "We talked about it a bit, in the beginning. He believed Capraro was being set up by an informant. I don't remember the guy's name, but it came up frequently in the trial."

I shrug my shoulders. I had no clue who the informant was either. I didn't stick around for any of it, the investigation or the trials. I finished school the month after the murder and moved to Boston...and then to Ohio...and then to New York...and then back to Massachusetts. I never wanted to be around any of it. I couldn't.

"Anyway, this informant was trying to connect Capraro with some mob lawyer from Providence. Said the lawyer ordered the hit."

"A lawyer from Providence? You don't mean Joey Casella...."

"Yup," Sophia nods, "that name sounds right. You know him?"

"Yeah. I even had dinner with Dad and him a few times. Joey a mob lawyer?" I shake my head. It doesn't make sense. "Even so, why would Joey order a hit? He was my Dad's good friend."

"Maybe he owed him money."

"I remember hearing my father owed some Vegas casinos a lot of money, but what would Joey Casella have to do with that?" I drain my last sip of wine. Sophie refills my glass. "A mob lawyer," I repeat for my own edification. "Soph, do you think my father was really in the Mafia? I mean, I know he had muscle, but the mob?"

"I don't know, Anna. He certainly was connected. But Greg once said your father and Capraro were more like the gang that couldn't shoot straight. But what does it all matter now? It's been almost thirty years."

I attempt another bite of my dinner, but my throat closes up. I put the fork down again and push the dish away. I begin to twist the gold ring I wear on my right ring finger. The ring features a small, gold Roman coin. It belonged to my father. He wore it on the pinky finger of his right hand.

"I'm not sure. Finding those articles…seeing his name again and again in the paper over all those years…remembering those horrid headlines—Gangland-style Murder—I don't know, Sophie, suddenly it matters." I take a measured sip of wine. "Do you think Greg would let me have access to his trial transcripts?"

I can tell by the look that flashed across Sophie's face that I had put her in an awkward position. "I can ask him," she replies reluctantly. "But really, Anna, why? Why do you want to open that Pandora's box?"

It was a fair question; a protective question. My eyes mist with the love I feel for my cousin, and for the joy of knowing the love she holds for me.

"Because I think it's time I learn who my father really was. And maybe it will answer questions I have about myself."

"How do you mean?"

"About the way I move through the world. Look at the relationships I've had. With very few exceptions I've fallen for liars, cheaters, and drunks. God, look at what I just went through with Edie." Sophie nods sympathetically. "There's a pattern, and maybe it has to do with growing up Paulie's daughter. Really, Soph, I carry so much—and I can't believe I'm about to use this word—baggage." I roll my eyes and chuckle. "But it's true, Sophie, I do. And it effects every relationship I have: friends, lovers, even family." I could tell by the look in Sophie's eyes that my last two words, even family, resonated. She knew what I meant. I rarely visited her since her marriage to Greg. I also knew she didn't quite grasp the scope if it. And that was my fault; I didn't talk about it. Not that I didn't want to, but I couldn't.

"After my father's death, I ran—and I've been running ever since. When those archived articles popped up it was like a net dropped over me and I was snared into finding out the truth—the truth about my father." I shake my head. "God! It's no wonder I'm so fucked up."

"What are you talking about? You're incredible."

"No, really, Soph, I mean it." Tears roll down my cheeks and I can't stop them. "I've been getting flashbacks from my childhood today and

35

they're scaring the hell out of me. When I think of some of the things I did as a kid, man Soph, I was kind of odd."

"Kind of odd?" Sophia's expression is absolutely deadpan. I start to laugh in spite of myself. "That rubber pellet gun you carried? How you jerry-rigged your bike with a coffee can filled with pebbles and olive oil so if someone chased you, you could pull the cord, dump the slick, and they'd skid out of control?"

I guffaw. "I forgot about my bike! Man! That was the Aston-Martin of Huffys! Remember how I rigged the fender with a spring to create an ejector seat?"

Sophie is out of control with laughter. "And you'd paint it a different color every week to disguise it! Anna, you were *really* odd! And yet," she looks at me sweetly, "somehow you made it all seem so normal!"

She pops the last morsel of crusted bread into her mouth and washes it down with a swig of wine. "Say, whatever happened to that old vest you wore constantly?"

I cover my face with my hands. "Oh, God! You *remember* that old moth-eaten vest?"

"Remember it? I coveted it!" Sophie is laughing hysterically now too.

"God, Soph, whatever *did* happen to that vest?" I grab my stomach as it hurt from the laughter. "After I left for college Ma cleaned out my closet. I think it was in there!"

"Maybe Aunt Theresa gave it to the Salvation Army!"

"Oh man! Can you imagine someone buying that vest and discovering its secrets?"

Chapter Four

During the hour-long drive home to Brookfield I think more about my childhood. I knew our family was different. In the early 1960s having parents who were separated was an anomaly and the nuns at school always found ways to remind Anthony and me that we were from a "broken home."

"Oh, yar las name's Matteo, is it?" said Sister Mary Bridget in her heavy brogue. "I hope yar not a troublemaker like yar brother. But we expect yar to be, bein' from a broken home an all."

I chose to deal with my damaged status by embracing it. I'd brag about my father's girlfriends, his apartment, his latest Cadillac with the built in bar in the back. I'd show off my diamond rings and gold necklaces, all gifts from my father. When the nuns passed the basket in class for Catholic Charities, while other kids deposited pennies, nickels and dimes, I'd drop a silver dollar or a five spot.

What I'd hide was my mother's pain, her loneliness, her humiliation. I never talked about the middle of the night drives by his apartment to see if "her" car was parked there. And it usually was. I never mentioned how Ma's beat up old car didn't have heat and was missing part of the floor. Or how Ma had to work four jobs to pay the rent, to clothe Anthony and me. I never talked about this. I never talked about life with Ma. Instead, I lived vicariously through my father. He had it all, and I longed to live with him and have it all too.

But children don't understand that having it all sometimes comes with a price. My father had paid the ultimate price.

"...connect Capraro with some mob lawyer from Providence. Saying the lawyer ordered the hit."

"You don't mean Joey Casella...."

Joey Casella. I hadn't thought of him in years. Decades. Little girls often have crushes on older men and those older men are usually friends of their parents. I knew a lot of my father's friends. On special occasions like my birthday, first communion, and report card day, Dad would take me around to his friends.

"Anna, show Mr. Fragola your report card. Look, Dom. Look at all those A's."

Mr. Fragola nodded approvingly. "Keep up your studies, Anna." Mr. Fragola then reached into the pocket of his trousers and pulled out a wad of folded bills. He peeled off a five for every A on my report card. And so did Whitey, and Mr. Riccio, and Johnny-D. Straight As would net me thirty-five bucks a stop. And I got to keep it all.

"That's your money, Anna. Put it some place safe. No one needs to know," Dad would say.

By 'no one' I knew he meant Ma. And she never did know. Our living room had built-in bookcases with decorative glass doors on either side of the fireplace. The case to the right held all my Trixie Belden books, a few knick-knacks, and a non-utilitarian yellow vase. A small brass key locked the doors. It was considered my bookcase and so I was keeper of the key. The tall yellow vase had become my bank vault.

On my tenth birthday I made another sizeable deposit.

The school day seemed to drag on forever and I couldn't wait to go home and eat another piece of my Italian cream birthday cake. Since Ma had to teach until eight o'clock and we wouldn't be home from dinner at the Broadway until well after nine, she greeted me in bed that morning with cake.

"Happy Birthday to you. Happy Birthday to you," she sang as she carried the luscious cream cake lit with eleven candles—one for each year and one for good luck—into my bedroom. I made my wish and blew out the candles with one easy breath.

"Hurry and get ready. We'll have cake before you go to school." Later that day, all my friends were so envious when I told them I had had birthday cake for breakfast.

As I walked out of school that afternoon part of my birthday wish came true. There was Dad, leaning against his red Cadillac, waiting for me. Shouting a quick "See ya tomorrow" to my friends, I ran to him.

"How's my birthday girl?" he asked, kissing the top of my head.

"I had the best day ever! Ma let me have birthday cake for breakfast and look what Nicky Fragola gave me!" I held up my wrist, showing off my new I.D. bracelet.

Dad took my hand and inspected my present. "Hmm! That's very pretty. But how come it says Nick? I thought your name was Anna?" he teased.

"Dad! It's *his* I.D. You *know*..."

He laughed. "Better not let your mother see it. You *know*..." he mimicked me.

Dad was right. Ma thought going steady was a near mortal sin. I quickly removed the bracelet and dropped it into my brown leather book bag.

"How about I take my birthday girl to Palermo's for *pasticiotti?*"

My smile could have lit up half of Cranston. Now my whole birthday wish had come true! "Can I have my own espresso too? After all, Dad, I am ten years old now."

He nodded. "Just don't tell your mother. But before we go..." Dad pulled the small black comb from his back pocket and ran it through my bangs—a ritual that embarrassed me to no end as my friends gathered to watch and titter. And protesting got me nowhere. Dad would simply laugh and renew his vow to comb my bangs right up to and including my wedding day.

He held open the car door for me. I tossed my book bag into the backseat before getting in. He closed the door with a wink and a smile. "A gentleman always holds a door for a lady," he told me. He smiled and nodded courtly at Sister Paulette as he walked proudly around the front of his red Cadillac. Sister Paulette blushed ever so noticeably. I chuckled. Even a nun couldn't resist his charm.

Once settled behind the wheel we were on our way within moments. Dad took my small hand in his, holding it tenderly. His palms were soft and smooth like the fine cashmere sweater he gave me for Christmas. His nails were always neatly trimmed and polished with a clear sheen. Nick's father did the same kind of work as my father. Both were produce dealers and drove trucks "down South" to buy produce to sell "up North." Both loaded trucks with crates of lettuce and oranges and fifty pound bags of potatoes by the gross. Both unloaded their haul, hurling and stacking the crates and bushels into walk-in coolers. Both set up makeshift produce stands every Thursday and Saturday at the Farmers Market. And every Christmas season, Mr. Fragola and my father sold Christmas trees and wreaths at an abandoned lot on Gansett.

Yet, Nick's father's hands were rough and callused and cracked. My father's hands were not. There was never a splinter, a cut, or a callous. Even at Christmas, not a drop of pine tar marred his smooth, soft palms and manicured nails.

Dad eased his Cadillac into a parking space across from Palermo's Pasticceria. I loved Palermo's. It was a little bit of Italy in Cranston. Trompe l'oeil murals of Roma, Venezia, and Napoli adorned the walls. The café tables and chairs, both inside and outside, were home to many old Italian men who met each day to play *scopone* or *terziglio*. Their Italian playing cards were so pretty and colorful with suits of swords, batons, cups, and coins. Now and then the men would shout *"re bello!"* or *"sette bello!"* Opposing players would curse back, throwing down their cards in disgust.

"Hey, Paulie," several men called out to my father. Dad nodded his acknowledgment.

"Want in?" one man asked.

"No cards today. It's my baby's birthday."

"Buon compleanno! Happy birthday!"

I smiled and nodded my acknowledgment, mimicking my Dad's mannerism, as he ushered me inside.

"Gino," Dad called out to the owner. *"Per piacere porta alla mia Anna un pasticiotti del cioccolata e un espresso. È il sua compleanno."*

Gino Palermo was a small Old World Italian. He rushed out from behind the counter. He quickly brushed the flour from his hands onto his apron before grasping my hands in his. *"Buon compleanno, Anna! Espresso o café americano?* He kissed me Old World-style on both cheeks.

"Espresso, please, Mr. Palermo. I'm ten now," I boasted.

Mr. Palermo made quite the fuss, telling everyone who walked in: *"Oggi è il decimo compleanno della figlia de Paolo."* Within minutes my small palm was pressed with several ten-dollar bills. *"Grazie, grazie,"* I'd say and Dad would nod his pleasure at their generosity.

Mr. Palermo came to the table and whispered in my father's ear. Dad nodded.

"I have to see somebody, baby. I'll be right back."

"Roger Wilco," I answered, picking up my espresso cup.

"Remember, baby. Sip it. Savor the bean," he said as he headed to the kitchen in the back of the café.

"I will, Daddy."

I took a sip of my espresso, making sure my pinky finger was extended away from the cup. Someday I would wear a pinky ring, just like Dad. I placed the cup on the saucer and took a bite of my *pasticiotti.* The cake was moist and cool from the refrigerated case. The chocolate filling was creamy and not too sweet.

"Happy birthday, Anna," an unfamiliar man said as he placed a large gift-wrapped box on the table. The stranger sat in my father's seat. "Go ahead. Open it."

I looked towards the back of the *pasticceria,* but Dad was nowhere in sight. Neither was Mr. Palermo.

"Excuse me, sir. I think you'd better leave. My father's coming right back, and you're in his seat." My voice was controlled, but my insides were shaking.

The stranger flashed a smile. His smile was familiar in that it was quick and broad and engaging, not unlike my father's smile. Not unlike mine. And like my father he was a sharp dresser. Dark blue silk suit with a blue-gray, silk pocket square that matched his tie.

He stood, then took the seat directly across from me. I glanced again towards the back of the cafe. Still no sign of my father or Mr. Palermo.

"Open your present," the stranger said.

"I'm not suppose to take things from strangers," I said, which was

41

ridiculous, really, considering I'd just pocketed sixty bucks from strangers.

"I'm not a stranger. I'm a friend of your father. Really, it's okay."

I wasn't sure what to do. Everything inside me said "Run!" But what if he chased me? Maybe he had an accomplice waiting outside ready to snatch me. They'd push me into the backseat of a car and screech and squeal down the street and out of sight before my father even knew I was missing. I'd seen that many times on *Batman* and *Man from U.N.C.L.E.*

"Yo, Joey," my father called out.

"Hey, Paulie. I was just wishing Anna here a happy birthday. Brought her a little present."

Maybe Mom was right. Maybe I did watch too much television.

"Anna, this is Joey Casella. He's from Providence. He's a big shot lawyer there."

"Nice to meet you, Mr. Casella," I said. "Sorry if I seemed impolite before."

He smiled. "No, you were right. Never take anything from a stranger."

I nodded. "And thank you for the gift, Mr. Casella."

"You're very welcome, Anna. And you don't have to be so formal. Call me Joey. Everybody does."

"Even the judge?"

Joey laughed. I liked his laugh. It was hearty, full of life.

"Let's see what Joey got you," Dad said. "Open your gift."

I tore open the wrapping. "Mousetrap!" I screamed. "I've really, really been wanting this game!" I jumped from my chair and threw my arms around Joey. He kissed my forehead.

"Such a beautiful girl you are, Anna. I hope to have a daughter just as beautiful as you someday."

"You don't have any kids?" I asked.

He shook his head.

"Are you married?" I pried.

He flashed that smile. I noticed how his sky blue eyes gleamed against his tanned skin, how his thick and wavy black hair framed his handsome face. He was younger than my father, too. Maybe as much as ten years younger. "Haven't found the right girl yet. Maybe I'll just wait until you grow up, *bella!* Anna-bella!"

Annabella, Joey nicknamed me. Beautiful Anna. Little girls are supposed to be in love with their fathers. And I was. But at that moment I transferred some of that love to Joey.

I am so lost in thought I don't notice the traffic on the Pike has come to a halt. I slam on the brakes and narrowly avert hitting the car in front of me. "Oh shit!" I take a few deep breaths attempting to slow the pounding in my chest. Up ahead is a line of red taillights as far as the eye can see. I tune the radio to the Boston news channel hoping to catch a traffic report. Within minutes the sky report newsman announces, "An overturned fuel tanker on I-90 just past the Westborough exit has brought west bound traffic to a dead stop. HAZMAT is on the scene…"

Great. Just great. I'm going to be stuck here half the night.

Ten minutes go by with absolutely no movement. I turn off the engine so I don't waste precious, over-priced gasoline. Since I was lost in thought I've no idea exactly where on the highway I am. I figure I'm at least fifteen miles from the Westborough exit. The car behind me beeps its horn and I notice that there has been some movement. I start my car, move about two-car lengths before coming to a stop again. I leave the engine running hoping to be moving again soon. Several minutes later, we move another few car lengths. A few minutes later we move and stop again. The sporadic movement and short distances seem a bit odd. And then it dawns on me.

"Smart move!"

I pull into the breakdown lane and cautiously pass the long line of stopped cars. Within moments I see the sign, *Rest Area 1 Mile*. I continue on, stopping only to let another car in along the way. Ten minutes later I'm sitting inside the travelers center enjoying a caramel macchiato and eavesdropping on surrounding conversations. The number one topic: the "inconvenience" on the Pike.

Why is it that people take things like this so personally? It's not as if the truck driver planned the accident just to stick it to Mary Jo Somebody and Billy Bob Nobody. I try to block out the woman three tables down yelling into her cell phone, but she is way too loud and obnoxious.

"You're so-o-o right! You'd think these people could work a little faster to clean up that mess." Her laugh is piercing. "You're so-o-o right. State workers. All they think about is their next coffee break!" More hyena sounds. "You're so-o-o right!"

I wish I had the balls to walk over and say, "You know, lady? Get a fucking grip! It's not all about you, you self-righteous, self-absorbed asswipe!"

She clicks the phone shut, gathers her coat and purse and gets up from the table. As she passes by me she makes a big mistake. "God! Can you believe how long it's taking out there? I've been at work since seven this morning and I'd like to get home before I have to turn around and go back!"

Hard as I try I can't reel it in. "You're so-o-o right! You'd think the truck driver would have at least called you and said, 'Hey lady, just so you know, I'm planning on crashing my truck and dumping hundreds of gallons of gasoline on the Pike tonight, so you might want to leave your office earlier.' You're so-o-o right! How unbelievably inconsiderate!"

Aghast, she starts to speak, then wisely stops. She shakes me off like a bad chill. Asswipe! I chuckle to myself as she scurries away.

I amble over to the window to see if there is any movement. The highway resembles a lava flow. I head back to the Starbucks concession. Might as well have another cup of coffee. As I wait for the barista to work her magic I search the bottom of my purse for my cell phone. I hate this thing; hate being this connected to the world. But Rose talked me into getting it.

"You're on the road far too much. Just carry it for emergencies."

"Rose, I've lived all these years without a cell phone and survived just fine. Besides, if there's an emergency I'll use a pay phone."

"Anna, really, when was the last time you even saw a payphone?"

I scroll through the calls and a familiar number brings a smile to my face. Lisa.

Lisa Bell, nee Paradides, was my first true friend, my best friend. Her family moved to Cranston from Binghamton, New York when Lisa was fifteen years old. It's tough enough being the new kid in class, and it's even harder coming into a new school midway through your high school years. But Lisa walked into homeroom that day with grace and confidence. It was as if we had joined her class, as if we were the strangers in her world. From that first moment I saw Lisa I knew in my gut we would be friends forever; but I never imagined the journey we would travel. We've stood by each other through it all—boyfriends, break-ups, loss of virginity, miscarriages, and death, especially my father's death.

I check my watch: 10:27. It's too late to call Lisa. Not because she's in bed—Lisa's a night owl like me—I don't want the late night phone call to frighten her ten-year-old daughter, Katie. *To frighten her ten-year-old daughter, Katie.* My choice of the words causes me pause. Why frighten? Why not awaken, or disturb?

I pay for the coffee and then stop by the gift shop and buy a Reese's Peanut Butter Cup two-pack. I head to the far side of the travel center—far from weary travelers, far from obnoxious cell phone users, far from bored janitorial workers. Something is brewing deep inside me and I want to be alone with my thoughts.

I pull a notebook from my purse and write the phrase *frighten her ten-year-old daughter, Katie* at the top of the page. I open the package of Reese's and devour one peanut butter cup in four bites as I begin a word association stratagem I employ when facing writer's block. Frighten. To frighten is to startle. To startle is to scare. To be scared is to be terrified. Terrified. The word halts me. My palms feel suddenly cold. I eat the second peanut butter cup in two bites.

Okay. Let's keep going. A daughter is one's young child. What else? Nothing else comes to mind so I move on to Katie. Katie sounds like Kathy. Kathy is short for Katherine. Katherine Katerina. Katrina. Karen.

Karen. Karen Santorelli. My breathing becomes shallow and my heart begins to pound as I remember ten-year old Karen Santorelli. A few months after my tenth birthday ten-year-old Karen Santorelli was strangled to death, her body left in plain view near Clarke Brook. She didn't attend St. Stephen's, but everyone at school talked about it as if we knew her. It was Matty Cosco who brought it home.

"I'd be careful if I were you, Anna. That girl's old man is like your old man. You better watch out."

I was confused and scared at the same time. "What are you talking about, Matty? There aren't any Santorellis in the produce business."

"Who's talkin' produce? Don't you remember last winter when your old man got busted for gambling? Salvatore Santorelli got busted with him. Maybe he owed big money, and maybe somebody took his daughter for ransom. Your dad ain't no Elliot Ness."

I slapped Matty. Hard. "Don't you talk about my father that way. He got cleared on that bust. And your dumb dad ain't no Elliot Ness either. More like...like Elmer Fudd, M-M-M-Matty." I mimicked his father's stutter.

Matty took one step towards me as his friends fell in line behind him. I took the remaining three steps towards him, stopping inches from his nose. My friends fell into formation at my side like geese heading south in November.

Beep! Beep! The familiar car horn sounded. And like a knight in shining armor, my father pulled alongside the curb. I threw back my shoulders, nodded to my friends, stepped away from Matty, and towards my father's car.

"At least my Pop's no gangster!" Matty yelled out.

I was seething as I slid in the front seat next to my father. He reached for my hand, but I pulled it away and shimmied over against the passenger door.

"Something happen, baby?"

"No."

"You sure? Looked to me like a little rumble was brewing."

"It was nothing, Dad. Matty Cosco's a ditz, that's all."

Dad reached into his pant's pocket and pulled out three mini-Reese's Peanut Butter Cups. "Got these for you, baby."

I smiled. "Thanks, Daddy."

He reached for my hand again and this time I let him hold it. I let out a deep breath, his soft palm comforted me. I was safe.

We rode in silence for several minutes. "I have to make a stop before I drop you home," Dad said as he turned into the parking lot of Grasso's Meat Market. But rather than park in the lot, he pulled around back to the loading dock.

I hated this place. Men in white doctor's coats with dried blood and bits of animal flesh were unloading skinned cow carcasses. Hooks, like the size needed to catch a shark, pierced the animals' backs. The smell of death made me gag. I rolled up my window.

I watched my father talking animatedly with three men. One man, older than my father and similarly well dressed, kept jabbing his finger at my father's face. I heard my father's voice raise, then lower as the two younger men flanked him.

The old man came over to the car and looked through the driver's window. He smiled at me, nodding his head. His rotting, yellow-brown teeth grossed me out. It was the first time I ever saw panic in my father's eyes.

Despite the smell of decaying flesh I rolled my window down slightly to eavesdrop.

"*Vito...sta ottenendo impaziente,*" he said to my father.

"Tell him I'll have it next week."

The man looked through the car window again. "You heard about the girl? *Era l'età della vostra figlia.*" He flashed his rotting teeth. "Not next week, Paulie. Tomorrow." He tapped the car window with his withered index finger. I ignored him. "*Una ragazza molto bella.* It would be a shame."

I quickly rolled the window shut. I could smell the fear.

I slept fitfully that night. A wind-driven rain pounded against the window and the constant lightning lit the room as if someone was flicking the light switch on and off, on and off. The thunder crashed so loudly and intensely the room rattled in abeyance. Once the thunder and lightning passed over and the rain settled into a steady rhythmic patter I managed to drift off to sleep, only to be awakened moments later by the jangle of a

47

telephone.

I heard Ma's groggy voice. "Hello?…What?….Oh God!" I heard the receiver fall heavily onto the floor. I heard her footsteps pound hurriedly across the hallway. My bedroom door flew open. "Anna!" I bolted upright. I could see the fear.

The rain was still falling hard the next morning. I pressed out the creases that had formed on the backside of my jumper uniform, and then meticulously ironed back in the crisp pleats of the skirt. A Sisyphean task, for sitting in the car on the way to school would wrinkle the backside miserably. I slipped my uniform over my head and adjusted the white Peter Pan collar of my blouse. A quick check in the mirror and I was ready to go. I quickly folded the ironing board and placed it behind the laundry room door before going to the window to look for my father's car.

The asphalt street had disappeared under a steady, flowing river of rainwater. Cars hydroplaned as they rushed down the flooded street. Dad's car was nowhere in sight. I sat on the hallway stairs and waited. I could hear Mom in the bathroom at the top of the stairs primping for the day. I recognized the *ssshhh* sound and knew Ma was dousing her hair with so much Aqua-Net hair spray her coif could survive a hurricane. Anthony was not home which, lately, was not all that unusual. He spent most nights sleeping on the couch at his girlfriend Virginia's house. He spent most nights eating dinner there, too. I rarely saw my brother anymore, and when I did see him, Virginia was usually tagging along.

I was still waiting on the steps when Ma came downstairs. I scooted over to let her pass.

"Your father's not here yet?"

"I guess not if I'm still sitting here."

"Anna! Don't you dare start talking to me like that. I get enough of that from your brother." The look in her eye was warning enough to drop it.

"I'm sorry, Ma." I noticed, too, she looked more tired than usual. I guess neither of us slept much after that telephone call last night.

48

"Who called here so late?" I asked nonchalantly.

I saw the same panic in her eyes I'd seen last night. She took a deep breath, checked her wristwatch, and avoided my question. "Call the market and see if your father's coming."

"That's okay. I'll just take the bus." I flipped over the lapel of my blazer and showed her my city bus badge. Most kids pinned their badge on the lapel's face, right there for the driver to see as they rushed past and hurried to the seats at the back of the bus. I preferred to keep mine concealed. As I boarded the bus I'd flash my badge, nod to the driver, and sit in one of the side seats at the front so I could watch everyone on the bus. The driver always nodded to me too. He knew I had his back.

She checked her watch again. "I'll drop you off on my way to church."

"Really, Ma, that's okay," I said as I got up and went to pull an umbrella from the stand by the door. "The rain's slowing down. I can take the bus." The bus stop was a little more than a block from our house.

"No!" Her voice resounded more with fear than anger. "Not today. Go get in the car." I knew better than to argue. I slipped on my blue rain slicker and grabbed my book bag.

As we pulled out of the driveway I noticed a gray Chrysler sedan parked a few houses up from us. A man wearing a fedora sat behind the wheel. I started to mention it to Ma, but decided not to. She was nervous enough already.

"If your father doesn't show up this afternoon I want you to go to the principal's office and ask to use the phone. You call me, and either Tony or I will pick you up. *Capisco?*" Her eyes were dark and serious.

Now, it was my nature to question most things, but my gut told me to ask nothing and just agree. "Roger Wilco, Ma. I promise." I crossed my heart for emphasis.

Dad didn't show that afternoon, so I did as I was told. I went to the office, asked to use the phone, and called home. I could hear the familiar strains of intermediate level Dozen-A-Day piano exercises in the background as Mom spoke. "I told your brother to swing by the school just in case. He should be there any minute. You wait for him."

The front steps of the school were still damp from the storm. I sat down, my book bag resting in my lap, and waited for my brother. Car after car pulled up alongside the schoolyard. You could pretty much tell which grade the kids were in by the way they approached their parents' car. The littler ones—the second and third graders—ran excitedly, some waving a drawing or graded paper high above their head for their parent to see. The fifth and sixth graders, kids like me, mostly huddled in small groups: boys with boys and girls with girls. It was the older kids, the seventh and eighth graders who seemed the most self-conscious. The girls had an eye out for the popular boy or "crush" of the moment. The boys swaggered. Aware of the attention they drew from the girls, yet doing their best to not notice, all the while looking oh-so-cool.

Soon after the schoolyard cleared out the nuns emerged from the school, one by one, and crossed the street to the convent. The principal, Mother Benedictus, was the last to leave. She must have seen me out of the corner of her eye as she looked both ways before crossing. "Anna, what are you still doing here?" She came over to me.

"Waiting for my ride. My brother must have got held up or something. I'm sure he'll be here soon."

"Would you like to call home and check?"

"No, thank you, Mother. That's okay. I'm sure he'll be here any second."

"I think you should call your mother. At least come with me and wait inside. You can watch for his car from our sitting room."

Wait inside the convent? Now that would be a coup! None of us kids had ever been inside the convent before. This could be my big chance to find out if the nuns really were bald under those veils. Then again, what if they tried to recruit me or something? Life as a nun? A fate worst than death.

"Really, it's okay. Besides, my mom's teaching. She really doesn't like to be disturbed when she's giving lessons." Just then I saw Tony's green Corvair turn the corner. "There he is!" I jumped up. "See?" I pointed to his car.

Mother Benedictus crossed the street just as Anthony pulled alongside the curb. I walked over to his car and peered in the open window.

50

"Where've you been? Bene-doodoo was about to drag me into the convent to call Ma." Tony laughed. Every kid who ever attended St. Stephen's in the past ten years knew that nickname. I got in the car. "So where were you? At your girlfriend's house, or at the pool hall?"

"I don't gotta answer to you."

"Yeah? Well you're gonna answer to Mom when I tell her you kept me waiting for over an hour."

"Fuck you!" he whacked me hard in the arm.

It was the first time I heard the F-word. Me and my friends hinted at the F-word, but nobody I knew actually spoke it. And I'm not sure if any of us kids even knew what it meant; we just knew it was bad. Really bad.

Actually, I kinda knew what it meant because I had asked Nicky, just the other day during recess, if he knew what the F-word means.

"Yeah," he said proudly. "I'll show you." He looked around the schoolyard. "Let's go over there." He pointed to the alley behind the school building.

We stealthily made our way across the schoolyard without any of the nuns seeing us leave. I followed Nicky three-quarters of the way down the alley. He kept looking back over his shoulder, making sure no one saw us, or followed us. "Over here." He moved into the recessed doorway, the delivery entrance of Dicksen's Market.

He reached into his jacket pocket and pulled out the familiar blue plastic egg. Silly-Putty was the greatest toy. It could bend, bounce, stretch, mold–even lift comic-strip pictures right off the pages of the Sunday funnies! Nicky took out the flesh-colored wad and rubbed it furiously between his hands until it was a five-inch long rod. He held the rod with his left hand, and with his other hand he cocked it upright, then pulled it down again. "See? The putty's fucking." He kept repeating the action: erect, not erect, erect, not erect.

"That's fucking?" I lowered my voice as I said the word for the first time. "Are you sure? That doesn't seem so God-awful bad."

"That's what my cousin Rico told me." The putty was losing its shape so Nicky rubbed it between his hands again. "Yup," he began cocking the rod again, "Rico said this was fucking."

51

I didn't doubt that's what Nicky was told, but his cousin Rico was no Mr. Peabody. I just knew that fucking had to be more than rubbing and cocking some limp putty.

The next morning, Ma had to be to church at seven for the St. Rita Society novena. I was in my bedroom getting dressed for school when I heard her telling Anthony to "get up and drive your sister to school today if your father doesn't come. And don't you dare skip school again today. I know you haven't been going. I told your father letting you have that car was a mistake. I see it parked at the pool hall when you should be in classes." Oh, boy. This wasn't good. A quarter-to-seven in the morning and she was already in a lather.

My bedroom door pushed open. "Anna. If your father..." I tuned her out. I knew the wise response. 'Sure, Ma...Okay, Ma...Roger-Wilco, Ma.' Any one of those answers would do.

When Dad hadn't come by ten minutes of eight I went upstairs to my brother's room. I slowly opened his door. Nobody knocked in our house. "Tony? Ma said you should drive me to school. Dad didn't come." He pulled the bedspread over his head. "Tony? It's almost eight." I waited a few more moments. "Tony? Are you gonna get up?"

"Fuck off!" he bellowed from under the bed cover.

Again with the F-word. I decided not to push my brother. A ride to school wasn't worth a whack upside the head or a punch in the arm.

As I was crossing the street to get to the bus stop, I saw the gray Chrysler sedan with the man in the fedora behind the wheel. I kept an eye on him until the bus came, nearly ten minutes later. When the bus pulled away from the curb, I stood up and pretended to adjust my skirt, all the while keeping an eye on the gray Chrysler. It didn't follow us.

A young woman boarded at the next stop and sat across the aisle from me. She smiled politely; I nodded. She wedged her black pocketbook between her hip and the seat's arm and then opened the newspaper she had carried on tucked under her arm. She flipped through to the classified section; quickly scanned the listings until she found something of interest. She folded the paper in quarters, making it more manageable. My eye caught the quarter-page ad for Grasso's Meat Market.

You heard about the girl? The words of the old man with the rotting teeth rang in my head. *Era l'età della vostra figlia.* I didn't speak Italian, but I was around it enough to be able to piece together what was being said. The old man had said something about age— your daughter's age. *It would be a shame.* A shiver washed over me. Did the late night phone call that sent mom flying into my bedroom have some connection to the old man?

I looked at the newspaper ad again. The Grasso Brothers - The Best Butchers in Town. I closed my eyes, desperate to shut out images of skinned cow carcasses and bound human bodies hanging from meat hooks. Karen Santorelli's body hanging…

"Hey, you…. Hey girlie….It's your stop." The bus driver called to me. I opened my eyes and for a moment I had no idea where I was.

"You okay, hon?" the young woman across the aisle asked.

With trembling hand I grabbed my book bag and stood on unsteady feet. "Yes, thank you," I said to her. "Thank you," I said to the driver as I wobbled off the bus. As I walked the half block to the school I heard my intestines rumble. "Oh no," I muttered. A wave of nausea made its way up my neck; I felt light-headed. Chilled. My gut rumbled again, like violent waves coursing through me. I squeezed my buttocks. *Please, God, just a few more yards,* I prayed. Climbing the twenty-four steps that led into the school was like climbing Everest.

"Hey, Anna," Lucia called to me as I rushed by. "You okay? You look like you saw a ghost."

I ducked into the lavatory just as the fear exploded out of me.

When Dad didn't pick me up from school that afternoon I debated whether I should wait or take the bus. I really wanted to see him. I wanted to know who the old man outside Grasso's was. I decided to walk home. Maybe he was running late. If so, I'd spy him along the way.

I was more than halfway home when Palermo's came into view. Maybe Dad was in there having an espresso. I decided to stop in and check.

"*Buon giorno,* Anna. Where's-a you Papa?" Mr. Palermo asked, drying his hands on the white terrycloth towel tucked under the apron string that twice circled his thin waistline.

I shrugged my shoulders. I was hoping he could tell me. "Working, I guess, Mr. Palermo."

"Ah, I see. You come-a all-a by-a youself, *si?*

"Si." Since I was here anyway I decided to treat myself. "I would like a cannoli, *per piacere."*

I sat at the café table I always shared with my father. As I popped the last bite of sweet ricotta into my mouth Mr. Palermo came by my table to pick up the empty plate. *"Una momento,* Mr. Palermo." I fumbled with the crumpled bills in my blazer pocket. "Maybe I'll have one more for the road," I said producing a dollar bill.

"Bene. But-a you watch-a you figure. You big-a girl like-a you Mama." He didn't mean to insult me, but he did. I was out the door, sans cannoli, before you could say *pasticiotti.*

When I got home from school that afternoon, I found Mom in the kitchen reading the newspaper.

"How come you're not teaching?" I asked.

I was hoping to get her on another track so she wouldn't ask if Tony brought me to school. Not that I didn't want him to get into trouble; I didn't want to get my ass kicked by him for squealing.

"My three-thirty canceled," she said referring to her piano student. "I wish that kid would quit altogether. He's always canceling, and when he does show up he's never prepared, which is too bad. He has talent."

"Who's he?"

"Peter Veneziano."

"That little pantywaist?"

"Anna!"

"What? Just callin' it like I see it. Wearin' those stupid little bow ties."

Ma laughed in spite of herself.

"Why don't you tell his mother you won't teach him anymore? What's the point if he's not interested in learning?"

"Oh, you think it's that simple? His mother would be telling everyone at the PTA how I think I'm too good to teach their kids."

"His mother barely speaks English, Ma. And beside, you are too good," I said. "Look at the write ups you get in the paper when you sing or play a concert. And I'll bet you're the only PTA mom who stays up late at night punching raised dots in paper so blind kids can learn to play the piano. They're just jealous of you, Ma. And stupid Petey P's just too stupid to know how lucky he is to have you as his teacher."

She spoke not a word, but her moist eyes said plenty.

I went over and gave her a hug. She pulled me to her ample bosom and kissed the top of my head. "Go get out of your uniform," she said still holding me. "We'll go to the diner when I'm done teaching tonight. Eight o'clock." She kissed me again and went back to reading the newspaper.

I slipped quietly into the living room and pulled the small key from my uniform blazer pocket, unlocked the bookcase, and withdrew ten dollars from my "bank." I wasn't sure what I intended to buy, but I would know it when I saw it.

I went upstairs and changed out of my uniform, then waited until her four o'clock student arrived before I left the house. As I walked outside I half expected to see the man in the gray Chrysler. The coast was clear. I crossed the street, cut through a few backyards, and headed over to Fleisman's Five and Ten.

"Hey, Mr. Fleisman. Hey, Mrs. Fleisman," I called out to the store's elderly owners.

"Hay is for horses, Anna," Mrs. Fleisman reminded me as always.

I browsed up and down each aisle with Mr. Fleisman always a few paces behind me. Didn't matter who you were. To him, all kids steal.

"Are you making more potholders?" he asked. "I have new loops in. Thirty different colors."

"Naw. I'm just kinda looking around. My ma's birthday's comin' up," I added the lie to get him off my trail. It didn't work.

"Still making potholders, though?"

"Oh, yeah," I said. "It's good business." Shoot! Didn't mean to let that cat out of the bag. I sold my colorful cotton square potholders around the neighborhood for a quarter a piece. If Mr. Fleisman knew I had parlayed my potholder loom into a moneymaking venture he'd probably charge me more for the cotton loops. Jews were that way, at least that's what Johnny-D always said.

Then I saw it. It was exactly what I wanted. But rather than buy it and have to endure Mrs. Fleisman's inquisition, I decided to go to Woolworth's where no one knew me.

I headed for the door. "Thanks Mr. and Mrs. Fleisman. I'll be back soon. Just, you know, felt like looking around today. Just getting birthday present ideas."

Three blocks later I was at Woolworth's. I went straight to the toy section. I scanned the shelves. There it was. Right before my eyes. The Secret Agent Rubber Pellet Luger with Shoulder Holster. As I went to grab it from the shelf Ricky McKinney and his mother came down the aisle and stopped a few feet away from me. I decided to wait. As I feigned interest in an Etch-a-Sketch, Ricky came beside me and eyed the Luger. Since it was the only one on the shelf I grabbed it before he had a chance.

"Hey!" he said. "I was looking at that." He tried grabbing the pistol set away from me.

"Too late. Guess you ain't no Quick Draw McGraw." I held it out of his reach.

"Oh, yeah? Whatta you need a gun for, Anna? You a lezzy?"

I didn't know what he meant by that, but I knew it didn't sound good. Taking advantage of my stunned silence, he grabbed the gun from me.

I lunged for it, yelling, "Give it back!"

"No!" He held it behind his back. "Lezzy!"

I got in his face. "What did you call me?"

"You heard me."

Just then his mother came over. "What's going on here?" she asked.

I didn't give him a chance to breathe, much less speak. "I was gonna buy that toy, Mrs. McKinney, but Ricky grabbed it right outta my hands."

She turned to her son. "Did you take that from her, Ricky?"

"No! I mean, I was reaching for it, but *she* grabbed it away from *me*."

"So, which one of you had it first?" she asked us both.

"I did, Mrs. McKinney." She was a small, mousy-looking woman. Timid. I knew instinctively what I could get away with. "Surely you saw

56

me standing here when you were coming down the aisle. I *was* here first."

"Maybe there's another one?" Mrs. McKinney suggested.

"It's the only one," I answered firmly.

Mrs. McKinney turned to her son who was holding the toy gun tightly to his chest. "She's right, Ricky. She was here first."

"So what?" he answered indignantly. "Besides, what does she need the gun for? She's a girl."

I need it to shoot your ditzy little ass. "So are April Dancer and Honey West girls."

"Yeah, but they're the *good guys.* Bet their fathers' mug shots weren't on TV last week, Anna."

"Ricky!" his mother yelled in horror.

Anger spewed from my eyes with the intensity of Mount Etna. I squared my shoulders and stared him down. "What did you say?" I could feel the blood pounding in my temples.

"I said, 'Bet their fathers' mug shots—"

"—You're Anna *Matteo?"* his mother interrupted.

Before I could speak, she ripped the toy gun from her son's clutch and handed it to me.

"I'm sorry for my son's rudeness, Anna. " She slapped the back of his head. "Apologize to Anna, Ricky. Right now!" She slapped his head again.

He glared at me venomously. "I'm sorry," he muttered.

For the first time I felt the power that comes with being Paulie Matteo's daughter. But as quickly as that surge of homage came over me, so came the wave of shame.

Bet their fathers' mug shots weren't on TV last week.

The Saturday before my run-in with Ricky McKinney was the start of bowling season. St. Paul's, my cousin Maria's parish church, sponsored children's bowling from September to November and Maria had asked me to join her team.

"Aw, c'mon. It'll be fun! Cousin Anita's bowlin' again. She got Most Improved Player last year. And I got Janice DeAngelis to switch to our team, too. Nobody can beat her!"

It was true. Janice DeAngelis was the best bowler in the league. She took the trophy for Highest Score last year. Bowled a 187. None of the boys even came close. Yeah…Janice was cool.

Ma was upstairs taking a shower and Tony was still asleep. I opened the front door just as the paperboy was approaching the house. "Thanks, Timmy," I said as he handed the newspaper to me.

I went into the kitchen and filled the coffeepot with water. While the water heated atop the blue flame I carefully measured out ten teaspoons of Maxwell House. I snapped on the pot's lid just as hot water bubbled up the stem and into the basket. Within minutes the sound and smell of percolating pleasure wafted throughout the kitchen. I took out two coffee cups and saucers from the cupboard. Using a teaspoon I skimmed the heavy cream from the top portion of the milk bottle into the matching creamer, stirring in a little milk to smooth it out. I washed the dishes Tony left in the sink from his midnight snack and wiped down the crumbs he left on the counter. Was he this much of a *cafone* at Virginia's house?

Once the coffee was brewed I poured myself a cup, inhaling the aroma as if it was a bouquet of fragrant red roses. I stirred in plenty of cream, settled at the kitchen table and opened the folded newspaper. The headline in the bottom right-hand corner caught my immediate attention.

LOCAL MEN ARRESTED FOR BURGLARY

I scanned the first few paragraphs.

> Break-in at Kochman Jewelers in West Warwick…tried to escape from back entrance…alarm sounded…taken into custody were Mark Barbee, 39, of Cumberland….Angelo Capraro, 36, of Cranston….Paul Matteo, 46, of Cranston…Augusto "the Panda" Pandozzi, 37, of Providence. All were charged with first degree robbery, and second degree burglary.

"Holy Mother of God!"

> Storeowner David Kochman told police he was working late in

his back office and was surprised by three men. Kochman also said he was kept tied and gagged while they opened a safe. At one point Kochman worked the gag loose and was told that unless he was quiet he would be killed.

Barbee and Matteo were picked up on Route 3, troopers said, and Capraro and Pandozzi were nabbed two blocks after being pursued on foot by patrolmen.

I heard Ma's footsteps on the stairs. "Aw jeez! Aw jeez!!" I muttered as I quickly folded the newspaper and shoved it under the linens in the bottom drawer of the hutch. I heard Ma opening the front door. I scampered into the pantry. I heard Ma close the door. I was nonchalantly searching for cereal when she walked in.

"Morning, Ma," I said, pulling out the Wheaties.

"You're up early today. Oh! And you made coffee!"

"Yup. There's a cup and saucer for you on the counter."

Ma kissed my cheek as she walked by. "Newspaper come yet?"

I hated lying to her, so I chose avoidance. "Bowling starts today. We're determined to take Most Improved Team, if not First Place Team this year."

"What time do you have to be there?"

"Ten-thirty. I'll leave my bike at Aunt Josie's and walk to the church with Maria and Anita. The bus is picking us up in the parking lot at eleven." I filled a bowl with the Breakfast of Champions. "Tony was home again last night," I kept the patter going.

"Thank God! I thought I was going to have to start paying Virginia's parents room and board." She filled the cup with coffee and a splash of cream, then took a sip. *"Delizioso, cara mia!"* She took another sip, savoring the flavor. She sat at the kitchen table. A long, deep yawn freed itself from her overworked body. "I can't remember when I didn't have to rush on a Saturday morning! No weddings, no funerals, and my first pupil canceled. I'm totally free until eleven!" She yawned again.

It was great to see my mother so relaxed. Ever since Dad moved out she seemed extremely stressed and strained. The summer months had been particularly rough on her. A lot of her pupils had taken time off from their piano and voice lessons. And with Dad not living at home, money was tight. Now, I had nearly three hundred bucks in my yellow vault, but I couldn't tell her about it. She'd have a cow if she knew how I got that money. Plus, Dad made me promise not to tell her. I hated secrets.

Yup, Ma was in a great mood. If only I had thought to take the phone off the hook. The second I heard the *Ring! Ring! Ring!* I knew her good mood was coming to an abrupt end.

"No, Jeannie," I heard my mother say. "I haven't seen the paper yet….The news? What channel?"

If only I had thought to hide the television.

"I don't have time to watch the news this morning. Just *tell* me…. Jeannie?…Jeannie?" With a look of incredulity Mom showed me the receiver. "She hung up." Mom placed the receiver back on the hook. "Anna, go turn on the television. Find the local news."

"There's no news on Saturday morning, only cartoons." I said, hoping to dissuade her.

"Jeannie said Channel 4 has a local morning news show, " she said as she headed for the front door. "Sometimes that kid throws the paper in the bushes."

I really needed to get to Maria's, but I didn't want Ma to be alone when she hears the news of Dad's arrest. Reluctantly, I turned on the television set in the sitting room. The timing couldn't have been worse. No sooner did the cathode ray tube light up, there was my father's mug shot: front view and side view.

I heard the coffee cup shatter and turned to see cappuccino-colored rivulets streaming down the white wall. "I haven't suffered enough humiliation? Now this? How am I supposed to hold my head up in this city with your father's mug shot plastered all over the airwaves? How are parents going to feel bringing their kids to this house, *his* house, for lessons?"

"What's going on?" Tony said groggily as he came down the stairs.

"Dad's been arrested."

"Cool." He yawned.

"Cool?" Ma bellowed. "You think it's cool your father's in jail? That his mug shot is on the news?"

"The fuzz is always breakin' him for his card games. Don't sweat it, Ma. It's no big deal," he said full of machismo.

"No big deal?" Ma lunged at him. But Tony's reflexes were swift. He grabbed hold of her wrists before she could land a blow.

"Let go of her!" I shrieked.

"Why? Whatta you gonna do?"

Tony let go, not because of my words, but because I started swinging, landing blows on his back and shoulders. He grabbed me by the back of my neck. Ma crumpled to the floor crying, "Stop it! Stop it!"

But the rage roiling from deep within me blinded me to our difference in size. "Don't you ever lay a hand on Ma again." I screamed, kicking wildly at his legs. Tony's grip on the nape of my neck tightened.

"Let go of her." The commanding voice surprised us all. Dad was not a big man, but at that moment his frame seemed to fill the doorway, as though he had consumed one of Alice's potions. Tony managed to rake his nails across the nape of my neck before letting go. Dad was in his face in two quick strides. Were he five inches taller he would have been nose-to-nose with Tony. "If you ever lay a hand on your mother or your sister again, you'll have to deal with me in ways you never thought possible. *Capisco?"* His tone was low. Exact. Chilling.

"Now help your mother off the floor. And apologize to her, and your sister."

Tony was suddenly a boy again. He nodded deferentially. "I'm sorry, Ma." Tony could not look her in the eyes as he helped her to her feet. I waited for my apology, too. All I got was a nod in my direction.

Dad spied the coffee-stained walled and broken cup. "I'm sorry, Theresa. I thought I'd be out before all this hit the news." He turned to me. "Anna, pour us some coffee." Dad shepherded Ma to the kitchen table. Tony and I followed like sheep.

I brought over coffee for my parents and me, pointedly ignoring my brother. But despite what Tony had done to me and to Ma, he was still an Italian male. And there were rules.

"Anna, ask your brother if he wants coffee, and get it for him," Dad said firmly.

I swallowed my short-lived independence. "You want coffee?"

Tony smirked his 'yes'. The Man was back.

As I placed the cup in front of him I muttered inaudibly, "Flat top."

"What did you say to your brother?" Dad's frightening tone returned.

I boldly looked my father in the eye. "I said, 'It's hot.'"

Luckily, I was quick-witted. Been that way as long as I could remember. The first time my quick-wit got me out of trouble was when I was five. I had mumbled "Jesus Christ!" in a fit of anger.

"Did I hear you take the Lord's name?" Ma asked.

"No, Ma. I was praying," I said, not missing a beat.

"Paulie," Ma interjected, "the news report said you were in jail for burglary."

"Burglary?" Tony said with a mix of shock and awe.

Dad and I continued our stare down, but I was not about to blink first. I had had it with the Italian code. And then, for a fleeting moment, an almost imperceptible change in expression flashed across my father's face and I knew what he was thinking. In that brief moment, my father wished that I had been a son. A slight smile came to his lips. Dad turned his attention back to Ma.

"I had nothing to do with it, Theresa. You gotta believe me."

It took every ounce of self-control to not show the victory I felt. I had stood up to Paulie Matteo. And I had won.

"That's why Joey was able to get me out so fast. I was playing cards with Angie and Barbee last night. Ang's car wouldn't start, so I offered him a lift home. Barbee was with us because Ang had picked him up."

I saw the skeptical look in my mother's eyes. After all the stories and lies she'd heard over the years, she had learned to question everything. "So on the way home you decide to stop by a jewelry store in Warwick at ten o'clock at night? For what, Paulie?"

"You gonna let me finish?" Dad said angrily. "I didn't stop at the jewelry store. Ang asked me to go by DeLuca's. You know, that import store you like, with the good provolone."

"He wanted to go to the market in the middle of the night?" I asked. I was learning, too.

Dad shot a look in my direction. It was filled with anger for questioning him, and a twinge of respect and awe for not being fooled. He turned his focus back to Mom. "Carmine runs a crap game there. He owed Ang some money. Barbee went in with him to collect while I waited in the car. I didn't know they were planning to hit the jewelry store behind the market. They were setting me up as an alibi. I had nothing to do with it, Theresa. You gotta believe me," he repeated.

Ma said nothing, which was saying a lot. I didn't believe him either, though I desperately wanted to. But the newspaper story mentioned a fourth guy. Somebody called "the Panda." I wanted to ask Dad who the Panda was and how did he happen to be there? Instead, I committed his version of the story to memory, word for word. I might need it today at the bowling alley.

"Can I go now?" Tony sighed. I couldn't tell if the sigh was weariness or relief that our little family meeting was over.

"I gotta go too," I chimed in. "Bowling league starts today," I directed my explanation towards my father.

He excused us with a toss of his head.

Aunt Josie bolted from her rocking chair the second she saw me coming. She was down the porch steps and standing in the driveway before I was even off my bike. "Ah, Anna, Anna," she wrapped her arms around me. "I'm glad you still came. Are you okay? How's your mother taking it?"

"We're okay. Actually, Dad's still at our house. Joey Casella, his lawyer friend, got him out. It was all some sort of mix up, Aunt Josie. Dad didn't have anything to do with it." I figured I would nip this in the bud rather than be subject to one of Aunt Josie's famous inquisitions—Where'd you go? Who'd you see? What'd you do?

"I better go get Maria. We don't want to miss the bus to the bowling alley." As if on cue, Maria and Cousin Anita came out the back door of the house. I kissed Aunt Josie on the cheek. "See ya!" and ran to meet them.

Anita was babbling on and on about her latest crush, Gary Prescott. "Did you know he was made captain of the basketball team? And Angie Frisella's all jealous now because she thought he'd ask her to the dance next week 'cause she's head cheerleader and all. You should've seen the look on her face when I casually let it slip I was going to the dance with Gary!"

We were half a block from St. Paul's when Maria put her hand on my shoulder. "Hold up a minute," she whispered to me. Anita kept on walking and talking, oblivious to the fact we were no longer beside her. "You doin' okay?"

"I'm cool."

Maria stared at me intently. But I was Charlie Chan. Inscrutable.

As we waited to board the bus for the bowling alley, Father Riccardi pulled me aside. "I'm proud of you, Anna. You came today, despite the shame."

I looked him in his beady little eyes. "Why should I be ashamed? I didn't do anything wrong."

"That's right. You didn't do anything. That's why I pray for you and your mother everyday."

"You pray for my mother and me?" I said incredulously. "Don't you pray for my father?"

"Your father needs to come to confession first, Anna."

"What about 'Pray for us sinners now and at the hour of our death?'" It was the second time in my young life I had questioned my religion. The first time was in second grade Catechism class. Sister Aloysius was reviewing the previous week's lessons.

"Who can tell me what a sacrament is?" she asked.

That one was easy. I raised my hand.

"Anna?"

"A sacrament is an outward sign instituted by Christ to give grace."

"Very good. And who can tell me what free will means?"

Know-it-all MaryAnn Bellagio raised her hand. "Free will means we can decide for ourselves. God doesn't tell us what to do."

"Very good, MaryAnn. And who can name three of God's traits?" Both my hand and MaryAnn's shot up into the air. "Anyone? Anyone other than Anna and MaryAnn? Nicky, how about you? I'll give you a hint. Each word starts with the letter O."

"Umm...Ahhh...Yeah. Let's see, umm, God is...umm... omnipotent...and a...omnipresent ...and...umm...a....a..."

64

"Omniscient," I whispered to him.

"Yeah…omniscient!" he said proudly.

"And what do those words mean? Class?"

"God is all-powerful, ever-present, and all-knowing," we recited in unison.

Then we moved on to the story of Adam and Eve in the Garden of Eden and how Eve ate the apple even though God told her not to eat the forbidden fruit. "Eve did so by her own free will," Sister said.

I raised my hand. "If God is omniscient and knows everything, didn't He know Eve was gonna eat that apple? I think Eve was set up." As hard as he tried, Nicky could not suppress his laughter.

Raucous laughter broke out on the bus. "Girls! Boys! Behave!" Father Riccardi scolded.

"Just so you know, Father, my dad was set up," I said, as I stepped onto the bus.

"I'll pray for your father, Anna, but he needs to repent first."

I whipped around. "Jesus didn't judge Mary Magdalene. And you shouldn't judge my father." Father Riccardi looked pissed. I had dared to question him *and* I had the audacity to talk back to him. And I did so of my own free will.

None of the kids at the bowling alley said anything to me about my father. I was sure Matty Cosco was gonna open his big trap, but thankfully he didn't. If he had, he'd have found out how all-powerful my right hook was.

The next morning I waited outside for Timmy to deliver the Sunday paper. "When you collect this week just apologize to my mother for not delivering yesterday's paper and deduct it from what she owes you." I handed him a five spot. "This will more than cover it." On my way to school on Monday I threw Saturday's newspaper in the trashcan behind Fleisman's.

"Looks like traffic's moving again," a voice jolts me back to the present. A mass exodus begins so I wait a few minutes and sip my coffee, which has grown lukewarm. I debate whether or not to get another one for the road. Caffeine usually does not keep me up at night; in fact, it tends to have the opposite effect—like giving a hyperactive kid Ritalin. I decide against it, mostly because I didn't want to be eating Tums half the night.

The traffic quickly resumes its normal pace. I try to keep my focus on the road, but thoughts of Karen Santorelli, the man in the gray Chrysler, and the meat hooks at Grasso's Meat Market keep intruding.

Chapter Five

As I reach my house I feel the blood pulsating in my carotid artery. Pulling slowly into the dark driveway I hug the right edge thinking the movement and positioning will trigger the motion detector lights on my house. It doesn't work. I sense my palms getting damp and my skin clammy. I never realized how dark my driveway was before. I back out again and reenter, this time coming within inches of the stone wall. As I roll to a stop the lights go on. Before turning off the engine I switch on the high beams and scan the yard.

"Well, aren't we a little paranoid tonight."

Therapists will tell you that acknowledging your fear is the first step towards overcoming it. Try telling that to a ten-year old kid. How do you tell a child that the source of her fear and the root of her anxiety is someone she loves? In the 1960s talking to a shrink was what crazy people did. Back then, there weren't support groups for everything from Alzheimer's to Zoloft abuse. We hadn't raised our consciousness yet. And in an Italian family there are things about which you just don't talk, not outside the family, and not within. Thankfully, children are remarkably resilient. They find ways to deal and cope that make syllogistic sense in their naïve world.

"Kind of odd? Anna, you were really odd! ....Say, whatever happened to that old vest you wore constantly?"

"Oh, God! You remember that old moth-eaten vest?"

"Remember it? I coveted it!"

I hadn't thought of that vest and the secrets it held in years.

"Ma, please!" I begged for the third time, "Let me have a quarter for a new comic book."

"Why do you need a new comic?" Ma's voice was terse, her patience worn thin. Exasperation bordering on anger was coming through loud and clear. "Didn't Uncle Peter give you all those old comic books that were in his attic? Besides, what happened to your allowance?"

I did have plenty of money stashed in the yellow vase in the bookcase. I started saving every dime of my allowance and every dollar from Dad's friends, just in case. In case I needed getaway money. Or in case Ma needed to make ransom.

But I needed a quarter now, because while Mom was flipping through *Photoplay* magazine, the one with Elizabeth Taylor and Richard Burton on the cover, I saw the latest additions to my arsenal in the new *Casper* comic book. And I was not about to explain how my need for the new *Casper* comic book had nothing to do with the comic strip itself, and everything to do with the miniature camera and smoke bombs advertised on the back page.

I had to buy that camera so I could take pictures of the man wearing the fedora in the gray Chrysler, and other suspicious-looking characters, and tuck them in the envelope taped to the inside cover of my diary. The pictures and my diary entries would give the police a lead should I go missing one day.

The smoke bombs were for my vest—an old, green wool vest that belonged to Uncle Peter. I found it in his attic while searching through boxes of his old comic books. I knew better than to ask him if I could have it. The comics alone were gonna cost me a winter of shoveling snow off his driveway and front walk. With Uncle Peter, everything had a price. So I walked out of his house wearing the vest under my school uniform blazer. I wore my blazer all the time now. It hid my shoulder holster with the Secret Agent rubber-pellet Luger perfectly.

My plan was to sew the smoke bombs, along with a few matches, into the vest's hem. Should I be kidnapped and able to make a getaway, I'd need them as a distraction. Last week I stole a few of Mom's pills from the medicine cabinet—two Valium and two dexa-something-or-other. I pried open the capsules and mixed the contents together, then very carefully refilled each one with the deadly blend. I unraveled the hem on the vest and

68

sewed the capsules in place. Should I be taken alive, these would be my "L" pills—lethal—just like the spies carry. Better I do myself in than be killed by someone else, I figured.

"If only I had that vest on now," I say aloud as I scan the yard one more time before getting out of the car. With a rapid stride, I make my way to the front door of my house, unlock it, and step into a brightly lit living room. Thank God for timers!

"Jazz!" I call out to my old, deaf dog.

I hang my car keys on the hook and place the gift bag from Sophie on the kitchen counter.

"Jazz!" I call out again as I hang my coat and slam the closet door hoping to arouse my beloved watchdog whose sole "watching" duties these days consist of *West Wing* reruns.

During a dinner party last week I was in the kitchen getting a few beers and another bottle of wine when my friend, Robbie, came in laughing. "Anna, what's up with your dog? She's standing in front of the television as if she wants you to turn it on."

I looked at the oven clock. "She does. It's almost nine. *West Wing* will be on in five minutes. It's her favorite show."

"Your dog watches *West Wing*?"

"She has a discerning taste in television programming."

I handed Robbie the three bottles of beer and motioned toward the living room with my head. A small crowd had gathered to stare at my dog staring at the blank television screen. I found the remote control.

"It's show time," I said.

I turned the set on and switched over to channel 63 just as Sam Seaborn walked into C. J. Cregg's office. Jazz laid down in front of the set, intently focused on the show. Everyone cracked up laughing.

"Figures your dog would be a Democrat," Robbie chortled.

I look at my wristwatch. It is almost midnight. I feel a twinge of guilt that she had missed her show tonight. After a search of the house I find Jazz sound asleep in my office. "Hey girl," I call out. "Jazz! Jazz!" I stomp my feet. She raises her head and gives me a puzzled 'When did you get home?' look. I kneel down and kiss her Golden Retriever/Chow head. "C'mon, girl. Let's go out. Go do 'good girls.'" My code phrase for 'Go take a shit.'

While Jazz attends to her business, I head into the bathroom to be a 'good girl' too. After my business is complete, I open the medicine cabinet above the sink and grab the jar of Pond's Cold Cream, used by the women in my family for generations. I study my reflection in the mirror. "You really were an odd kid, Anna." I massage the cream onto my face and methodically tissue off my make-up.

Back in the kitchen I grab an apple from the refrigerator and a dog biscuit from the cupboard and head out onto the porch. "Jazz! Jazz!" I call out repeatedly. Eventually she hears me. "Good girl!" I praise her as she plods up the steps. We both pad into my office. Jazz is hopping to and fro, waiting for her reward. I give her the biscuit and place my reward on the desk.

In Judeo-Christian mythology, after Adam and Eve ate the fruit of the tree of knowledge of good and evil, God punished them by driving them out of the Garden of Eden and into the world where they would be subject to sickness and pain and death. During Capraro's first trial I did everything possible to avoid any knowledge of the courtroom proceedings. I never once went to court. I didn't read the newspaper accounts. Mom didn't attend the trial either, but Anthony and other family friends kept her abreast of the proceedings. Catching Haynes' awkward on-the-steps-of-the-courthouse interview was happenstance. I was out partying. The barroom television was on. My ears pricked when I heard Haynes' assuring the press that his client "will be found innocent of the murder of Paul Matteo."

Acquaintances sidled up like new best friends—eager for dirt or perhaps just thrill seeking; desperate for any clues about a life so unlike their childhoods. But I gave them nothing. *Omerta* is part of an Italian's DNA. By the time the second trial came around, I had moved to Massachusetts.

The message indicator on the telephone is blinking a steady "Someone

70

called! Someone called!" I pick up the receiver and punch in my latest secret code.

"You changed the code again? How am I supposed to get my messages if you keep changing the code?" Edie rightly complained.

Old habits, like old voices, die slowly.

"You have two messages. Press 1 to—"

Yeah, yeah, yeah. I press 1.

"Anna, it's Lisa. You'll never guess who I ran into. Peter Veneziano. He says hello. I got the distinct impression you and he play for the same league, different teams. Call me. Maybe I'll try your cell, too."

My laughter over her 'distinct impression' is short lived. Peter Veneziano. Petey Pantywaist. Petey P. If it is true that to forgive is divine, then Peter Veneziano has carved out his niche in heaven.

My thoughts are interrupted by Denise Diction. "Next new message received today at 10:52 P.M."

"Hey, Anna, it's Sophie. I just talked to Greg. He said no problem. But I hope you will really, really think about this, okay? So let me know what you want to do. Great seeing you! I love you tons!" Click.

...that's my memory of Uncle Paulie. Kind of like the Invisible Man. One minute you see him, then you don't.

The Invisible Man. H.G. Wells' classic is a cautionary tale of hubris. Although Wells' Griffin wrapped himself in rags while Paulie Matteo draped himself in Italian silk, both men fell victim to their own impudence. As H.G. Wells slowly reveals Griffin's true nature, we discover the destructive effects of his invisibility on those around him and the chaos that ensued. If transcripts of Angelo Capraro's trial and conversations with Greg Haynes were to reveal my father's true nature, what destructive effect would that discovery have on me? The moral of Wells' story is straightforward: Science devoid of humanity results in destruction and suffering. What would be the moral of Paulie Matteo's story?

I decide to travel the Road to Damascus and fire off an e-mail to Sophie.

71

Hey Cousin, Great night. Stirred many memories. And speaking of
stirring, please tell Greg I'd like to stir the cauldron. Talk soon!
XXX, Anna ;-)

I pick up the apple on my desk and laugh aloud. I bite into the crisp, tart Pink Lady. The apple doesn't fall far from the tree.

Had I been born a boy, a son of Paulie Matteo, I have no doubt that I would have charted a far different course. Despite the Movie-of-the-Week version of *Mafia Princess*, there was no place for a girl in my father's world other than that of mother, wife, daughter, *comare*. I know my father saw through the veneer of Daddy's Little Girl and into my core. He knew I was smart, charismatic, and loyal. He knew I possessed an acute sixth sense that enabled me to be sufficiently leery. What he didn't know was that I could be cruel.

Peter Veneziano knew. For it was only a matter of time before my adolescent fascination with law enforcement twisted like a mobius strip revealing its underside.

Browsing the bookshelves at Aberdeen's Bargain Basement had become a Saturday ritual. I had developed into a voracious reader and my personal library had grown to well over one hundred books. Ma was quite the reader, too. Once she realized I had outgrown Trixie Belden, she introduced me to some of the authors she admired, like Agatha Christie and Taylor Caldwell.

I had just finished reading Meyer Levin's *Compulsion*, a fictional account of the infamous Leopold and Loeb murder of fourteen-year-old Bobby Franks in 1924. Nathan Leopold and Richard Loeb were teenage boys who considered themselves to be so intellectually superior they believed they could execute the perfect murder. So it was not surprising that Colin Wilson and Patricia Pitman's one-volume *Encyclopedia of Murder* caught my fascination. I pulled it from the shelf and skimmed the introductory material.

"Why should anyone want an encyclopedia of murder?" the author Pitman pondered. For "within the covers of one murder-file, an entire way of life is illuminated….every subtle strand in a nexus of family and class relationships is applied…in any murder trial…"

I squatted next to the bookshelf, flipping through page after page of wanton disregard for human life. It was the illustration pages that caused me pause. There were women. Henriette Caillaux, Yvonne Chevallier, Styllou Christofi, Adelaide Bartlett, Constance Kent, Marie Lafarge, Louisa Merrifield, Edith Thompson, Nora Tierney, Dorothea Waddingham. I had not thought of women as murderers before. Sure, I knew the story of Massachusetts native Lizzie Borden.

> *Lizzie Borden took an axe*
> *And gave her mother forty whacks*
> *When she saw what she had done*
> *She gave her father forty-one.*

What kid didn't know that rhyme? But Lizzie Borden was an anomaly, or so I thought until today, looking through the *Encyclopedia of Murder*. Chevallier had pumped five bullets into her unfaithful husband; Adelaide Bartlett poisoned her polygamous husband; Marie Lafarge also poisoned her husband. But not all the women were not driven into crime by passion. Dorothea Waddingham and Bella Gunness were each driven by greed; Pauline Parker, together with her friend Juliet Hulme bludgeoned Parker's mother. At the trial, letters were entered into evidence showing the teenage girls believed themselves to be geniuses. "I am apart from the law," Hulme had said.

I scanned the list of illustrations and turned to page 161: Nathan Leopold and Richard Loeb. I studied the picture of the two young men. They looked like any two boys you'd see walking the Brown University campus—well-groomed, intelligent looking, boy-next-door types. The kind of killer you don't see coming.

"Hey, Anna. Whatcha reading?"

I didn't have to look up. That high-pitched voice and lisp belonged to only one person. "Hey, Petey."

"You come here often?"

What an original, I thought sarcastically. "Often enough."

"I'm glad I ran into you. Have you picked a reading buddy yet? 'Cause, if not, I was wondering if maybe you'd like to partner with me."

Yesterday, Miss Gualtieri, our eighth grade English teacher, thought it would be a "good exercise to establish a reading buddy. Sort of like a one-on-one book discussion group. You'll decide together which book you'd like to read, set up a schedule for completing the reading of the book, a date to discuss the book, and schedule time together to write your joint book report," she instructed us.

My classmates scurried about selecting best friends with whom to do the assignment. I looked over at Lucia, but she was jockeying to work with her crush, Timmy Bloom. MaryAnn snagged Nicky before I had a chance to breathe in his direction, which left Ricky McKinney, Matty Cosco, and Peter Pantywaist Veneziano. No way was I working with Ricky or Matty. And I did everything to avoid Peter who was looking my way, shrugging his shoulders as if to say, "Would you mind partnering with me?"

I laid the book on the bottom shelf and then stood up. Most of the boys in our class seemed to have gone through a growth spurt during the summer months between seventh and eighth grade. Not Petey P. I still towered over him by a good five inches. I looked down at him. I had to admit he did have the sweetest, most gentle blue eyes. If only he wasn't such a pantywaist. Oh, what the hell. At least he was smart. If I partnered with one of the other two, I'd end up doing all the work myself.

"Sure, Petey. Why not? You gotta book in mind?"

"I like most everything. But I love suspense-type novels."

I smiled. "Now you're talkin' my language!"

During the course of our book project I discovered that Peter—as he preferred to be called—was actually very nice, although incredibly shy. We shared a love of books, we both thought Aberdeen's Bargain Basement was primo, and we both thought Barbra Streisand was the greatest singer on the face of the earth. Peter entertained me with his rendition of *Marty the*

Martian and I blew him away with my performance of *The Minute Waltz*.

"Wow! Anna, you sing as good as Barbra! You must get that from your mother. I heard her sing at my Grandma's funeral last May. When she sang the *Ave Maria* she made me cry."

"Do you still take piano lessons? I haven't seen you at my house in a while, come to think of it."

"No," he said with hesitation.

"Why'd you quit?"

I think my prying made him a tad uncomfortable. "My dad retired so he said we had to focus on the necessities; especially if I wanted to go to college."

I had heard Peter's parents were older. Ma once referred to Peter as a change-of-life baby. I wasn't sure what that meant, but I figured it maybe had to do with his parents being Italian immigrants. Peter did seem to have difficulty adjusting to a change in language. When he came to St. Stephen's in the middle of our second grade year he spoke virtually no English at all. I still recall how nasty the nuns were to him.

"Yar mixin' yar words all up thar, Peter. Tare's no room far broken English in this class," Sister Bridget reprimanded him. And I remember thinking she had a lot of nerve. All the years she's been in this country and she still butchered the language with that brogue. It was my first lesson in hypocrisy, a word that I found kept coming to mind the more I learned about Catholicism.

"I really miss my piano lessons, though. I try to keep up, you know? Practice the exercises your mother taught me." He smiled again. "I bet you're great at the piano, too. How cool, having your mother for a piano teacher."

I smiled and nodded, not wanting to dispel his illusion that I, too, was a virtuoso like my mother. I was a decent pianist, but I couldn't grasp reading music. It was a sour note between Ma and me, and not worth the frustration it put us both through. So I plucked away on my own. Writing the alphabetic equivalent next to each note on the staff, then erasing them as soon as the piece was committed to memory so no one would know my inadequacy.

Later that night at the Broadway Diner I mentioned Peter's dilemma to Ma.

"I always wondered why he quit all of a sudden, and just when he was getting focused. That boy had natural talent."

"For what it's worth, Ma, he says he practices the exercises you taught him every day."

Ma smiled.

Peter and I began meeting for lunch each day in the school cafeteria, and I found myself really looking forward to our time together. I didn't belong to any of the cliques, and Nicky had betrayed me by asking Maryann Bellagio to the Spring Fling. Not that I wanted to go with him, but did he have to go with Maryann Blow-job-io?

"Well, look at who we've got here. Lizzy Lezzy and Caspar Milquetoast," Ricky said as he and Matty took the table directly behind us.

"C'mon, Peter, let's go," I suggested. "I don't want to get into it with those jerks." I stood and picked up my tray. Peter followed suit.

"Dig those lezzy shoes she's wearing!" Ricky taunted. "All she needs is Petey's bow tie and she'd be a full-on, bull-dyke lezzy!"

Lezzy shoes? My new brown leather high top shoes with the thick zipper up the front were absolutely fab! What does Ricky Mc-Ninny know about style anyway? Jerk head!

"Yeah," chimed in Matty.

My hand went instinctively under my blazer. Damn! I'd quit wearing the Luger last winter, after that awful night outside my father's apartment. So instead I used the only weapon at my disposal. I flipped Ricky the bird. "Climb it, Tarzan." I threw back my shoulders and walked away resolutely. Peter, on the other hand, was tippy-toeing away like a mouse that had spied a cat laying in wait for unsuspecting prey.

This was the second time Ricky had called me a lezzy. Only now I knew what it meant. Lucia Barone had told me after Ricky called me that the first time. "It's gotta do with girls who fight a lot and end up in prison. They cut their hair real short, and wear men's clothes. Then they start kissing the other girls in jail."

I never wore those brown shoes again.

76

Peter had taken to joining me on Saturdays at Aberdeen's. We were way in the back of the store where Mr. Aberdeen had used paperbacks for sale. "Peter, I've been thinking. What do you say we get Ricky McKinney."

"What do you mean?" he asked.

I handed him a worn copy of *Compulsion* I'd found. "Ever read this?"

Peter perused the summary on the back cover. I watched his expression change from casual interest to confusion to concern to fear.

"Anna," Peter looked rightly worried. "What are you thinking of doing? Are you thinking of…" he couldn't say the word he feared might be what I had in mind, so instead he chose a word less savage, "…harming Ricky?"

I saw the fear in his eyes, and I had to admit it was empowering. At this moment I knew I was a Matteo through and through. "I don't know. But if I did want to…" I paused for effect "…harm him, would you do it with me?"

"I don't know."

"Well, think about it. Because if something does happen to Ricky, and you're not in on it, you'll still know who was behind it. And that's not a good position to be in either, Petey P." There was cruelty in the way I said the nickname he so abhorred. I pulled the book from his hands. I was surprised and a bit awed at how effortlessly my mind was heading down this dark course.

"You know, Petey, the real guys, Leopold and Loeb, the guys who inspired this story almost got away with it. It was one mistake, one small mistake —Leopold's glasses fell out of his jacket pocket—that got them caught. You see, the secret to getting away with it is to study the mistakes other people made."

I lowered my voice for effect. "Remember that day you saw me here? The day you asked me to be your reading buddy? You asked me what I was reading. I never told you." I took one step closer to him. "But I'm gonna tell you now. I was reading the *Encyclopedia of Murder*. And I bought the book that day." I took another step towards him, forcing him to back into the bookshelf. "And I read it every night. I study the cases. Study how they did it and why they got caught. I study their mistakes." I leaned in and whispered in his ear. "I won't make a mistake."

77

Peter burst into tears. He began to plead. "Please. Anna, don't. I don't want to be a part of it and I promise I'll never say a word to anyone. Please..." He was sobbing uncontrollably now. I tried to put my arms around him, to calm him, but he screamed and ran towards the front of the store. I ran after him, calling to him. He ran past Mr. Aberdeen who tried stopping him, but Peter twisted away.

Mr. Aberdeen grabbed my arm. "Everything okay there, girlie?"

I wriggled out of his grasp. "Please, I gotta go after my friend."

I saw Peter tearing up the block. I ran after him, calling his name at the top of my lungs. "Peter! Please, stop! Stop! I'm sorry! I'm sorry! I didn't mean it. Please stop!" I don't know if he slowed down because of exhaustion or because he was willing to give me another chance. But I was grateful to him and thankful to God that he did stop.

By the time I caught up to him I was crying so hard I couldn't catch my breath. And then, like the angel he was, he put his arms around me and said, "Just breathe, Anna. Breathe."

I begged for his forgiveness. "I don't know what came over me," I sobbed. "I got caught up in this twisted scenario in my mind. I'd never hurt you, Peter. Never." I was crying so hard I began to choke. "I'd never hurt you or Ricky or anybody. You gotta believe me. I'm not like him...I'm not like him..."

There, but for the grace of God....

I finished writing my senior thesis the week my father died. It was entitled *The Dialectics of Alienation: Karl Marx and Jean-Paul Sartre,* an audacious undertaking for a twenty-one year old.

Alienation—the word itself has a mournful sound to it. Feelings of loneliness, helplessness, and insecurity are often synonymous with, or characterized as, alienation. Its plea is clear: I feel cut off from others, and I would rather not be. It is a sense of being rejected by others upon whom one should like to depend or, more often, one must depend.

In the preface I stated that alienation was the general human condition, a problem of human destiny; that for centuries philosophers sought after answers to questions concerning alienation in the groundwork of economics, politics, even mere existence. And while some philosophers attempted to unravel the problem by examining its syllogistic framework, others searched for methods or systems of analyses.

Like Socrates, Kant, Hegel, Marx, and Sartre, I purported that dialectical reasoning was the hidden key that could unlock the secrets and mysteries of the universe. Johann Gottlieb Fichte first introduced the triadic formation of the dialectic as consisting of a thesis, an antithesis, and a synthesis. Hegel described this form as Being, Nothing, and Becoming. He reasoned there was a "necessary conflict" between the contradictory terms Being and Nothing, and that Becoming passes through the conflicting terms, confronts each of them on its own level and in its own degree, and finally transcends their opposition by creating something new. Thus the thesis and the antithesis are two related entities, in which through their coming together generate a third entity, the synthesis.

My parents were the oppositional base of the triad. Ma was a college graduate; Dad was a seventh-grade dropout. Ma directed the choir at St. Stephen's Church; Dad conducted the gambling hall at the Cranston Businessmen's Club. Ma gave of herself to better others; Dad took from others to better himself.

Even in death, they were diametric. By the time the cancer was detected, Ma had less than three months to live. She cycled through the first two stages, denial and anger, with lightning speed. And with the grace that defined her existence, she skipped bargaining and grieved privately. Then, with the ease in which she marveled audiences with a glissando passage, she glided into a deep peace within herself. And being the great maestro, she directed us to a path of peace within ourselves.

I was thankful for the peace she found in her final days, for peace had eluded Ma most of her life, particularly since she had chosen to spend half of her life with the antithesis of her being.

"How did you and Daddy meet?" is a question most children ask their parents. I was surprised to learn my mother had married the proverbial boy next door. "His family moved here from Pawtucket when your father was

79

thirteen years old," she explained. My father was the youngest of five boys and Ma was the oldest of five girls. It was a statistical inevitability that one of the Matteo boys would marry a Franconi girl.

"I remember I was riding my bike up and down the street. As I passed your father's house, he was sitting on the railing of his front porch smoking a cigar. And I remember I was self-conscious every time I passed him, because the day before a boy had yelled out, 'What a spread!' It's not that I was heavy, like I am now, I was shapely like you," she said with a proud smile. "So, as I was passing your father, sitting there on the porch, puffing that cigar like a big shot, I made sure my fanny was on the seat! And I said to myself, 'I'm going to marry him.' I was only eleven years old, but I knew. I had a feeling in my gut."

Ma always worried about what other people thought of her. Maybe it started with the boy's sarcastic remark about her ass, or maybe it was simply life with Paulie Matteo. I never understood her concern. Never once did I hear anyone then or now talk about my mother with nothing less than adoration and admiration. She was loving, generous, and loyal. Intelligent, multi-talented, and elegant. Most of all, she earned respect by virtue of her intrinsic goodness, and not by reason of intimidation. Just as one could consider my father satanic, one could consider my mother saint-like.

There, but for the grace of my mother....

Aunt Jeannie once commented, "How is it that you and Anthony came from the same womb?" I've often pondered that remark. Anthony and I were, indeed, the fruit of her womb. Our bodies had developed and formed within her inner sanctum. Yet, we both were seeds of his loins. But once spawned, it was the proximity to that womb that molded our characters.

The amount of time I spent with Ma while I was growing up was proportional to the amount of time Anthony spent with Dad. My time with my father was limited to rides to and from school, stops at Palermo's, and shopping sprees at Aberdeen's. Anthony, on the other hand, worked with Dad at the produce company, he went down south with him to pick up fruits and vegetables for the produce company, and later as an adult, Tony ran the blackjack table at the Cranston Businessmen's Club.

I was much more than my mother's daughter. I was her companion, her pal, her confidante. And while the vast amount of time spent with my mother shaped my ultimate character, it exposed me to adult concerns a child should not have had to face.

"See ya tomorrow, Timmy," I said to my friend as he headed into his house.

I continued down the street singing the latest Monkees' tune when, from half a block away, I saw the pile of clothing on our front lawn. I stopped in my tracks and took a deep breath.

"Oh, man! Ma's throwing Dad out of the house again," I muttered.

Tears welled in my eyes. Dad had been home for a whole month this time. I knew it was too good to be true. My father had moved out and moved in and moved back out again at least a dozen times since I was born. I think I spent more time with him in his car than I did in our home.

Yeah, I didn't have to be home to know what took place today. I'd seen it all before. At some point in time between when I left for school and when I came home, the bedroom windows flew open and Dad's clothes went flying down onto the ground below. And each article of clothing was accompanied by hysterics and crying. "Go...go to your whore...Go to your *puttana*...." Man, was I thankful not to be home for the drama today.

After graduating with a Bachelor of Fine Arts degree in the 1940s, Ma continued her vocal studies in New York City with Metropolitan Opera diva Karin Branzell. She was well on her way to a career in opera when the war ended. But when Paulie came marching home again, so did my mother. Now she performed at the Matteo Opera House regularly. And Anthony and I had season's tickets to *Don Giovanni, La Traviata, Mefistofele.*

As I stood looking at Dad's suits, shirts, shoes, and poker chips strewn on the front lawn, a car slowed down. "Having a yard sale?" a woman's voice peeped sincerely through the slightly open car window.

I was tempted to say yes. To get rid of it all—even make a few bucks.

81

Maybe if all this stuff belonged to someone else I'd never have to see it on the lawn again. Instead, I gingerly opened my blazer, just enough for the butt of my Luger to be visible. "I think you should move on." The woman's eyes widened in disbelief. The car sped off.

I knew Ma would be downstairs in her basement studio giving piano lessons, so I bolted up the stairs to their bedroom and waited by the window for Dad to come and retrieve his belongings. I didn't have to wait long.

The red Cadillac pulled in front of the house. I watched Dad get out of his car. He stood on the front lawn shaking his head and...I focused in...laughing. He was laughing. And he kept on laughing as he loaded his suits, shirts, and shoes into the trunk of his car. He laughed as he picked up each poker chip—one by one—from the blades of grass. As he slammed the trunk shut he looked up towards the bedroom window. Our eyes met. He stopped laughing. I gave a slight wave and he raised his manicured hand to his lips and blew me a kiss. My sixth sense told me he would not be coming home again.

I got my sixth sense from my mother. She called it a feeling in her gut. "I've got a feeling in my gut that Jeannie and the kids will stop by today," she'd say. And they would. "I've got a feeling in my gut my six o'clock will cancel." And her student would call and cancel his or her piano lesson.

A week after Dad left, Ma's gut told her that Dad was living in the new apartments on Park Avenue. "The ones with the fancy skylights," she told me as I changed out of my pajamas and got dressed to go do our first drive by. It was after ten p.m., but Ma had a feeling in her gut. Sure enough, there was Dad's red Cadillac parked outside apartment 3D. A few nights later we went back again. As we slowed our approach to 1067 Park Avenue, apartment 3D, we saw a yellow Ford parked next to his red Caddy. I made of mental note of the license plate, 583 RHP. The yellow Ford was there the next night, and the following night, and most nights after that. With each sighting of that yellow Ford next to Dad's red Cadillac, Ma's torment increased exponentially.

I recalled Ma's story about when she was eleven, seeing my father for the first time and having a feeling in her gut that she would marry him. And then I thought about Grandmama's story about Ma when she was eleven. It

82

was the middle of the night and Grandmama was jolted awake by her daughter's panicked screams. She bolted out of bed and found "Theresa in the bathroom huddled over the toilet, crying hysterically. She held out her hands to me. Her fingers were covered in blood." Grandmama described vividly how Ma's pink nightdress with delicate hand-embroidered roses was soaked through with dark bile and blood. "Eleven years old," she said. "The youngest person to ever have a bleeding ulcer." Maybe Ma should have listened to that feeling in her gut.

Within a few weeks, our nightly reconnaissance evolved into a stakeout. On the way to what I thought was our usual drive-by, Ma stopped at the Broadway Diner. I waited in the car while she went inside. Two minutes later, Ma came back to the car with coffee for her, hot cocoa for me, and a neatly tied, white box filled with a half-dozen assorted pastries.

Ma was no longer content with seeing if "her" car was parked outside Dad's apartment. She wanted to see "her." We took our position outside apartment 3D. Shortly after one a.m.—after the pastries were gone and Ma's coffee had grown cold—the apartment lights went out. We waited, our eyes fixed on the door. Nothing happened. No one emerged. The owner of the yellow Ford remained a mystery. We kept our lookout for the next twelve nights. And each night nothing—that is, until the thirteenth night.

An old familiar pain clutches my intestines. I pace up and down the hallway, trying to walk it off—back and forth, back and forth. On the third pass by my office Jazz joins in, pacing one step behind me.

The hallway is a gallery of family photographs going back seven generations—from my maternal great-great grandfather to my great-nieces and great-nephews. Their eyes follow me like an El Greco portrait with each pass.

Every family has a notable physical feature that carries through the generations—an aquiline proboscis, a protuberant ear. I stop in front of the formal portrait of my mother taken the day she made her First Communion. Young children don't really understand that they are a melding of their parents. Aunt Josie would say, "Anna, you look just like your mother!" And I'd look at Ma's Rubenesque figure, the gray halo that framed her brow, and I'd think that Aunt Josie needed new glasses. That is, until the day I found Ma's First Communion picture when I was twelve years old.

It took a lot of pleading that day before Grandpapa finally agreed to teach me *scopone*. He kept the special playing cards in the right-hand drawer of the credenza. As I pulled open the drawer a young girl's portrait came slowly into view—a bouquet of flowers was nestled in her small hands, she wore a dainty locket around her neck, her dress fell just off her shoulders revealing creamy skin. Her hair was styled in long ringlets, her mouth was pouty, her nose straight. And then I saw her eyes. They were my eyes.

"Where did this picture of me come from?" I called to Grandmama who was in the kitchen preparing Sunday dinner.

"What picture?"

I took the portrait from the drawer and brought it into the kitchen. Grandmama was at the table rolling out dough for ravioli on a large wooden board that served just that one purpose. She wiped the flour from her hands on a *mopine* before taking the photograph from my hands.

Grandmama smiled. "This picture? That isn't you. That's your Mama, on the day she made her First Communion."

"Are you sure? It looks like me."

"That's because you have the Franconi eyes."

Years later when Grandmama learned that she was terminally ill, she asked each of her grandchildren which of her belongings they would like to have. I asked for the picture of my mother.

I study Ma's young face. There is nothing youthful about my mother's eyes, nothing innocent. They are serious and somber. I catch my reflection in the glass of the picture frame. I have the Franconi eyes.

On the thirteenth night I saw my father through my mother's eyes. We got to our post a few hours earlier than usual, about eight-thirty. Neither

Dad's car nor the yellow Ford were there. I was surprised by the look of disappointment on Ma's face. I thought she would be relieved. I was. I wanted to go home and watch *Laugh-In.* Then it hit me—Knowledge is power. Sister Paulette had told us that in class yesterday. If the cars were here, then Ma knew what was going on. The empty parking spaces had rendered her powerless.

"Drive up alongside that building," I said, pointing to the apartment cluster up the hill. "If we park along the back side we got a clear view of the lot."

I watched Ma's face as she considered my suggestion. It's one thing for a betrayed wife to want to seek the truth; and her means to that end— though questionable—are understandable. But it's another thing for a child to be witness to those means. I knew she was weighing this. I had a feeling in my gut. But Sister Paulette was right. Knowledge is power, so I decided to help Ma out. I nonchalantly untied the string and opened the pastry box. I bit into the soft, moist cruller. *Que sera, sera.*

Ma drove up the hill and parked alongside the building. I was barely through the cruller when I spotted Dad's Caddy, followed by "her" yellow Ford. As the cars moved into position side-by-side, Ma started the engine and tore down the hill. She wedged her car behind theirs, threw it into park, got out and steam-rolled over to the Ford just as the driver's door opened.

I got a glimpse of red hair as Dad bellowed, "Gloria, get back in the car!"

Gloria. The yellow Ford had a name.

"Theresa, what in hell are you're doing here? How did you find me?"

"What, you think I'm too stupid to figure out you'd move into the best?"

"Oh, right. The college graduate. You're so smart." His voice dripped sarcasm.

I shifted my focus to Gloria. All I could see in the dim glow of the streetlights was her profile. Her nose was long and straight just like her red hair, which rested below her shoulders. I saw the glowing red tip of a cigarette. I saw long, painted fingernails. I saw my mother's body obscure my sight line as she furiously pummeled the driver's window with her fists.

85

Dad was behind her in a flash. He nearly lifted Ma off the ground as he pulled her from Gloria's car. Ma was having a conniption fit as Dad kept pushing her towards our car. "Get out of here!" he said ferociously, shoving her against the hood. I wanted to get out and help her, but I was frozen. It was the first time I feared my father.

He went over to the yellow Ford, opened the driver's door, and helped Gloria from the car. He was gentle, wiping tears from her cheek as he led her into apartment 3D. It was the first time I hated my father.

We didn't go back that next night or the night after that or in the weeks that followed. Maybe seeing "her"—Gloria—was enough, I thought. Maybe now, I thought, Ma would try to make some peace with this. I thought wrong.

"Anna, get up!"

Oh, Ma, I thought, *not again, not tonight. I'm tired and it's cold outside.* "Ma," I started to complain, but the sound of banging drawers and slamming doors shut me up. I tried to block out her yelling at everyone and no one. But Ma was an opera singer—she could *PROJECT.*

"You've made a fool of me for the last time, Paulie Matteo…parading that *puttana* all over town.…" Had I not heard all this so many times before, I'd have thought Dad was here, taking her verbal scolding. With the rise in volume I knew we were headed into Act One, Scene Two, "…she's a pig.…she's a home-wrecker…well, she can have him…"

No, this was not good. And I had a feeling in my gut that it was gonna get even worse.

I quickly dressed and headed downstairs. Maybe I could talk her out of going tonight. Ma was at the closet putting on her overcoat. I opened the front door wide, giving her a full view of the wind-driven snow.

"I don't know, Ma. Doesn't look like the plows have been out yet."

She threw my parka at me. "You too? You too?" she screamed nonsensically. Me too what? I wanted to ask. But I kept quiet. Ma's anger was so intense tonight that I feared what might happen.

"I gotta go to the bathroom," I lied. "I'll be right out."

I carried my parka upstairs with me. I sat on the toilet, listening for the front door to open and close or, more likely, slam. Snow had been falling since early evening so I knew I had a few minutes while she cleaned off her car.

Slam! I heard my cue.

I ran into my bedroom and strapped on my shoulder holster. I filled the chamber with rubber pellets, tucked the Luger in place, and put on my overcoat.

Ma was furiously scraping ice and snow from the windshield, spewing resentment after resentment at having to be doing this in the middle of the night. I grabbed the brush and cleared the hood, all the while praying she would calm down a bit before we took to the icy roads.

She didn't.

One good thing about it being one o'clock in the morning, there were no other cars on the road as we skidded through the first red light.

"Why the heck don't they sand the roads?" I yelled, while in my mind I screamed, *Why the hell don't you slow down!* Maybe she read my mind, or maybe her sanity was somehow restored; whatever the reason, she did slow down. We rode in silence the rest of the way. We didn't even stop at the Broadway Diner for donuts. Oh, man, this definitely was not looking good.

I swear Ma could spot "her" yellow Ford, license plate 583 RHP—583 Red-Headed *Puttana* as I now called it—at five-hundred paces. She pulled up alongside "her" car. Gloria's car. The lights inside apartment 3-D were off. Ma turned to me; her eyes bore into mine. "Stay in the car." She spoke slowly and firmly. I nodded.

Ma got out of the car and stood next to it for several moments.

"Please change your mind. Please change your mind. Please change your mind," I prayed softly, unceasingly.

Ma stepped up to the apartment door. Her cupped hand raised as if in slow motion. Her knuckles tapped the door. *Rap-rap-rap. Rap-rap-rap.* I was surprised by how gently she was knocking. *Rap-rap-rap.* The outside light came on. I saw the window curtain move as Dad peeked out to see who was knocking on his door in the middle of the night. The outside light went out.

Ma's rapping turned into hard knocking in its evolution to full-blown banging with her fist. "Paulie, open this door! Open this door! I know your whore is in there. *Open this door!"*

The light outside 3-C came on. The door opened slowly. I unbuttoned my overcoat and placed my hand on my Luger.

"Everything all right, ma'am?" 3-C asked.

3-D's door flew open. "Mind your fuckin' business!"

3-C stepped back inside and closed the door quickly.

"I want to *talk* to her. I want to talk *to her,"* Ma said as she tried pushing past my father.

But he pushed back—roughly. Ma's feet slid out from under her. Her left arm went out in an attempt to break her fall. She landed hard on her wrist and cried out in pain.

I reached for the door handle. *Stay in the car,* her voice echoed in my head. My father and I watched as she struggled to get up. But she couldn't get her footing on the icy walkway and she fell again. She reached out her hand to him. All he offered her were his words.

"I want a divorce, Theresa," he said matter-of-factly.

Ma crumpled back on the ground. Her fingers tore through her hair. "No....I won't....you can't...." she sobbed mournfully, her chest heaving with each deep, guttural wail.

The door to 3-D slammed shut.

The light outside 3-C went out.

I got out of the car and ran to my mother. She was clutching her wrist to her chest. "I think it's broken," she said.

"Let me take a look, Ma." She held her wrist with her right hand. It had swelled to twice its size and was more black and blue than flesh colored.

"You son of a bitch!" I jumped up and pulled the Luger from its holster and fired at his apartment. "I hate you! I hate you!" I screamed with every snap of the trigger until I had emptied the chamber of pellets. "I hate you!" I smashed the gun against his door.

"Anna, stop! Stop! Anna!" I don't know how long Ma had been calling to me to stop before her voice came into my consciousness. I felt prickling waves course through my body, like the tingling of a numb hand as feeling starts to return to it. My eyes wanted to explode with tears, but I refused to let them burst forth. I looked at my mother huddled on the ground, her overcoat coated thick with snow. In the dim glow of the streetlights, I saw her cheeks were stained with tears that flowed not from her broken wrist, but from her broken heart.

I searched my coat pockets for a handkerchief and dabbed the tears from her cheeks. "I hate him, Ma."

"Don't say that, Anna," her voice was surprisingly gentle. "You love your father, and that's okay. This here," she pointed towards his apartment door, "this is between us." She let go of her hold on her broken wrist and brought my head to her lips. She kissed my forehead. "Help me up now."

It was a bit of a struggle getting Ma to her feet as the walkway was thick with ice. I helped her to the car and held the door for her. She winced and moaned with every movement. "Are you sure you can drive?" She nodded. Before getting in myself, I took off my knit hat and packed it with snow. "Here, Ma," I said as I got in the car. "Keep this on your wrist until we get to the hospital."

Two weeks passed before I saw my father again. He didn't talk about that night. And he didn't mention the gun outside his door.

Four frames down is a photograph of the cousins' reunion two years ago. Sophie is to my left. Next to her is Greg, followed by Anita, Jimmy, Frankie, Patsy, Marco, and Angela. To my right is Edie, followed by Maria, Patrick, Sonny, little Tony, and girl-Toni. We all hadn't been together in more than a decade. It was a fun night, filled with remember whens, laughter, and more laughter.

Soph, look at the relationships I've had. With very few exceptions I've fallen for liars, cheaters, and drunks.

Edie. My years of paternal surveillance came in handy. At first I chose to believe her lies about my suspicions. "You just don't trust me," she'd say. And I'd feel guilty because it was true. I was not a trusting person. So I gave her every benefit of every doubt. But I had a feeling in my gut. And the more I tried to push it away, the stronger the feeling got.

"I'm going for a drive. Maybe head to Quabbin and hike for awhile," Edie spoke to me through the closed bathroom door.

"Wait a sec. I'm almost done." Less than a minute later I opened the door. "Want me to come with you?" I asked as I washed my hands.

"Nah. I just want to be alone for awhile. Sit under a tree, read a book."

At first I didn't think too much about the lunch she packed to take along, or the blanket, or the mini-cooler. But an hour later when I went to get a bottle of Pellegrino from the refrigerator, I noticed the six-pack of beer was gone. And I got a feeling in my gut. I tried to dismiss it. I turned on the television. Flipped through dozens of channels. Turned off the television. I set up my laptop. Tried to write. Shutdown my laptop. Couldn't write. Couldn't write because I could not shut out the images in my head. Edie's constant checking of her cell phone to see if anyone had called; the way their eyes locked and lingered last week when we all went out to dinner; the whispered comments to one another when they thought no one was looking.

I got in the car. Turned it on. Turned it off. I sat for several moments trying to talk myself out of it. But I couldn't. Knowledge is power.

As I headed down Route 9 towards Quabbin Reservoir I had another feeling in my gut. I hooked a U-turn and picked up Route 19 heading south. Thirty minutes later I was at Bigelow Hollow in Connecticut. I drove into the park and down to the lake. It was a favorite spot of ours. I saw Edie's blue Honda and "her" white Volkswagen parked side-by-side.

I take the reunion picture down from the wall and put it in my briefcase. Tomorrow I'll have Walt Ashton, the local photographer, digitally remove her image. "C'mon, Jazz, let's go to bed."

Chapter Six

A hundred bonfires blaze just above the surface of the three rivers that course through downtown Providence. The cobblestone and brick walkways that weave along the water's edge are bustling with tourists and residents who come each night to witness the WaterFire. I fall into step on the cobblestone path illuminated by the string of fire, my gait ebbs and flows to the melodies resounding in counterpoint with the sounds of urban life. Black-clad figures in gondolas float quietly by tending to the crackling flames flickering firelight on the Venetian-style, arched footbridges. The fragrant scent of burning cedar and pine fills the night air.

I look up at the statue of the Independent Man atop the State House, a bronze sentry of the ideals upon which the city was founded. In the distance is Lady Justice, perched atop the State Supreme Court building— blindfolded, fair-minded, impartial.

At first, I don't make much of the cloud descending from the sky towards the courthouse. But then I notice it begin to swirl, faster and faster until it funnels, changing in color from white to brown to dark gray. Electricity sprays from the funnel cloud and the sparks ignite the courthouse below. Within moments, Lady Justice is shrouded in flames.

"Help! Fire!" I scream. But the once humming riverwalk is empty, except for a lone figure leaning over the footbridge railing peering into the water below. She is holding onto a rope and my thoughts are momentarily distracted from the fire as I wonder why she is fishing in the fiery river?

"Help me, please," I call out, running to her. I begin to cough and choke. My eyes burn and tear as the air, once filled with the sweet scent of cedar, has become putrid and sulfuric in odor.

The figure, a woman of Asian descent, is pulling hand over hand on a thick rope. A fishing net emerges from the river below. She grasps it gingerly and, crouching, places it carefully on the bridge. She unfolds the

91

netting, as if peeling an onion, revealing a Chinese vase. "Ah, early Qing Dynasty. From Palace of Heavenly Purity in Forbidden City. Belong to Son of Heaven." She glances towards the Hall of Justice now enveloped in flames, where the prodigal, the avaricious, the wrathful meet along the River Styx.

"I will help you," she says. She places the vase that once belonged to the Supreme Authority, the mediator between the heavenly and earthly realms, back inside the netting and carefully lowers it into the water. She waits a moment, then raises the vase from the depths once again, lowers it onto the footbridge and removes the netting.

She hands the elaborately hand-painted porcelain vase to me. I run towards the courthouse. The large vase is heavy with water and I am careful not to spill its precious contents. Lightning bolts explode from the black funnel cloud igniting everything in my path. The ground shakes from the voltage coursing through it and I stumble forward, struggling to regain my footing without dropping and shattering this witness to antiquity.

I reach the front steps of the State Supreme Court, but they don't extend far enough to reach Justice's perch. I run around the building looking for another set of stairs, but there is no other way to reach her. I run back to the front of the building and begin my ascent. As I climb the steps, they begin to build upon themselves, extending beyond the entranceway, upwards farther and farther.

The acrid air and thick black smoke fill my lungs, making it nearly impossible to climb the hundreds of steps before me.

Panting and wet with sweat, I reach Lady Justice. And with my last ounce of strength, douse her with the water from the vase. As it splashes onto the scales of justice she holds in her hand, the clear water changes into a blood-red, viscous liquid. It drips from the scales and onto my face.

Chapter Seven

Up! Up! Time to write! Write for you! Amy Tan's words release me from my dreams and I am grateful to be awakened. I reach for the pad and pen on my nightstand and try to recall the images that had filled my dreams. Lady Justice. Fire. Blood. But as quickly as they had entered my dreams, they vanished from my waking mind.

Time to write! Write for you!

"All right, already!" I say as I roll reluctantly out of bed. I try to rouse Jazz curled peacefully at the edge of the bed. She opens one eye, telepathically transmits, "You gotta be kidding!" and falls back to sleep immediately, as only a dog can do.

As I shuffle towards the kitchen, the recollection that Sophie had given me Starbucks' new Komodo Dragon blend kick-starts my gears. Ah! A new coffee blend! Ever since that first cup of espresso on my tenth birthday, I had been hooked. As the bag opens for the first time, the vacuum seal releases the ambrosial roasted bean into my olfactory center. Mmm! Do I detect a slight hint of nut? My palate can distinguish coffee blends like a wine connoisseur can discern a pinot grape from a syrah. I grind the beans to a fine grain, fill the coffeemaker to the eight mark, and carefully spoon eight rounded teaspoons of Asian-Pacific gold into the filter, plug it in, and flip the switch. Within moments the murmur of heating water slowly crescendos into a resolute chant. The transformation begins—water into wine.

I unwrap the tissue paper protecting the mug Sophie bought me. Its simple message makes me smile: I Write, Therefore I Am. Sophie must have been talking to Amy Tan. I rinse out the mug, dry it with the *mopine,* and put it in the cupboard along with the other sixty-seven mugs I own. I grab my *Sex and the City* cappuccino cup and fill the Thermos with hot water to warm it before I transfer the coffee. As I head to the dining room to boot up my iBook, the ringing telephone startles me.

"Who the hell is calling this early?"

I check the caller I.D.—Private. It must be Sophia. I let the phone ring two more times as I try to slow down my rapidly beating heart. A call this early is never good news. "Please, God, don't let it be about Aunt Jeannie."

"Sophie? What happened? What's the matter?"

"Whatever happened to 'Hello' or 'Good morning, Sophie?'" Her smart-ass tone calms me immediately.

"It's five-forty in the morning, Soph. No call this early is ever good news."

"Unless, of course, it's from you favorite cousin. Hey," she says in her rapid-fire delivery, "I didn't wake you, did I?"

"No, I'm up and making coffee. So slow down; I haven't had any yet."

"The Komodo Dragon?"

"Absolutely! God! It smells incredible! I can't wait to taste it!"

"You're going to love it!" Sophie is the only person I know who shares my love of coffee. "But what's up with the new packaging? It's hideous! What were they thinking?"

Sophia was right. Starbucks' new bags were absolutely awful. White, bland, tasteless. The old bag design—the cocoa-colored background, the forest green, copper, and sky blue—superbly illustrated the environment that had nourished the beans inside.

"Obviously, they weren't. Gotta be a new marketing director onboard. It always happens that way. A new decision-maker enters the picture and the first thing he does is make a very visible change. Something that screams: Take notice! I'm in charge now!"

Sophie laughs. "You're right! And that fool hired a product designer who most likely pours tap water over instant coffee crystals, for all he knows about coffee!"

Our laughter soon turns to a thick silence that hovers over us longer than the time it takes to brew a cappuccino. I clear my throat. "Something tells me, Cousin, that you didn't call me at oh-dark-hundred to diss Starbucks. What's on your mind?"

"Anna, I couldn't sleep all night thinking about our conversation," Sophie says uncharacteristically slow. "You know I trust your judgment, but I'm worried about you reading those trial transcripts. Some of the…the stuff, the details…are going to be disturbing. I mean really, Anna, after all these years, why open that wound?"

"Because the wound never closed, Sophia. And now something deep inside me is picking it raw, and I don't know what that 'something' is."

"I guess I'm worried that it will become so raw it will fester. Are you really, really sure you want to do this?"

Dear, dear Cousin Sophia. How I wished I could reach through the phone lines and wrap my arms around her. "Yeah. I'm really, really sure, Sophie. I need to heal that open wound once and for all. Maybe learning the truth is the salve I need."

"Okay, then. I'll do…we'll do, Greg and I, whatever we can to help."

"Thank you, Soph." A moment of understanding silence passes between us. "So," I break the silence, yet add a deliberate pause, "you ready to tell me which aging newscaster's ass you're working to save?"

"Nope. So quit asking!"

"Oh, all right! But one day you're gonna slip, and I'm gonna be ready with pen and paper in hand to catch all the dirt!"

Minutes later I am lost in the rapture of the Komodo Dragon. And since a fine coffee should be savored, I wrap a shawl around my shoulders and head out onto the porch rather than to my computer. The crisp autumn air is refreshing. I inhale deeply, hoping it will clear the congestion welling in my sinuses.

The cool morning air mixed with the rising steam from my coffee mug work their magic and my nose begins to drip. I go inside for a tissue. Finding the bathroom tissue box empty, I head down the hallway to the dining room where a nearly full tissue box rests on the table next to my Muse. I grab a handful. Amy's eyes snag mine. *Time to write.*

"Oh, all right."

I gather the printed copy of the pages I wrote yesterday, along with a yellow legal pad and pencil. Back on the porch I read over the previous day's writing. I hear the words in my head, but they are merely sounds

95

devoid of meaning. I reread the text. Nothing. The words are not making any sense.

"Where the hell was I going with this?"

I read the pages yet again, and still I've no clue as to what I was thinking or where I was heading in the storyline yesterday. "Maybe it's just bad writing," I tell myself. Maybe. But I don't think that's it. I think I am, once again, just not into writing this seven-year-old albatross.

Time to write. Write for you.

"You know, Amy, sometimes you really annoy me."

I pick up the legal pad and pencil. Okay. What's the crux of the story? Generational family secrets. I print the words 'family secrets' at the top of the page. Now, what are family secrets?

I unconsciously tap the pad rhythmically with the pencil's eraser end and the sound reminds me of my mother, tap, tap, tapping the piano's edge with a yellow number two pencil, keeping a metronomic beat for her young students struggling through Dozen-A-Day piano exercises.

"Okay, Anna, focus," I tell myself.

Family secrets. Family secrets are skeletons in the closet, are 'ills that flesh are heir to.' I write this down. Secrets are hurtful. Secrets cause harm. Secrets wound. I add this to the page.

I need to heal that open wound once and for all. Maybe learning the truth is the salve I need. Salve. I write that down and continue the word association. A salve is an ointment. An ointment, a balm. A balm is an oil…an oil, an unction. An unction is an anointing. An anointing, a laying on of hands. A laying on of hands is a blessing. A blessing, a sanctification. To sanctify is to purify, to free from sin. Salve. Salvation.

I'll pray for your father, Anna, but he needs to repent first. Father Riccardi's voice enters my thoughts. To be saved, one must first atone, I write. Atonement…redemption… deliverance… liberation.

Are you really, really sure you want to do this?

Yeah. I'm really, really sure. For the truth shall set me free, I write.

I go inside, refill my cup and settle at my computer. "Let's try it again," I say to Mac. I scan the hard drive and locate *Newmanuscript.doc*. Click. I scroll down to where I left off.

Being a girl in a third generation Portuguese family comes without its entitlements. I'm not entitled to the boat, not entitled to the sea, not entitled to breaking my back from dawn to dusk rigging masts, yards, and sails, lifting and hauling traps while the sun and the wind brown and leather my skin.

Instead I have to work in town, serving the fish my father and brothers catch to *them*—pretty boys with matching accessories, 6'3" Diana Ross wannabes in sequined gowns. And to those tourist couples from the "I" states: Iowa, Indiana, Idaho—the men in Bermuda shorts with sandals and black socks reaching not quite up their pasty white calves, and their fat-assed wives who wear polyester shorts with "Ask me about my grandchildren" T-shirts, with their big hairdos, dry and thinning from bleach and dye and over-teasing.

I stare at the cursor. Blink. Blink. Blink. Its hypnotic pulse draws me into the page. I place my fingertips on the keyboard. Blink. Blink. Blink. No words come into my head. Blink. Blink. Blink. Nothing flows through to my fingers. Blink. Blink. Blink. I've entered a void. V-O-I-D. I type. N-O-T-H-I-N-G....N-I-L....N-A-U-G-H-T. "Why is this story such a struggle?" I shout in frustration.

Write for you.

I look at Amy smiling at me from the book's jacket. "You know, Amy? I've had just about enough of you. I've had enough of your nagging, and I've had enough of this stupid story. I'm done. Done with both of you."

I close the file and drag it to the trash, then shut down my laptop, pack it away in its titanium carrying case, and stick it in the closet in my office. I gather my talismans from the dining room table. The dictionary and thesaurus go back on the desk in my office and Amy Tan goes back on the bookshelf.

No! No! Write! Write for you! Write for you! She repeats over and over and over.

"No!" I scream back. I grab her from the bookshelf and stare at her

97

smug, smiling face.

"That's right, smug!" I yell at her. "Just because you're able to spin your family history into spellbinding fiction doesn't mean I can. I've nothing to write, Amy, nothing to say. Nothing. Nil. Naught."

I open the bottom drawer of my desk, toss her in and pile an unopened ten-pack of yellow legal tablets on top of her before slamming the drawer shut.

Write for you! Write for you! Her muffled voice cries out to me as I leave the room in a huff.

Chapter Eight

Days pass into weeks without a word from Sophie, or Amy. Thank God for the latter. I'm able to feel like a total failure well enough without Amy's help, thank you very much. But why hadn't Sophie called? Did Greg have a change of heart? Was it too much to ask of him? In all the years they've been married, he and I exchanged maybe a hundred words, and the bulk of that being, 'Hi, Greg, It's Anna. Is Sophia home?' And now I'm asking him to share information that shows my father was a gangster and that he, the brilliant attorney, got his murdering client acquitted. And maybe Sophie doesn't know how to tell me that he's had second thoughts.

I pick up the phone and start dialing her number. Midway through, I hang up. I'll send an e-mail instead. I click on AOL and type in my password. Moments later the AOL-guy informs me I have mail. I scroll through, deleting along the way unsolicited offers for Cialis, Viagra, penile performance enhancers, and the myriad other offers that in no way relate to me. I stop midway through and have a chuckle. Sophia.

> *Hi Anna,*
>   *Sorry it's been so long, but Greg's secretary has been combing the office for the files. She thinks they got rid of them during the last move. But Greg still thinks the files are somewhere. Call Greg's office when you get this. He says he remembers a lot and he's willing to sit and talk and tell you whatever he can.*
>   *Love you!*
>   *XXX Soph*

Shit! Sit and talk? Yeah, right. "So, Greg, tell me how my father's body was found riddled with bullets on the side of the road and how your murdering son-of-a-bitch client had nothing to do with it?"

I start to dial Sophie and once again, hang up midway. Now what? I simply cannot sit and talk with him. I don't trust my emotional reaction to what I'll learn. I need privacy…seclusion…sequestration from the players involved.

I click on Reply.

> *Hey, Soph, thanks for letting me know. I need to*
> *think about Greg's offer. I'm crossing my fingers*
> *the files will turn up. I'll call you soon.*
> *XXX, Anna*

Within moments of clicking 'Send,' the telephone rings. Private.

"That was fast," I say.

"What was fast?"

"Lisa?"

"Yeah. Who did you think was calling?"

"I had just sent an e-mail to…oh, never mind! Doesn't matter. How are you?"

"Unbelievably great! Wait'll you hear! I've gone back to work, and you'll never guess where I'm working!"

"Oh, I don't know…the zoo?"

Lisa chuckles. "Close. The Providence Playhouse, two blocks from the zoo."

"You got a theater job? Oh, Lis, that's fabulous! What are you doing?"

"I'm the managing director of the children's program. Can you believe it?"

"I'm thrilled for you! And how lucky are those kids to have you! God knows how that little theater company we belonged to in Cranston saved my life."

"Saved the both of us. I don't think either of us would have survived adolescence without it. How's the writing?"

I sigh deeply as the air goes out of me. "Did you have to ask?"

"I'm sorry. In a slump?"

100

"In the dump. Literally. I actually trashed the file this time."

Silence.

"Anna, please tell me you didn't do that."

"'fraid so."

"And have you emptied the trash yet?"

I thought for a moment. "No."

"Good. Then I want you to promise me that as soon as we hang up you'll grab that file from the trash and save it."

"Lisa, please don't make me promise. It belongs in the trash. It's crap." I indulge in a little self-pity bordering on self-loathing.

"First of all, Anna, you are incapable of writing crap. Maybe parts of it aren't working and need to be changed. But aren't you the one who coined the phrase: The best part of writing is the rewriting? And second of all, that story has been hanging around for a reason. You just haven't figured out the why of it yet. Now, I'm asking you to please promise me you will retrieve that file." The last five words are enunciated in that firm, do-as-I-say staccato beat women seem to acquire shortly after childbirth.

Shit. I hate it when she's right. "I promise," I pledge with resignation.

"Good. Now what else is up? I know there's something you haven't told me."

"You think you know me, huh?"

"Sometimes better than you know yourself, my friend."

It was true. Lisa had a better sense of my core being than I did. Sometimes she knew what I was thinking before the synapses in my brain relayed the message to me. I tell her the whole story—from my on-line discovery, to my dinner with Sophie, right up to the e-mail I just sent. "I just can't see myself sitting and talking with Greg about this. I need to read those transcripts on my own."

"My God, Anna, it's no wonder you've been on my mind!" She pauses. "Okay," Her intonation—Oh-kaay—and the pause that follows, makes me wary of what's coming.

"So…" she says. Here it comes. "Let's say you get those transcripts and you read them. Then what?"

"What do you mean?"

101

"Once you find all this out, then what are you going to do? It's a helluva story."

"It's a helluva story? Lisa, it's my life!"

"I know that, Anna, but I know you. You can't hold this in. It's your nature to work things out through your writing."

It's my nature? Sure, it's true that writers write about what they know—their friends, their observations and speculations about strangers, their families. "Committed gossips," Jane Smiley calls us. She wrote, too, that story is life reworked by thought. The operative word being reworked. Enhanced. Transformed.

"I can see it now, Lisa. Like my last novel didn't get me into enough deep shit with my family. Can you imagine what exploring and exposing these secrets will do? I can't even finish that other novel. And the family secrets in that story are nothing compared to my own."

"Then maybe it's time you explore your story. Even if you just write it for you. You've carried your childhood and your father's death like a millstone around your neck long enough."

"What are you saying?"

"I'm saying you've got issues. And maybe delving into your family story will help resolve them."

Even though I knew she was right, I could feel my blood boil, and not metaphorically. "Not everyone had the perfect family life, Lisa." I regretted my words the millisecond they came flying out of my mouth. "I'm sorry, Lisa. I didn't mean to say that. I love your folks, you know I do."

"I know."

"It's just I've been overwhelmed by childhood memories these past few weeks. In some ways, I thought of my father as this fabled figure. Even after he was murdered, after those blaring headlines—Gangland-Style Murder of Matteo, Mob Connection in Matteo Slaying—I still didn't completely think of him as that kind of man. Then, I read those articles on-line connecting him with mob enforcers and arsonists, and suddenly it's like I never knew the man. But the truth is, I did know that man.

"And I knew the men mentioned in those articles, too. He'd bring me around to those men and they'd give me money and presents. And in

102

bringing me to those men he put me in harm's way. So as a kid I'm dealing with it by carrying a rubber pellet gun, and smoke bombs in my vest, and changing the color of my bike every week to throw off these imaginary villains who, I see now, weren't imaginary at all.

"I've been flooded with feelings of anger and hurt and guilt." Tears begin flowing down my face. "I feel so guilty, that for the longest time I never took my mother's side when he was being so horrible to her." The words choke out through uncontrollable sobbing.

"Oh, Anna, Anna…Ssh…Ssh…It's okay…" Lisa tries desperately to soothe me, to break through the physical distance between us. "Sweetie, why don't you come stay with us for a few days? We can stay up late after Katie and Matt go to bed, and drink tea and eat cinnamon-raisin toast, and talk and cry together."

I breathe in deeply through my nostrils trying, unsuccessfully, to stop my nose from dripping onto my upper lip. "Hang on. I need a tissue." Three tissues later I'm back on the phone. "I'm really sorry. Lisa. I didn't mean what I said about your family."

"Not another word, Matteo. You hear me?"

"I hear you, Paradides." A quick, short burst of laughter breaks through my disconsolation as the tension begins to subside and my blood flows calmly again. "Maybe I will come for a few days. Let me think about it."

"Okay. I'm going to call you later. I have to pick up Katie from field hockey practice, but I'll be back home in a few hours. We'll talk then, okay?"

"Okay. Thanks, Lisa, I love you."

"I love you too, sweetie."

As I grab another tissue from the box on my desk my eye catches the Two Months-at-a-Glance erasable calendar that hangs in my office. Oh shit! Lunch with Rose, 12:30. I glance at my watch: 11:52. Shit! If I skip a shower, I can maybe make it on time. I sprint to the bathroom. A sponge bath will have to do.

Eighteen minutes later I'm out the door and headed for the Salem Cross Inn. Rose is already seated in the tavern. "You look tired," is her greeting.

"Why thank you. You look pretty beat yourself," I return the compliment.

"This conference is exhausting. I was glad for the break today. You can digest only so much chicken and shoptalk before you feel like screaming, 'Could I just have a Big Mac and some banal conversation, please?'"

"Well, my friend, we could head down the road for a Big Mac if you'd like, and I'll do my best to restrict my conversation to dull, trite, and hackneyed statements."

Rose has a great laugh. It wells up from deep within and hovers in the air like a hummingbird. "How's the novel coming?"

"It's not." I grunt. And before she has a chance to chastise me I launch into the events that have occupied my mind for the past three weeks. When I finish my diatribe, Rose is staring at me in stunned silence. "Sorry, Rose. Not the dull, trite conversation you had in mind, eh?" My attempt to lighten the air fails dismally.

"Anna, I had no idea your father was murdered. You've never said a word."

"Well, it's not exactly icebreaker conversation."

"I think you're right about reading the transcripts first before you talk with…Greg, is it? It will give you distance and perspective."

"I know. But what if the files are gone? Pandora's box is open."

Rose nods in agreement. Maybe it's because she, too, is a writer. She understands there is no turning back. "You know, you could always get the trial transcripts from the court."

I fall back in my chair. Why didn't I think of that before?

"Rose, you're a Godsend. Just for that, I'm buying lunch."

"You were buying lunch anyway. It's your turn."

"Right!" I snap my fingers. "Damn! I knew we should have gone to MacDonalds!"

Immediately upon returning home I phone the Providence County Clerk's Office and inquire as to how to request a set of trial transcripts. The clerk, Ann Shapiro, is extremely helpful. "Send a letter detailing as much information as possible. The dates of the trials, the defendant's name and address, and any other information that may help us locate the indictment."

The dates? Shit! I don't know the trial dates. I suppose I could call

Greg and ask him. Or I could do my usual avoidance and call Sophia and ask her to ask him. Or I could be the ultimate chicken shit and send an e-mail. Impersonal. Non-confrontational.

"Non-confrontational?" I voice my thought. "Greg's been nothing but helpful and willing to talk. I'm the one with the fancy footwork. 'I float like a butterfly, I sting like a bee.' I'm Cassius Clay; I'm Muhammed Ali." If anyone had to fear confrontation, it should be Greg. I pick up the telephone. "It's time to stop dancing, Matteo."

Sophia answers on the third ring. I tell her about Rose's suggestion that I request the transcripts directly from the court. "But, I don't know the dates of the trials. Do you think Greg would remember?"

"Let me ask him. He's home."

As I wait, I am aware that my hands are ice-cold—a physical reaction I have whenever I am anxious. I cradle the phone between my shoulder and jaw so I can rub my hands together vigorously.

"Hi, Anna, Sophia said you needed some information."

My body temperature plummets and I begin to shiver. "Yeah, hi Greg. I want to request copies of the trial transcripts from the court. The clerk said I needed the trial dates. I was wondering if you remember them?"

"Well, as I recall, the first trial was in November of '78. And the acquittal trial was a year later, late November into early December. As for the exact dates, I'm not sure. But that should be enough information."

"Thank you, Greg."

"You know, Anna, getting copies of transcripts is expensive. It could run hundreds of dollars. Give me a little more time to track things down. I can't believe we don't have the files anymore."

Greg's been nothing but helpful. "That's okay, Greg."

"Debbie, my assistant, says they threw out all the old cases when I moved the office last year. And I never represented Capraro after the acquittal. But I can't believe we don't have something I can legally show you."

"Really, Greg. It's okay." *Can't you hear I'm letting you off the hook?* I want to scream at him.

"Anna, even if everything is gone, we can talk about it. I've got a pretty

105

good memory."

"I'm sure you do, Greg, and I appreciate your help. I really do. But I think I'm still going to try and get the transcripts." I am shaking so hard the telephone almost slips from my hand.

"And I'll have Debbie keep looking, too. Whatever I can do, Anna, let me know."

"Thank you, Greg." I can barely get the words out.

"Shall I put Sophia back on?"

"No, that's okay. I'll call her later." My entire body is quivering and I struggle to get the receiver back on the hook.

"Breathe, Anna. Breathe." I tell myself.

Sitting at my desk I attempt to type the request, but I've little control over my icy, shaking hands. My fingertips, their nail beds now a bluish-purple hue, glide jerkily across the mousepad to click on the new document icon. Document 1 fills the screen like a white, blank canvas. I bury my hands in my armpits to extract some warmth into them. A deep, chattering yawn wracks through my body, a familiar and welcome sign that my system is working to right itself. Huddled in my office chair, I yawn repeatedly over the next several minutes and with each releasing breath, my temperature begins to rise as oxygen flows through my bloodstream. My fingernails are back to their natural pinkish hue. I rub my hands together and begin to type.

Chapter Nine

From my office window I see the mail carrier's car moving slowly down the road towards my neighbor's house. I hear the letterbox door creak open and slam shut a moment later. I slip on a pair of shoes as the car pulls up to my roadside delivery box. I head outside and walk the gravel driveway to retrieve the mail. "Thank you," I call to Jeff, my mail carrier. He waves his hand before coasting down to the next house.

On top of the pile of mail are two dog biscuits for Jazz. Amidst the collection of bills and requests for charitable contributions is an envelope from the Providence County Clerk's Office. I move the envelope to the top of the stack. My heart pounds as I hurry into the house.

Jazz is waiting at the door for the treats she is sure Jeff has left for her. I give them to her, one at a time, as I deposit all but the clerk's letter on the countertop. My suddenly ice-cold hands cautiously open the envelope, as if Capraro himself might pop out.

> Re: People vs Angelo Capraro
> Index 77-4927, Indictment 77-274-9
>
> Dear Ms. Matteo:
> In response to your inquiry of November 2th, I find one set of trial transcripts. The trial dates are February 14th, 15th and 19th, 1979. Please note the charge on this case appears to be arson. I do not know if this is the case you are interested in obtaining. The defense attorney for this case was Gregory Haynes.

Arson? I specifically said they were murder indictments. February 1979? I listed the trials dates as November 1978 and 1979. Shit! The letter goes on to detail the costs of obtaining the records. I call the clerk's office and ask to speak with M. Perry, the signatory on the letter. I'm immediately transferred to Marie Perry's office. I explain my confusion about the arson transcripts. "I was looking specifically for the two murder indictments."

"And he was found guilty?"

"No. The first trial ended with a hung jury. The 1979 jury acquitted him of all charges."

"Well, that explains it. If a defendant is not found guilty, the trial transcripts are sealed."

The air went out of me like a hot air balloon that had returned to earth. "There's no way I can access these records? Aren't they public information?"

"Only if the party is found guilty. Are you interested in obtaining the arson transcripts?"

"No, thank you, Marie. I wanted the other cases. Thank you, though, for your time and help."

Damn it. I call Sophia and relay the news. "I'm so frustrated!"

"Then come and talk with Greg. Really, Anna, he has an incredible memory. He can tell you what you want to know."

"I can't." *And don't push me.*

"Why are you being so resistant? Greg wants to do this. He wants to talk with you."

"I'm sure he does, but I just can't, Sophie." I fight to keep my voice even.

But Sophie won't give up. "Why?"

"Because I know me," I say emphatically. "I'll have a breakdown right in front of him. I know he's your husband, Sophie, but in my mind, Greg Haynes is the lawyer who got that fuck who killed my father off. It was his client who gunned down my father and left him to die in the road like an animal. How am I supposed to talk with him about that? How am I supposed to ask him what evidence came out at the trial? And how was he able to so brilliantly squash it? What loopholes in our criminal's-rights-system-of-justice was he able to leap through to make his case?" My body begins to shake as my diatribe continues: "Everyone knows Capraro did it.

And he got away with murder because he had a great lawyer who knows how to work a fucked-up legal system that doesn't gives a shit about victim's rights. The justice system is a game of chess and Greg's the Grand Master." Sobs wrack through me. "I can't talk to him about this, Sophie. Not now."

Sophia voice is soft. "I understand, Anna. You don't have to say another word. We'll find another way." She pauses a moment. "You know, Pat O'Connell's a good friend of ours. He was one of the prosecutors. We're going to see him this weekend. Actually, he's going to be at our house for a party Friday night. I'll talk to him. I bet he would be willing to talk with you. He might even still have files."

Sophie is true to her word. That Monday I have an e-mail from her.

> *Anna...I spoke with Pat. He'll see what he's got. I'm on my way*
> *out of town. I'll call you when I get back.*
> > *Love you! Sophie*

There is also an e-mail from Rose.

> *I've been thinking about you. Call me and let me know if you were*
> *able to get the information you wanted. — R*

I call Rose and bring her up to speed.

"I wonder if the newspaper has an archive department with back editions that aren't on the Web?" Rose says. "If so, you could research the stories filed during the trial. From what you've said it sounds like it was a high-profile case. I bet they covered it in detail. You may learn a lot from the newspaper about what went on in court."

"Rose, remind me to kiss you next time I see you!"

I hang up with Rose and immediately call *The Providence Journal*. "What we have archived is available on projo.com. Those records go back to 1983," says the editorial assistant.

"I know. What I'm researching goes back to the mid-to-late Seventies. Do you have a research archive?"

109

"Not really, but you may want to give the Providence Public Library a call. They most likely won't have the actual newspapers, but they might have microfilm. Hold on a moment, I'll get you the phone number for their research department."

I call the library next. "Yes, back editions are on microfilm," I am told.

Ralph Waldo Emerson wrote, "Once you make a decision, the universe conspires to make it happen." A cosmic ball had been set in motion. Maybe I was meant to read the news coverage of the trials before I read the actual files. Maybe those news accounts will prepare me for the sordid details. Like Rose said, with knowledge comes perspective. And if it turns out the files are gone and I have to talk with Greg, I'll be able to handle it. And maybe then Greg and I can have that heart-to-heart I've been avoiding for twenty years. The universe did its part, and now I had to do mine. I call Sophia to arrange my trip to the Providence Public Library around her schedule.

"SAF Media Group. May I help you?"

"Hello Michelle, it's Anna. Is Sophie available?"

"No, Anna, I'm sorry. She and Greg left for Belize this morning."

"Belize? She mentioned she was going out of town, but Belize? And they didn't take you and me with them?"

Michelle's laugh is like her voice—low, husky, sexy. She could make a fortune with one of those 1-900 phone lines.

"When is she expected back?"

"Not until after Thanksgiving."

"After Thanksgiving? That's like ten days from now!"

"Would you like to leave a message? She does call in every day."

I think for a moment. "Yeah, Michelle, I would. Tell Sophia I decided to accept her Thanksgiving dinner invitation and I want to know what I can bring."

"But she's not due back until after Thanksgiving," Michelle spoke steadily, as if I hadn't understood.

"I know. She really didn't invite me, but for a couple of minutes she'll worry that she did, and she'll feel awful for running off to Bay-leeeeze without me!"

Michelle laughs and wishes me a happy holiday.

Now what? I really don't want to wait until Sophia is back to research those articles. I check my calendar. Wednesday is clear. Grabbing a blue marker, I draw a star—my code for personal day—in the box for Wednesday, November 17. I pick up the phone again and leave a message for Lisa, telling her I am planning to come on Wednesday and that I would like to stay at her house for a day or two.

I pour a glass of Chianti and sit in my wicker rocker on the porch. Lisa....A daughter at field hockey practice, a husband who comes home every night. Even in adulthood, my life is so very different from her's. As a child, I never realized just how very different family life was in the Matteo house—until I had dinner with the Paradides.

W̲e were hanging out on Lisa's front porch enjoying an after school snack of tea and cinnamon-raisin toast when her mother pulled into the driveway. She called to us as she emerged from "the boat," our nickname for their green 1968 Ford Country Squire station wagon. "Girls, come give me a hand, would you?" The back of the boat was piled high with brown grocery bags. Lisa and I carried the brimming bags into the house depositing them on the kitchen table, counter, chairs—wherever there was space.

"What's with all the food?" I whispered to Lisa. "You guys having a party?"

Lisa shrugged her shoulders, as if to say, 'Whattaya mean?' "My mom likes to shop for the whole week," she added nonplussed.

This was one week's worth of groceries? There had to be at least a dozen bags here. Sure, now that Anthony was married and it was just Ma and me at home, there was less food to buy. But even when Anthony was home, I rarely remember more than four, maybe five bags of groceries each week.

Mrs. Paradides unpacked and stored the contents of each bag with precision. Every item had its place in her full cupboards. I helped fold the empty brown bags, which Lisa then gathered and stowed in the utility closet off the kitchen.

"Anna, would you like to stay and have dinner with us tonight?" Mrs. Paradides asked.

I froze. I'd never eaten dinner at anyone's home before, other than the occasional Sunday dinner at Grandmama's. But that was family. And although I'd been to the Paradides' home dozens of times, I never felt the ease and comfort Lisa did when she was at my house. I felt more like the proverbial stranger in a strange land.

The other dilemma was that Mom and I always ate dinner together after she was finished teaching. If I had dinner here now, what would I do about dinner with Ma later?

"Lisa," Mrs. Paradides called to her daughter, "I asked your shy friend here to stay and have dinner with us. But she doesn't say anything. Maybe you should ask her, too?"

"C'mon, Anna, stay," Lisa begged as she entered the kitchen. "We can get our anthropology homework done before dinner. And you can hear my new Jethro Tull album!"

Hmm! Jethro Tull certainly was a selling point.

"You like Greek food?" Mrs. Paradides asked. "I made Spanokopita."

Spano-what did she call it? I shrugged. "I don't think I've ever had it before."

"You like spinach? Cheese?" I nodded. "Then you'll like Spanokopita. A Greek spinach and cheese pie. But instead of piecrust we use phyllo, which makes it very light and flaky."

"Really, Anna. My mom makes the best!" Lisa boasted.

"So, tonight you try it," Mrs. Paradides insisted. "Go and call your mother. Ask if it's okay that you stay for dinner."

Greek food would be different. And hanging more with Lisa would be great, too. Oh, what the heck. I just won't tell Ma I already ate dinner. "Okay, thank you, I will stay. But," I had to think fast, "I don't have to call my mom, Mrs. Paradides. She knows I'm here"—which was a lie—"and besides, she's teaching. And she really hates being interrupted when she's giving lessons"—which was the truth.

PAINTING THE INVISIBLE MAN

Lisa and I went up to her bedroom. It was so elegant, so grown-up. Her double bed had an antique brass headboard and footboard that once belonged to her grandparents. Her bureau was solid oak; also an antique. And then there was the rocking chair in which her mother, her mother's mother, and her great-grandmother gently nestled and suckled their babies.

I still had the frilly, white furniture set Ma bought when I was nine years old. My walls were covered with posters—Peter Fonda from *Easy Rider*, Omar Sharif who I wanted to marry some day, and a psychedelic peace sign—as well as umpteen pullout pages from *Teen Beat* magazine.

"Look!" Lisa said excitedly as she pointed to the back of the door. "It came with the album!" Lisa closed the door and revealed the only clue that this was indeed the room of a teenage girl. I studied Ian Anderson's face—the way his hair flowed down his shoulders, the soft-looking texture of his beard, his creamy long and tapered fingers caressing his flute.

"He's got gorgeous hands," I said.

"He's got gorgeous *everything*," Lisa gushed.

We plopped on her bed and whizzed through the chapter on aborigines and answered the four questions at the end. We were grooving to *Thick as a Brick* when her mother called up to us. "Lisa, your father's home. You and Anna come downstairs now."

I loved Lisa's dad. Although Mr. Paradides was a corporate lawyer, in his soul he was an actor and a poet. His rich, baritone voice was strong and bold, yet melodious and gentle at the same time. As Lisa and I descended the stairs he opened his arms like a king welcoming his gentry. "Ah! Two of the fairest stars in all the heaven!" I couldn't help but giggle, I so adored him, my Romeo.

The coffee table in the living room was set with a plate of cheese and crackers dotted with black and green olives. Mrs. Paradides, wearing a floral bib apron, carried a tray holding a pitcher of ice tea and two glasses, plus two mixed drinks—which I later learned were Manhattans—one for her, and one for him. Mr. Paradides sat in one of two winged-back chairs that flanked the fieldstone fireplace.

113

"Thank you, my dear," he said as Mrs. Paradides handed him his drink.

Lisa poured us each a glass of her mother's fresh-brewed iced tea. "Thank you, my friend," I mimicked him as Lisa handed me the glass of aromatic tea with hints of lemon and mint.

Lisa took her place on the couch. She looked at me and shook her head. "Anna, you *can* sit down," she said with amused, loving, exasperation. I joined Lisa on the couch.

"Help yourself to some hors d'oeuvres," said Mrs. Paradides. "Try the Kalamata olives, Anna. The black ones. They're imported from Greece."

"Yes, ma'am. Thank you. I will." I filled the small plate with olives, cheese and crackers and returned to my spot on the couch. I was awed and amazed by Mr. and Mrs. Paradides interaction. The way they spoke to one another; how Mrs. Paradides refilled her husband's drink; how he got up and gathered more hors d'oeuvres for the plate they shared.

"Your father's not here yet?" Ma asked as she came up from her studio. She'd been downstairs most of the afternoon practicing the music for tonight's service. "Is your brother home yet?"

I shook my head.

"He's getting more and more like his father everyday. Call Virginia's house and tell him to get home. It's almost six o'clock."

I could feel the annoyance brewing inside her because I was feeling annoyed too. They know this is a big night for Ma. Every year she composes all the music for the Christmas Eve Midnight Mass. For months she's labored over every note, and drilled her choir until they sounded like a heavenly chorus of angels. They know she likes to have dinner by six so she can rest a few hours before she has to be at church. They know she leaves at 10:30 to get everything set up for the guest musicians who join the choir for the Christmas carol portion of the service. And they know that with all Ma has to do on Christmas Eve, she still prepares the traditional Italian Christmas Eve dinner.

114

PAINTING THE INVISIBLE MAN

It was one of the few nights of the year when Ma cooked, and this one meal made up for all the ones she didn't. She made *pasta alia e olio*— vermicelli with olive oil, garlic, anchovy, and walnuts. There were three pounds of jumbo shrimp, lightly dusted with flour and sautéed in olive oil until they curled and turned pink. Sometimes Dad would bring smelts and *calamari* from Nunzio's Fish Market in Providence. And we ate this feast on "the good dishes" and with "the good silver."

"I got the water on for the pasta," I said. "And the shrimp's cleaned and ready to cook. Maybe we should start without them?" I couldn't believe the suggestion came out of my mouth. Christmas Eve dinner was the one night we were together as a family. It was tradition; our only family tradition.

"I'm off to my dressing room to shed this wretched suit," Mr. Paradides' voice snapped me back into the moment. "I shall return to dine with my lovely ladies anon."

He smiled and winked at me. I giggled again like the schoolgirl I was.

While we 'lovely ladies' were setting the dining room table for dinner, Lisa sidled up to me. "You okay, Anna? You've hardly said a word during cocktails."

I chuckled at her use of the word 'cocktails,' which was a good thing, as it covered my lie. "I'm great."

Mrs. Paradides came in with a simmering platter and placed it at the center of the table. "It sure does smell delicious," I said, trying to present a normality I did not feel.

Mr. Paradides returned as promised, free of his "wretched suit" and dressed casually in a pullover sweater and slacks. "Allow me," he said as he pulled my chair from the table and held it for me.

"Thank you, kind sir," I said, adding the Matteo nod. He did the same for his wife and his daughter.

Once our plates were filled and grace was offered, Mr. Paradides turned his attention to us. "Now, tell me girls, what happened at school today?"

Lisa spoke for the both of us, which was another good thing as I was

115

lost in thought, trying to envision this scene in my house. Not only was there no father seated at the head of the table, our dinner table was booth number four at the Broadway Diner. And I sure couldn't imagine Anthony pulling the chair out for us. More likely he'd pull the chair out and away, leaving me to fall on my ass—or arse, as Mr. Paradides most likely would pronounce it.

Dinner was followed by dessert—homemade baklava—light, flaky, gooey, and sweet. Lisa and I cleared the table as Mr. and Mrs. Paradides tended to the dishes. She washed; he dried.

We went back upstairs to Lisa's room. As soon as the door closed, I turned to her. "That was really strange."

"What was?" Lisa asked.

"That…you know, the hors d'oeuvres, the drinks, dinner in the dining room. Tell me the God's honest truth, Lisa, you guys do that every night?"

I couldn't tell if Lisa was perplexed, shocked, or embarrassed by my question. "Of course. Don't you?"

"No. Never."

"Never? You don't eat dinner with your mother?"

"I eat dinner with my mother, sure, but we usually eat at the Broadway."

"Every night?"

"Pretty much. If not the Broadway, we go to Dino's."

Lisa was truly shocked. "You're not kidding me, are you."

Now I was clearly embarrassed. "Why would I kid about that? My mother teaches until eight or eight-thirty every night. It's just easier for Mom and me to eat out."

"You don't *ever* have dinner at home?" She looked at me like I was from another planet.

I shook my head. "Lisa, I honestly cannot remember the last time we ate at home, other than like, you know, holidays…Christmas. And trust me, Christmas Eve dinner with my father and Anthony, before he got married, was never like this." And that's because it was also tradition that Dad would start a fight with Ma shortly after dinner so he could leave and be with Gloria.

Lisa put her arms around me and held me tight for several seconds. She kissed my cheek and looked into my eyes, speaking volumes without saying a single word.

Mom was just finishing teaching when I got home. "I'm famished," she said. "Ready to go eat?"

"Yeah, I'm starving," I lied.

As Mom and I sat across from each other in booth number four talking about our days, I realized our dinnertime wasn't all that different from the Paradides'. And in some ways it was better. There weren't any dishes to wash.

Chapter Ten

The night before my providential trip to Providence, I gather my photo albums to visit the ghosts of my past. Inside the album labeled 1973-75 are pictures from my freshman year of college. There are several photos of me and Nancy Purdue, my hot-shit roommate from Tyler, Texas. There's a group shot of the Dorm Dykes, a now regrettable appellation we gave ourselves, taken the night we won the right to establish the Gay Student Organization on campus. And there are pictures from Fathers' Weekend. Amidst the candid shots is a professional photograph of Dad and me. I am wearing a black, floor-length gown with lace bodice and sleeves, and Dad is dapper as ever in his custom-made blue silk suit with matching tie and pocket square. I touch his handsome face with my fingertips.

A child's relationship with a parent has a natural evolution, with stages of change and development that unfold as the child cycles through maturation. My relationship with my father flowed more like a rural stream impeded by beaver dams. When the Fathers' Weekend Planning Committee tapped me to emcee the talent show as Groucho Marx—an impersonation that started as a prank I pulled on Nick (with Lisa as Charlie Chaplin) and instantly became a part of my repertoire—I found myself in a quandary. Like most girls on campus, I was caught up in the excitement of "a wild weekend with my Daddy," as Nancy would drawl.

I met Nancy's ten-gallon-hat-and-cowboy-boot-wearin' Texas oilman daddy during orientation. My dorm-mates fathers also included a Marriott, a Kraftt, and a pharmaceutical company president. Paulie Matteo on the Smith College campus? Oh, yeah. He'd fit right in.

But, the main reason I was hesitant to ask him to come for Fathers' Weekend was that I had learned to minimize my losses.

"Daddy, I'm in a dance recital…"

"Just tell me when, baby, and I'll be there."

118

"Daddy, I'm playing Lucy in *You're a Good Man, Charlie Brown....*"

"Just tell me when, baby, and I'll be there."

"Daddy, I'm graduating next month...."

"Just tell me when, baby, and I'll be there."

But, he never was there. And so I had learned to, as Tony was fond of saying, never calculate juvenile poultry.

But Nancy, being a Southern Daddy's Little Girl, was insistent. "Just aa-sk him," she drawled. "If he doesn't show up, then you'll be my Daddy's other little girl."

"How's my baby?" Daddy asked.

I laughed. He'll be calling me his 'baby' when he's combing my gray bangs with a toothless pocket comb. "I'm great, Daddy, but," I hesitated. "I've something to ask you."

"What is it, baby? You need money?"

Money. Even if I did need it, I wouldn't ask him for it, or Ma for that matter. The only time I ever talked money with my father was when I wanted to go to college. "Just tell me how much you need, baby, and I'll write you a check," he said. And he did.

"No, Dad, I'm fine. I still have plenty of money in my account." I drew a deep breath. "The reason I'm calling, Dad, is that next month the college is having Fathers' Weekend. I was wondering if you would come. I mean, you wouldn't have to stay all weekend, maybe just come for the dinner on Saturday."

"What else is goin' on that weekend?" His question surprised me. I was expecting the "Just tell me when, baby..." response.

"Well, Friday we're having a talent show. Actually, I'm the Master of Ceremony. I'm doing my Groucho Marx." Dad loved my impression. He'd wiggle his eyebrows at me and ask me to do a bit whenever we were together. "Saturday night is a formal dinner dance. And Sunday is a brunch. So, if you want to just come on Saturday, that would be great."

"Count me in, baby, Friday and Saturday. And maybe Sunday I'll come up, too, and we'll have lunch. I hear you got some great restaurants in Northampton."

I take the picture of Dad and me out of the photo album and wedge it in the mirror's frame in my bedroom. That weekend was a new beginning for my father and me. Whatever worries I had about Paulie not fitting in were quickly dispelled. I had underestimated the Matteo charm. Mr. Purdue, my professors, even Dean Whitman fell under his spell.

On Friday night after the talent show Judy, our dormmate Linda, and their fathers joined Daddy and me at Pasquale's for espresso and dessert.

"So, Paul," Mr. Purdue said, "I hear Coppola's coming out with *The Godfather II*. What did you think of the first one?"

"Daddy!" Judy was horrified.

"What, darlin'? I'm sure Mr. Matteo here knows I meant no, like his people say, disrespect. I was merely wondering what he thought, is all. You know, being Italian."

"Mr. Matteo, please, excuse my father." Judy looked as if she were wishing the floor would open up and swallow her.

My father's face gave away nothing as to his thoughts. He was the consummate poker player. But I knew that if he started subtly twisting his pinky ring that meant his blood was boiling. He'd turn that ring as if it were a hot water shut-off, trying to get his temper under control. Dad rested his elbows on the table, his hands clasped. I watched his hands…and then, almost imperceptibly, his thumb and forefinger began turning the ring "righty-tighty."

"I liked the movie," he answered, his voice even.

"See," Mr. Purdue said to his daughter.

"May I ask you a question then, Mr. Matteo?" Linda interjected.

"Call me Paulie," Dad interrupted with a charming smile.

Linda was smitten. "Paulie. I'm taking a sociology class, Society

120

Through Film. We talked about *The Godfather*, even had a screening of it. Don't you think, though, the movie perpetuates a myth that all Italians are gangsters?"

Now I was wishing the floor would open up and swallow me.

Paulie flashed the Matteo smile. "Well, not all Italians are gangsters. Someone's gotta pay the piper." Everyone broke into tension-releasing laughter. "But, to answer your question: Like it or not, us Italians gotta accept it's part of our heritage. Men like Capone, Anastasia, and Vito—you know, Genovese—these men were proud men. They didn't come to this country lookin' for handouts. They made their own way. They were businessmen, doin' what they had to do to provide for their families. You want criminals? Look what happened last year. That Watergate thing. Erlichman, Liddy, the Attorney General there," Dad turned to me, "*Come si chiama?*"

"Mitchell," I tell him.

"Yeah, Mitchell. Even that Fibby, Gray, proved to be a crook. Place your bets, my friends, the President himself will fall before this is over."

"Fibby?" Judy whispered to me.

"FBI," I whispered back.

And had we placed those bets we would have won. Six months after my father's prediction, Nixon resigned.

Dad arrived just before noon on Saturday. True to form, he came bearing gifts—a magnum of champagne and a pocket full of mini-Reese's Peanut Butter Cups. "I thought we'd all enjoy this with dinner tonight," he said as he pulled the magnum from the backseat of his latest Cadillac.

As we walked around the campus, Dad and I talked for the first time about his service during World War II. I learned he was a glider pilot with the 101st Airborne Division, "The Screaming Eagles," he said proudly. I learned he was saved from near-certain death, having been shot down over England just days before the invasion at Normandy. He spent three months in a British hospital with a broken back, a broken arm, and multiple contusions.

He tried his best, too, to learn more about me that weekend. He asked if I smoked pot, asked if I was a virgin. "I'm not judging you," he said, adding

121

almost sheepishly, "I'm the last person to do that. I'm no angel. I just want you to be, you know, careful." I admitted to smoking some pot, but my sex life was my own business, especially since I was a card-carrying Dorm Dyke.

And since he had opened the door, I decided to push my way into his life a little further. "How come you and Ma never divorced?"

His answer was straightforward and sincere. "Because I love your mother."

And I knew he was telling the truth.

Mother Benedictus knocked on the classroom door before entering. She never said a word, simply wagged her finger for Sister Paulette to join her in the hall. Moments later, Sister Paulette came back in and pointed to me. "Anna, get your belongings and go with Mother."

As Mother Bene-doodoo and I were headed down the hallway, I saw my father standing outside her office. My stomach sank. Something's happened to Ma.

"Thank you, Sister," he said as he reached for my hand. "Anna will be back at school tomorrow."

I waited until we were out of the building. "Is Ma okay?" I was sick with worry.

"Oh, baby, she's fine. Just fine. As a matter of fact, we're gonna surprise her." He opened the car door for me. "Careful throwing your book bag in back." I looked before I tossed and saw a huge bouquet of gladiolus on the seat. Daddy smiled at the look of astonishment on my face. "They're your mother's favorite flower," he added proudly.

And then I remembered. Ma was singing at the Museum of Art's Morning Musicals in Providence today. "We're going to Mom's concert?" I could barely contain my joy.

Daddy nodded. He was beaming.

"Oh, Daddy, thank you! Thank you!" I threw my arms around his neck.

"Careful there, baby. We don't want to have an accident and miss the recital!"

Thirty minutes later Dad and I were seated in the third row of the museum concert hall. I waited somewhat patiently through a Rachmaninoff concerto and a string quartet. But the moment the program leader came onto the stage to introduce Ma, I began bouncing gently with excitement.

"We are honored to have Mrs. Theresa Matteo perform for us today. Mrs. Matteo will be singing Schubert's *Die Krähe*, followed by *Es muss ein Wunderbares sein* by Liszt, and she will end her program with Brahms' *O liebliche Wangen*. Please join me in welcoming Mrs. Theresa Matteo."

A gentle applause greeted my mother as she walked onto the stage. "Look how beautiful your mother is," Dad whispered to me. She was breathtakingly beautiful. She wore a lavender dress with a floral overlay tailor-made for her by her good friend, Mrs. Giamatti. Her lavender suede heels matched her dress perfectly. Ma nodded to Mrs. Buonpietro, her accompanist. As the opening bars filtered through the music hall, Ma stood regally beside the piano, her hands clasped just below her breasts.

It was the first time I heard my mother perform in a formal setting. Her rich contralto voice was mesmerizing as it caressed every note and phrase. Even though I couldn't understand the languages in which she sang, I was moved by the emotion in her voice. I glanced around the concert hall. Everyone was under her spell. And then I looked at my father. His face was filled with awe. Tears flowed gently down his cheeks. I took his hand in mine.

It is customary at formal concerts to hold one's applause until the end of a performer's full program. And no sooner had the last note escaped my mother's lips, the audience rose to its feet en masse, shouting "Brava! Brava!" No one clapped louder than my father.

As Ma nodded her thanks to the appreciative audience her eyes set upon us. She smiled first at me, and then her eyes locked on her Paulie. And the current that flowed between them was born of a commingling of two souls.

123

During spring break that year, Daddy invited me to join him and Gloria in Las Vegas. We flew first class—compliments of the casino, I later discovered. As we approached the registration desk at the Stardust, Dad whispered to me: "Be sure to sign your name Anna Renzi. If you want room service, just sign for it. Anna Renzi. Always Renzi, got it?"

As Anna Renzi, I had my own room, was given two hundred dollars in house chips, and just about anything else I desired. Whatever I wanted was on the house. All I had to do was sign my name: Anna Renzi. I decided to test it out. I called room service and ordered a bottle of Chianti. It was delivered within ten minutes. The tab read "house charge" so I signed, Anna Renzi, and tipped the waiter five bucks.

The next night I called room service. "This is room 409. I'd like a bottle of Tanqueray, a bottle of Kaluha, and a bottle of Stoli. Hundred-proof. Renzi. Anna Renzi." Again, the tab read "house charge." I signed it Anna Renzi, tipped the waiter ten bucks, and promptly packed the bottles in my suitcase to take back to school.

While in Vegas I spent most of those four days by the pool with Gloria. I had to admit I kind of liked her. She adored my father, tended to his every whim, and had a temperament in balance with his. I thought about how I met Gloria. About how, had I not followed a feeling in my gut that day, I would not be sitting by Caesar's pool today.

Three years ago, Dad had suffered a heart attack. It was determined he needed open-heart bypass surgery, a relatively new procedure in the early 1970s. Ma was banned from the hospital, but Tony and I were allowed to go. We settled in for the long wait the day of the operation. The surgery would take eight to ten hours. I brought my schoolwork, but couldn't concentrate.

Tony seemed particularly fidgety. He kept getting up to go get yet another cup of coffee, or to make a phone call, or to get another pack of cigarettes. Each time he'd leave he would not come back for twenty minutes or so. About three hours into his mini-disappearing act, I had a feeling in my gut. "Hey, Tone, where you been getting this coffee? I wanna get another cup. This one's kinda cold."

He jumped up. "I'll go get it for you."

"You sure? I don't mind going." Actually, having my brother wait on me was great. And I was certain it would come to an abrupt end once Dad's hospital stay was over.

"Nope, I'll go. You want a Danish or somethin'?"

"Yeah. That would be great!" I was going to soak this for all I could get out of him.

But, I had another reason for sending him on this mission. As Tony headed down the hallway I followed stealthily, around the corner and down another hallway. He stopped short and went into a room. I hung back a moment, then ducked into a nearby telephone booth. I kept the door propped open and took the phone off the hook and pretended I was on a call. As soon as I heard Tony's footsteps again in the hallway, I made my way down to the room he had been in. It was another smaller lounge. I peeked inside. I saw the shoulder-length red hair, the red fingernails wrapped around a magazine. "You must be Gloria," I said.

She peered up from the copy of *Redbook.* A look of shock crossed her face. She nodded and a small smile formed on her red lips. She stood and extended her hand. "And you must be Anna. I recognize you from the picture your father has on his dresser."

I don't know what surprised me more, that she seemed pleasant or that Dad had a picture of me in his apartment. I sat down next to her. "Let's all wait together," I said.

I was surprised that Gloria and I could talk so easily. I shared my concerns about my father's care once he was home from the hospital. She assured me she would be by his side. "And you come and visit him whenever you want."

I laughed. "Well, you're going to have to get my father to extend that invitation. It's not up to me, or to you, really."

When Tony came back with our coffee he nearly dropped the cups on the floor. "What the…?"

"Don't get mad, Tony," I said.

"Anna, get back to the other lounge. Dad doesn't want this."

I rolled my eyes at Gloria. "Oh well. He's not exactly in a position to do anything about it himself right now, is he Tony?"

"Anthony, sit down," Gloria said. "It's time Anna and I met."

Daddy's open-heart surgery opened our lives a little more. After his discharge from the hospital and during his recuperation, he agreed to let me visit him at his apartment. Over the years I'd been to his apartment building more times than I could possibly count, but it was the first time he let me in.

Of course, true to the oppositional nature of my parents' relationship, my newfound openness with my father meant keeping yet another secret from my mother. And not because Dad had asked me to, this time it was of my own volition. I really enjoyed spending time with Dad and Gloria, having dinner at his apartment, going to Palermo's together for an espresso. But I felt I was betraying my mother and it began to eat away at my gut. I turned to Aunt Jeannie for advice.

"Just tell her the truth. You mother loves you and wants you to have time with your father, even if that means spending time with her." Her. 583 Red-Headed Puttana. The woman I now called Gloria.

Aunt Jeannie was right. Ma took the news calmly, one might say even graciously. "I appreciate knowing you don't want to go behind my back." And when she asked me, "What's she like?" I knew there was no turning back. I had to stay the course of truth.

"She's nice."

Ma said nothing. She simply nodded. Maybe it wasn't the answer she had hoped to hear, but in my truthfulness Ma knew she could trust that I would never lie to her again. She was given the respect she deserved at last.

Chapter Eleven

On the morning of November 17th, I pack Jazz's bowl and a few days worth of dog food and treats into an old, blue gym bag that has officially become Jazz's travel bag, and toss two days worth of underwear, socks, and clothing into my black leather overnight satchel. "C'mon, girl. Wanna go for a ride?" It never ceases to amaze me how my deaf dog always seems to hear those specific words. She also apparently hears, 'Wanna treat' with no problem, too. With the energy of a young pup, Jazz runs to the door and hops side to side exuberantly until I open it. Her bum bounces up and down as she tears top-speed down the walkway and to my car. A little over an hour later, Jazz and I pull into the driveway of Lisa's house. I beep the horn announcing our arrival.

While I am retrieving the overnight bags from the trunk of the car, I hear the side door of the house open. Peering over the trunk's hood, I'm surprised to see Katie come running towards my car.

"Jazzy!" she screams gleefully. Jazz jumps from the car and hightails it to her young friend. "Hi, Miss Matteo." Katie gives me a quick hug.

The side door to the house opens again and I see my oldest and dearest friend—tall, thin, and regal as the day we met, and holding the ever-present teacup in hand.

"No school today, Katie?"

"Katie has 'a real awful-bad headache' today," Lisa rumples Katie's hair as she affectionately imitates her daughter. "Just too 'real awful-bad' to go to school. But, something tells me Jazz is going to cure her real quick!"

I laugh and give Lisa a bear hug.

"Can Jazzy and I play in the yard, Miss Matteo?"

"Absolutely!" Katie and Jazz tear off together. "You know, Lis, she really can call me Anna."

127

"This coming from the woman who, to this day, still calls my mother Mrs. Paradides?"

In the time it takes to extract my bags from the trunk, Katie and Jazz are in the backyard playing fetch with a stick. "Yup, she's feeling better," I remark.

Lisa rolls her eyes. "What can I say?" She takes my satchel and we head inside.

"Not much. Remember that time you called into school and told Sister Monique," I switch over to a dry, raspy voice, "'I'm too sick to come to school today.'" Lisa starts to laugh. "And then Sister Monique said, 'Oh? And what's Anna's excuse?'"

"How many days did we skip that year?"

"I don't know about you, but I skipped like sixty-six days. It's a miracle I graduated." We enter the house. "Wow!" I look around Lisa's kitchen. Simple elegance. Calm colors, open kitchen cupboards with board-and-batten siding. "Your kitchen is beautiful!"

"Matt's done a lot. All those years building theatrical sets in college has paid off." Matthew's detailed carpentry reflects well-crafted simplicity. The rest of the house has the same unassuming character.

"Whatever happened to that great bedroom set you had when we were kids?"

Lisa grabs dramatically at her heart. "Oh, wasn't that the best? I loved that bedroom set! If only the bed were queen size. It's in Katie's room, now. Sometimes when she's in school, I go and take a nap on it."

"Your home is truly lovely, Lisa."

Lisa smiles. "Thank you. I love it too." She turns one of the stove's knobs and a blue gas flame ignites under the stainless steel teakettle. "How about a cup of tea?"

I look at my watch. "I hate to dump and run, but I'm anxious to get to the library."

"I know," Lisa says with understanding. "Go ahead. We'll have plenty of time to talk this evening, once Matt and Katie go to bed. "

I start towards the door, then stop and turn to her. "Lisa, don't wait dinner for me. I may be there a long time."

128

"Take whatever time you need," she interrupts. "Jazz's food is in the bag?" I nod. "How much does she get?"

"One cup. And don't buy into her 'starving dog' routine. No table scraps. Promise?"

"Maybe."

"Great." I roll my eyes, knowing it's a lost cause.

Lisa places her hand on my shoulder. "I still think I should come with you, Anna. I can get someone to stay with Katie. My sister-in-law lives a few blocks away."

Tears spring into my eyes as I am touched by her concern. I take her hand and hold it. "I need to do this alone, Lisa, but thank you. You are the dearest friend. Really, I'll be fine," I assure her.

I stop at the newsstand next to the Providence Public Library and buy three, two-packs of Reese's. Armed, I take a deep breath and head inside. I fill out a microfilm request form for December 1976, January 1977, October and November 1978, and November and December 1979. As I wait for the librarian to retrieve the microfilm, I ignore the "No Food, No Beverages" sign and quickly eat a package of peanut butter cups, hiding the evidence in my pocket just as the librarian returns with the microfilm.

"Here you are." She is an attractive woman, about my age. Her smiling is fetching, quick. She places several rolls of microfilm and a microfilm reader-printer direction sheet on the counter. I look at her hands. They are strong, caregiver hands, and sans wedding ring. "The viewing room is straight back," she points behind me. Her eyes dart to the crumpled orange wrapper peeking out of my pocket. Suddenly, I'm five again, caught red-handed with my hand in the cookie jar.

She stares at me as though sizing me up, as if she is trying to discern if the contents of the microfilm I've requested correlates to my apparent need to sneak eat. I hang my head, feeling vulnerable, exposed.

"I've got a thing for Reese's too," she says with the compassion of a knowing addict.

129

I look at her trim body. "Really," I say with a smile. "You hide it well." I reach into my other pocket and slide the distinctive orange, yellow, and brown package across the desk. "Enjoy."

"Thank you, no. But you're kind to offer," she says. Her melodious voice is gentle. "Something tells me you may want it later."

"Trust me," I glance at her nametag, "Jacqueline, I'm well prepared." I pat my coat pocket.

Her face brightens with that luminous smile. "Thanks," she whispers as she scans the room before palming the goods, tucking the contraband alongside her computer terminal. "The viewing room is the farthest door. Is there anything further you need?"

"Anything further, father? That can't be right. Isn't it anything farther further?" The Groucho Marx lines escape my lips before I can reel them in. It was a bit I did on Fathers' Weekend. And from that night on, Dad would ask me to do that shtick every time we were together.

Jacqueline's laugh is rich and deep. Hearty. "That was good. From *Horsefeathers*, right?

"A Reese's addict *and* a Marx Brothers fan? If you tell me you love Starbucks - - "

"Grande caramel macchiato, extra shot."

I clutch my chest with both hands. I've hit the Trifecta! I think I'm in love. "Me too. Extra foam."

Again, that brilliant smile beams towards me. She glances at my request form. "Are you Anna Matteo, the writer?"

I nod and squash the urge to disparage myself.

"I was at the In Her Own Words anniversary celebration, the year you read *Pillow Talk*." Her smile broadens. "Are you here researching another story?"

"Of sorts," I say. Suddenly, I am aware that my hands are icy cold. My nerve begins to plummet along with my body temperature. "I better get to this," I say rather abruptly.

I begin to hurriedly gather the rolls of film and the instruction sheet. The paper, along with two rolls of microfilm, slips through my fingers. Jacqueline comes out from behind the desk. "Let me help you with all that."

"I'm fine. Really."

Jacqueline nods, yet her slight smile tells me she doesn't believe me.

Midway to the viewing room I turn back. As I reach the front desk, Jacqueline is busy with another patron. I plop the assemblage of film on a nearby table. Reaching into my coat pocket, I pull a business card from my wallet and—as Jacqueline watches from the corner of her eye—I slide it under the Reese's pack next to her computer. A slight smile crosses her lips.

Even though the viewing room is empty, I head to the farthest machine. Per the instruction sheet, I flip on the power switch, turn the film advance knob to *Off*, set the gauge to 16mm, open the threader, load and thread the film past the glass, and close the threader. I take an audible, deep breath and push Load. I turn and turn the film advance knob until I find what I'm looking for.

TUESDAY, DEC. 21, 1976

Body Riddled by Bullets Identified

CRANSTON—Police have identified the middle-aged man found shot to death last night on a desolate road in Cumberland as Cranston produce dealer Paul Matteo of 1067 Park Avenue. Matteo had been shot several times in the head and body, according to Providence County sheriffs' deputies.

"Okay," I say as I take a deep breath. I advance to the next day and skim the article, looking for new information.

WEDNESDAY, DEC. 22, 1976

FBI Joins Matteo Slaying Probe

PROVIDENCE—The FBI is among several law enforcement agencies that have joined the Providence County Sheriff's Department investigation of the murder of Paul Matteo....

An autopsy by Medical Examiner Dr. Francis Kreiger revealed that Matteo died of an undisclosed number of gunshot wounds in the head, neck and chest. The type of gun used was not determined. According to deputies, Matteo had gambling connections. They would not comment whether or not they thought the murder was an "execution." There were no signs of struggle in the area where the body was found, deputies said.

Matteo's body was discovered by an unidentified passing motorist. Krespi said the body was still warm when found. Police were trying to determine if Matteo was shot at the location or if he was shot elsewhere and his body moved there. Cranston police found the dead man's car, a 1975 Cadillac, parked in the 500 block of Phenix Avenue, but a check of the neighborhood reportedly turned up little information. Police said there were no signs of a struggle in or around the car.

It was not known where Matteo was last seen alive, and his family had not reported him missing. Matteo was separated from his wife, the former Theresa Franconi.

I advance the film to December 24, 1976, the day of my father's funeral. Above the headline, *IRS Investigates Matteo Dealings*, is a picture of the funeral procession. Captured in this moment in time is the long row of black limousines parked curbside in front of St. Stephen's Church. The rear door of the hearse is wide open with the pallbearers standing nearby, watching and waiting as the coffin is being rolled out. Tears drip down my cheeks.

"Get the (bleep) out of here!" is all viewers heard on the evening news that night. The visual footage of the Paulie Matteo funeral had been blocked by my cousin Vito, who pushed a handful of snow into the camera lens.

Tony and Uncle Peter supported Ma as she struggled up the steps of the church she so loved to say a final goodbye to the man she had loved since she was eleven years old. I followed behind, walking stoically alongside Virginia. I never saw Ashton Croupier, the Channel 10 news reporter, coming. He thrust his microphone in front of my face. "Have the police given you any clues as to who did this to your father?"

Before the insanity and rudeness of the moment could register in my brain, Frank Riccio wrestled the microphone from the reporter's hand as Johnny D shoved the cameraman into the snow bank. My father's friends then flanked Ginny and I, ushering us into the church vestibule.

Monsignor O'Reilly waited at the foot of the altar as the bronze-colored casket came down the aisle. He had agreed to perform the funeral mass, a sacred last rite of passage for devout Catholics, out of love and respect for my mother. Paulie had not step foot in this church since his mother-in-law's funeral several years ago. The fluid and melodic opening strains of Schubert's *Ave Maria* filtered down from the choir loft as the priest blessed my father's coffin, sprinkling it with holy water. Carlene Rayburn, a soprano in Ma's choir, began: "*Ave Maria, gratia plena...*" It was a song we all loved, but no one loved it more than my father.

When Grandmama died, Ma honored her mother's passing by playing the funeral mass and singing the musical offering, just as she had done for her father. Ma's parents had nurtured her talents, and it was a fitting goodbye. I sat in the church pew with my father. As Ma's rich voice colored the melody and caressed the Latin lyrics...*Ma-ri-a...gra-ti-a...ple-na, Ma-ri-a...gra-ti-a...ple-na...*Dad began to cry. And when his tears turned to sobs for the mother-in-law he dearly loved; I held his hand in mine.

I knew Ma wanted to sing one last time for her beloved Paulie, but her grief was overwhelming. As I listened to Carlene, I bowed my head and cried. A hand reached out and touched mine. It was soft, familiar. I opened my eyes. My hands lay in my lap, one resting upon the other. I closed my eyes again and felt his soft hand reach across the dimensions that would separate us until I died. He held my hand in his hand one last, comforting time. "I love you, Daddy," I whispered.

An army of men fell into formation alongside the front steps, shielding the funeral procession from the persistent press as we exited the church. Ma, Tony, Virginia and the kids, and I rode in silence to the cemetery. The ground had begun to freeze, and so the burial service was held in the small cemetery chapel. Chairs were stationed alongside the casket for the immediate family. We sat in a row: Ma, Anthony, Virginia, their kids—Little Paulie and Tess—and me. Since Paulie was a World War II veteran, the funeral director had arranged for a Veteran Honor Guard. The casket was draped with an American burial flag and three military men in dress uniform stood solemnly by.

I felt a hand on my shoulder and turned to see Lisa standing behind me. I raised my hand across my chest and placed it on hers. I was no longer alone.

After Monsignor O'Reilly finished the final blessing, two members of the Honor Guard began the precise ceremonial folding of the flag as the mournful strains of Taps reverberated through the small stone chapel. The flag was presented to Ma. And then my father's own army of men, dressed in black silk suits, made their way past the coffin. As I watched Johnny D., Frankie Riccio, Whitey, Mr. Fragola, Joe "Boots," Lenny "Aces High" Marzulli, and the others paid their last respects, I noticed there were two people absent—Joey Casella and Gloria.

It was Ma's last act of grace towards Paulie. The night before the wake, she called Gloria. "You've been a part of his life all these years. I know Paulie would want you there. And I want you to know I welcome you to come to the services."

She didn't.

I fought tears as I followed my family back to the waiting limousine. Ma, Virginia and the kids, and I got into the back. Tony sat up front next to the driver. As the limo made its way to the main gate, Tony snapped. He screamed and cried and thrashed about like a child, nearly kicking out the front windshield. "Go back! Go back! We left Daddy! We can't leave Daddy there!" Ma and Ginny tried to calm him as I tended to his children.

Tess cried, "What's the matter with my daddy?"

I wrapped my arms around her and Little Paulie. "He'll be okay, honey. Your daddy's very sad. That's all."

But Tony was never the same again.

I wipe the tears from my cheeks and pull the Reese's from my pocket. I tear open the wrapper. *This is the only pack you have,* I remind myself. I eat one cup as I take several laps around the room, determined to settle myself down. I sit back at the machine and take a deep breath. *Think of this as if you are researching a story. As if you are a journalist on assignment,* I tell myself. I close my eyes and focus on my breathing. *Keep it nice and steady, take long, deep breaths.* An eerie calm flows into my body. I open my eyes and advance to the next news article.

FRIDAY, DEC. 31, 1976

Investigators Pursue Gambling Debts As Possible Motive In Gangland-Style Murder

Assistant State Attorney General Michael T. Reiser said yesterday that he "hopes by early next week to have a complete report from the various law enforcement agencies" regarding the gangland-style shooting death of Cranston-native Paul "Paulie" Matteo. The State Task Force on Organized Crime assumed full responsibility for the investigation of the slaying.

The Task Force will focus on determining whether Matteo was gunned down for nonpayment of syndicate gambling debts by a "hit" man fulfilling a contract put out on Matteo by crime overlords. There are $130,943.50 in unsatisfied judgments against Matteo on file at the Providence County clerk's office dating back to 1966, including one for $71,475 filed by the Stardust, Las Vegas, Nev., from 1972. Of the six judgments, one for $7,933.87 was filed the day after Matteo's body was found. Filing that judgment was Providence attorney, Joseph P. Casella.

I load the film for October 1978. As I peruse several days worth of news looking for the first murder trial, I come across an unexpected article involving Angelo Capraro.

MONDAY, OCT. 9, 1978
FBI Informant Links Capraro To Fire

James Hedrick, the prosecution's star witness in the arson trial of Angelo Capraro testified today the defendant told him he "'never dreamed" the Rowe Furniture "would burn that fast." Hedrick said he had two conversations with Capraro hours after a blaze destroyed the furniture store at Elmhurst and Phenix Avenues.

Defense attorney Gregory Haynes argued whether the tapes could be admitted as evidence. Hedrick, who is serving a three-to-five year sentence at Maximum Security Facility in Cranston for assaulting his wife with a tire iron, said a tape recorder in a car supplied to him by the FBI recorded the conversation.

Hedrick recalled Capraro saying, "You see that job over there?" referring to the charred shell of the furniture store across the street from where the men had their conversation, "It looks like a pro job." The witness said Capraro also was concerned about whether "somebody'd seen my car" parked across the street from the store the night of the fire.

I skip down to the last paragraph.

Hedrick testified he signed a form giving the FBI permission to tape his conversations two weeks before the fire. Sources said the FBI was attempting to get information about the 1976 Paul Matteo murder. Hedrick, a longtime friend of Capraro, ended up getting the arson information, instead. Capraro faces separate charges of murder and kidnapping in the Matteo slaying. Hedrick is expected to be the prosecution's final witness.

Like a bloodhound trailing a scent I hunt, through the next few days of news determined to find the outcome of the arson trial. The glaring headline, **Hung Jury Gains Capraro Mistrial,** releases a Tourette's-like stream of obscenities. "Motherfucker-son-of-a-goddam-bitch! Nothing sticks to this fuck!" That scumbag Capraro was Teflon before John Gotti was Don. I continue reading the news account.

> Shortly after noon Thursday, the jury in the Angelo Capraro arson-conspiracy trial asked State Supreme Court Justice Arthur Pisoni "if there are still such things as hung juries." Three hours later it proved there are.
>
> The jury foreman told Pisoni the jurors could not decide whether the defendant was guilty of burning down Rowe Furniture as part of an "arson-for-profit scheme." During its two-day deliberation, the jury became deadlocked "on the same three or four points," the foreman told the judge. After ascertaining there was no way the jury was going to reach a decision, Pisoni discharged the nine women and three men and tentatively scheduled a new trial for Nov. 16.
>
> Three times during the morning, the jurors asked to have portions of the tape replayed. During the trial, Haynes proposed that Capraro had "boasted about setting the fire in an attempt to obtain some merchandise" from another alleged FBI informant without paying for it immediately. The jurors asked, too, that Pisoni explain the procedure in case there are two equally plausible hypotheses based on the facts. Pisoni told them they "are required to assume the hypothesis indicating innocence is correct."

I lean back in the chair and take the last peanut butter cup from the package. Two equally plausible hypotheses. "There it is. There's the loophole, and Greg led the jury right through it," I say aloud to myself. "Son-of-a-bitch he's good." I read on.

> Three hours later, the jurors reported they could not reach a decision. Capraro is also charged with murder in the 1976 gangland-style slaying of Cranston produce dealer Paul Matteo. Haynes said he wants Capraro brought to trial on the murder charge before he is retried on the arson charge. "Jurors in the arson trial might be prejudiced by an outstanding murder charge."

A search through the next several days leads to what I'm looking for. A shudder courses through me as I read the headline.

TUESDAY, OCT. 24, 1978
Matteo Murder Trial to Start

Angelo Capraro apparently will be tried on murder charges before he is re-tried on arson charges. County Judge Lewis Bell confirmed Monday that he has scheduled October 30 as the start of jury selection for Capraro's trial on the murder charges.

That decision pleased defense counsel Gregory Haynes, who has pushed hard to have a jury decide the murder charges first. The arson charges were considered the stronger of the two cases.

Both cases depend on FBI informant James Hedrick and both allegedly involve tape recordings. The defense counsel wants the murder trial to come first. "I think the fact that the murder is pending is going to unduly prejudice 12 jurors," stated Haynes.

God forbid the jurors see Capraro for the low-life, scum-of-the-earth, dirt-bag he is. I remove October and load in November 1978. It isn't long before I find the first article about the trial.

THURSDAY NOV. 2, 1978
Matteo Slaying Motives Offered

A state Organized Crime Task Force prosecutor told a County Court jury today that Angelo Capraro could have slain Cranston produce dealer Paul Matteo either over gambling debts or out of personal revenge. Assistant Attorney General Patrick O'Connell offered two possibilities. "One is the defendant was upset because he had done eight years in prison because of Paulie Matteo." The prosecutor contended Capraro, while in prison, sent a letter to Matteo's family asking for money, but "didn't receive anything."

The second possibility was that Capraro murdered Matteo because the victim owed "at least $7,000 or $8,000" to Joseph Casella, a Providence attorney. O'Connell said Casella filed a judgment for the money in the Providence County clerk's office Dec. 20, 1976, the same day Matteo's bullet-riddled body was found lying along Albion Road in Cumberland.

The prosecutor implicated Casella and Massimo Pandozzi, a friend of Capraro, in the slaying, although neither has been charged.

The key evidence against Capraro, according to O'Connell, will be tape recordings made of conversations between Capraro and FBI informant James Hedrick a few days after the killing. "You're not going to hear the defendant say. 'I did it, I pulled the trigger.'"

In his opening statement, defense attorney Gregory Haynes told the jurors the tape recordings in no way prove Capraro guilty. On the tapes, Haynes said jurors will hear Capraro lament to the FBI informant: "You know what the worst thing about this is, Jimmy? I paid Paulie Matteo $100 I owed him the day before he was killed." The defense attorney questioned whether a man would repay a debt to a person he was to murder the next day.

Haynes said his client is a man "concerned about a frame." Matteo owed several debts other than the one to Casella, Haynes said, including more than $100,000 to various casinos in Las Vegas..

Be sure to sign your name Anna Renzi. If you want room service, just sign for it. Anna Renzi. Always Renzi, got it?

This is room 409. A bottle of Tanqueray, a bottle of Kaluha, and a bottle of Stoli. Hundred-proof. Renzi. Anna Renzi.

TUESDAY NOV. 14, 1978
Lawyer Denies Hiring Gunman

Organized Crime Prosecutor Patrick O'Connell claims Capraro shot Matteo in a complex plot that may have involved Matteo's debt to Providence attorney Joseph P. Casella. In his opening statement, O'Connell carefully avoided saying Casella knew anything about the shooting. But defense counsel Gregory Haynes didn't hesitate in asking Casella whether he ordered the killing of Matteo. "Are you aware the prosecutor has alleged that you ordered the death of Mr. Matteo?" Haynes asked.

"Yes, I am and it's ridiculous," replied Casella.

Later, Casella said that he made more than $100,000 in 1976 and would not kill anyone over a $7,000 to $8,000 debt. "If I was going to kill somebody, do you think I'd put a judgment on the record for everybody to see?" Casella asked rhetorically.

In his opening statement, O'Connell outlined that theory and focused on the connections between Capraro, Casella, and a man named Massimo Pandozzi.

"Pandozzi threatened Anthony Matteo, saying he was a debt collector for Joseph Casella and his father had better pay up or else." O'Connell said. Casella conceded that he did fight with Matteo. "Paul was a friend," said Casella, "I never spoke to anyone about the loan. It was private, between friends." Casella also said the fight did not mean they disliked one another. "After the fight, I had a party at which Paulie was present," Casella said.

The next headline nearly stops my heart.

THURSDAY NOV. 16, 1978
Capraro Jury Hears of 'Last Ride'
On Wednesday, jury members heard a voice, purportedly that of Angelo Capraro, talking about what a man does "on his last ride."

"They do the normal amount of begging and pleading," the voice on the tape recording says in a matter-of-fact tone.

Capraro continues on the tape to claim that a man about to die offers money, partnership and an apartment. "He had the opportunity to do all that before," Capraro appears to conclude.

Tape recordings of conversations, which the prosecution claims are between Capraro and his friend-turned-FBI informant James Hedrick, were played for the County Court jury. Whether those tapes reveal Capraro as the killer of Matteo will be up to the jury.

140

Numerous passages on the tapes appear to incriminate Capraro. Others, however, seem to depict Capraro as a man worried that he is being framed for the Matteo killing. Several passages appear to be open to two interpretations: that Capraro was talking about himself as the killer or that he was talking about a theoretical killer. The Capraro voice says: "He had no heart; none whatsoever." Whether that is a reference to Matteo on the "last ride" or to the theoretical killer is difficult to judge.

The obscenity-filled conversations between Hedrick and Capraro show Capraro as a man concerned because Matteo's son, Anthony, was talking with the police. Capraro calls Anthony "that dog." At one point, Capraro tells Hedrick, "He was spared and he owes it to me. He was spared." Capraro mutters something and then suggests Hedrick take Anthony Matteo out for a drink and "just lug him."

Capraro recalls for Hedrick that the Matteo family treated him badly. "I did eight years in the can (prison) and I wrote to his family and asked for money. I thought I'd at least get a coupla thousand. I got sh--," Capraro appears to say. "Is that justice? When I asked him for help, he turned me down."

The conversations took place in Hedrick's car. When they arrive at the location where Matteo's car was found on December 20, 1976, where Organized Crime Task Force prosecutors believe Matteo was kidnapped, Hedrick begins a conversation:

Hedrick: Right here? You snatched him right here?

Capraro: "Yeah, right there; right there. The spot was beautiful."

At another point, Capraro adds: That was done so perfectly that f---ing night —perfectly.

A few moments later Hedrick is heard asking Capraro: What does a man do on his last ride?

Capraro: They do the normal amount of begging and pleading.... They offer you money, to make you a partner, to give you their apartment. Too late. Paulie could of done all that before.

Hedrick: He promised the money that night?

Capraro's response is indecipherable.

141

Hedrick: You could of been his partner?

Capraro: Sky's the limit.

Hedrick asks whether the job—snatching and shooting Matteo—took an hour.

Capraro: That's right, maybe less.

Hedrick: And they don't know who it is?

Capraro: (laughing) That's right.

"Just think," says Hedrick a little later, "You could of got anything. You could of been his partner; you could of lived in his apartment."

Capraro: Yeah, and probably f---ed his *gomatta* too.

The two men also discuss their own theories of who killed Matteo. They talk of a Providence connection, of a Las Vegas hit, of "out-of-town guys" and of a local killer. "Paulie owed money to bad people," Capraro says, adding, "Not that I knew this was going to happen, but I knew something was going to happen." Capraro also tells Hedrick, "I'm Mr. Clean."

"Whoever did it," Capraro says, "isn't joking around. I told Tony, 'Your father's f---ed a lot of people.'" Capraro adds, "He's gotta right to go out and revenge his father's death."

Capraro also tells Hedrick that Matteo didn't have to die. "As sharp as Paulie is, he didn't believe they'd send somebody to kill him. Paulie handled a lot of money in his days to become a scumbag like this. All Paulie had to do was throw a f---ing bone," Capraro said. He adds, "I'll tell ya the truth. He did it to himself, the f---." Whoever killed Matteo, said Capraro, "made money. A f---ing big payday."

Several times, Capraro tells Hedrick that he's being framed for the killing. "I'm scared about a f---ing frame, Jimmy, because one day he dies and the next, I just turn the plates in and they (FBI) got my car," Capraro said.

My stomach begins to lurch and I fear I will vomit. Gripping the table I try to pull myself to my feet, but my legs are weak and won't hold me up. I collapse back in the chair. An agonizing shriek, like the pain-wracked howling of a cat being eviscerated by a coyote, escapes from deep within me. I grab my stomach as pain shoots through my abdomen. My worst fears about my father on that night had been confirmed. For months after his death, my imagination created scenario after scenario of his last moments in that car. Did Capraro hold a gun to his head the entire ride? Did he pistol-whip him? Taunt him? Torment him? Did my father plead for his life? Did he breakdown and weep like a child?

The door creaks open and a young man peeks in. "Are you all right, Miss?"

My face is soaked with tears. Rivulets of brown-black mascara and eyeliner have made their way down my cheeks and onto my blouse. I wave him off, choking out the words, "I'm fine." The door closes gently, as if he is relieved he does not have to be a party to the madness inside the room.

I try to breathe deeply, to calm myself down. I blow my nose, quickly filling the last tissue from the pocket-sized pack. I reuse every tissue in my pockets until they are reduced to shreds. "Great," I huff. In desperation, I turn to my shirtsleeves. "What are you, three, Matteo?" I say aloud. But what's my option? Make my way to the women's room, which would entail stopping at the desk and asking Jacqueline where it is?

The sound of voices outside the door draws my attention away from my disgusting shirt. "Thank you," I hear a woman say. The door opens and I notice the young man peering over Jacqueline's shoulder as she enters. She nods to him before closing the door in his face. I fumble for my jacket, which has fallen onto the floor.

"I thought you might need this." Jacqueline places a large tissue box on the table next to the microfilm machine and a gentle hand on my shoulder, hindering me from putting on my coat and covering up my filthy deed. From her position beside me, she is able to see the screen, to read the words that sent me into this emotional hellhole. Her hand grips my shoulder and I feel her compassion. "Would you like a glass of water, Anna?"

I bury my head in my hands, trying desperately to prevent the next tidal wave of tears from pushing through. But the levee breaks, and I am once again drowning in sorrow.

143

Jacqueline wraps her arm around my shoulders and tenderly strokes my forehead. "Let it out, Anna. Let it out."

It seems an eternity before I settle down, before the tears subside and my breathing is less shallow. "I'll be right back," Jacqueline says. She returns a few minutes later with a bottle of water and the Reese's I had given her earlier. "I'm off work in about thirty minutes. There's a Starbucks two blocks from here on Washington. Why don't you go there for awhile and have a cup of coffee? Get away from here for a bit. And when my shift's over, I'll help you go through this film and print out whichever articles you want." She adds softly, "Maybe you've read enough for today." I nod, unable to find my voice.

Jacqueline spies my sleeves. She grabs a handful of tissue from the box. "Here, take these with you. I don't want you starting in on your slacks." I am totally embarrassed, yet I can't help but laugh. Her deadpan delivery was the antidote I needed. Jacqueline tries to restrain herself, but soon the two of us are laughing uncontrollably.

Her suggestion was wise. Several minutes later I'm sitting in Starbucks, sipping a mug of Sumatra blend. The place is teeming with college students from Roger Williams University and business professionals in need of a java jolt to get them through rush hour traffic. I notice a young man at the counter fumbling through his backpack.

"I know I grabbed my wallet," he says with a mix of confusion and embarrassment. As he rifles through his bag, a textbook falls to the floor. The woman in line behind him shakes her head, annoyed. The young man picks up the book, placing it and the backpack on the counter. A frantic search through his pockets produces a dollar bill and a handful of change. The harried woman behind him begins mumbling inaudibly under her breath.

"How much are you short?" asks a gentleman in the adjacent line.

"Ninety cents," the cashier answers for him.

The man extends his Starbucks card. "Take the whole thing out of here."

The young man scoops up his money and tries to hand it to the gentleman, but he refuses. "I hope you find your wallet," he says before

144

turning on his heel and heading for the door.

The kindness of strangers...people whose door to their hearts is never locked. People who give of themselves and ask for nothing in return. Was Jacqueline's kindness towards me sincere? If my gaydar is on target, she's a sister. Did she comfort me and offer her assistance because she expects something of me in return? Or is she truly one of those people who grace this world by their very presence? My gut told me she was the latter. The kindness of strangers—inexorable proof of the interconnectedness of souls.

Since I couldn't bring a caramel macchiato back into the library, I purchased a ten-dollar gift card for her. "You didn't have to do that," she says as I place it on her desk.

"I know. I wanted to."

Over the next hour, and with Jacqueline's help, I flip through roll after roll of microfilm. We work side-by-side in a silence that speaks volumes. I locate several more articles and decide to print five of them. Jacqueline gathers the print-outs and slides them into a large manila envelope. Before she can hand it to me, I give her a hug. Not a quick one, but not one that lingers either. "I couldn't have gotten through this without you."

She smiles shyly. "Are you heading back to Massachusetts?"

"No. I'm staying at my friend's house. I sure hope she and her husband didn't hold dinner for me," I add, clarifying my friend's status. I can tell the reference is not lost on Jacqueline as her eyes brighten. *Okay, Matteo, take the plunge.* "Maybe we can have dinner, or lunch sometime? You know, when I'm wearing a clean shirt."

Her laugh comes from a place of genuine sweetness; there is no judgment behind it. "I'd like that, Anna." She reaches into her blazer pocket and pulls out a slip of paper. "Here's my home phone number. And you can always reach me here at the library."

It is nearly nine o'clock when I get to Lisa's house. Jazz greets me at the door as if I had been gone for a week, which I suppose may be the case to her as one year in our life is equal to seven for a dog. I'm kneeling on the floor, petting my beloved dog's belly when Lisa comes into the kitchen. "Hey, you," she says.

"Hey." I get to my feet. As I take off my jacket, Lisa notices my mascara-stained, snot-covered shirt. "I knew I should have come with you."

"It was all right, really."

Lisa gives me a theatrical glare. "Anna, your shirt looks like it was made by Kleenex." I laugh heartily. "All you need is a little box emblem over the breast area," she adds. My laughter quickly turns to hysterics. "I've heard of drip dry, Anna, but *really!"*

Every time I catch my breath, spasms of laughter roll over me. I clutch my stomach. "Stop! Stop!" Jazz, confused by my display, starts growling at Lisa, which just makes me laugh even harder. "Jazz," I sputter, "stop growling. It's okay." But Jazz either doesn't hear me, or doesn't believe me. She closes in on Lisa.

"Anna, call off your dog!" Lisa is scared, yet she can't stop laughing either.

"Jazz, no!" I say and try to catch my breath. But no sooner do I, the laughing starts all over again. "Jazzy, Mommy's okay." I grab Jazz, who's now baring her teeth at Lisa, by the collar and pull her towards me.

"That's what you get for mocking my clothes."

Once the three of us settle down Lisa asks, "Did you have any dinner?"

"Well, if you call three packages of Reese's Peanut Butter Cups and a Starbucks dinner, then yes, I did."

"How about I warm up some lasagna?"

"Nah. I'm not that hungry. Actually, tea and cinnamon-raisin toast would be perfect."

I run upstairs to change into my comfy-cozys while Lisa fixes our favorite childhood snack. Minutes later, we're sitting in her kitchen sipping tea and munching cinnamon-raisin toast. It is as if we were seventeen again.

"I threw my shirt in your clothes hamper."

Lisa looks appalled.

"Kidding!"

Lisa chuckles momentarily, and then takes a sip of tea. Her eyes study my face, my demeanor. "You seem surprisingly calm," she says with a hint of doubt about the veracity of her observation.

I blow gently on the hot, fragrant liquid with hints of mango and lemon before taking a quick sip. "I'm better now. But, as you saw from my shirt, I was a mess earlier. I really wasn't prepared for what I read."

"Sweetie, there was no way to prepare," her voice is gentle. "That's your father's murder you were reading about."

"I know." I run my finger through my hair from crown to nape and slowly try to massage the tension from my neck. "I guess I had this idea in my head that I could read those articles and maintain a writer's perspective. Wrong!" I snort and chuckle. "I was howling like a wounded animal; sobbing so loudly that this young guy pokes his head in the room and asks if I'm okay." I shake my head in embarrassed disbelief. "Of course, I said I was fine."

"Of course," Lisa agrees sarcastically.

"Don't be a smart-ass." I take a bite of toast. "You'll be pleased to know he didn't believe me either, because the next thing I know the librarian comes in with a box of tissues."

"She didn't know you preferred your shirt?"

"Ha, ha," I say dryly.

"At least she didn't pull the tissue out from her sleeve like old Miss Fiske at CJ High. "

"God! Old Miss Fiske—the epitome of the spinster librarian. I can still see her flabby upper arms swaying to and fro when she'd write on the blackboard." Lisa guffaws at the memory. "One day, she was writing a sentence, and the flab of her upper arm was swinging so fast, I thought it was gonna hit her in the face and knock her out!" Lisa is slapping the table from laughter. "Jacqueline, I suspect, has triceps of steel. She looks to be in great shape."

"Jacqueline? Hmm!" Lisa eyes me impishly.

I smile with a dash of braggadocio. "Actually, she did give me her phone number."

"Even in grief, Matteo, you manage to charm 'em!" Lisa smiles proudly at me.

I impart to Lisa all that transpired with Jacqueline. She takes my hand. "That was very sweet of her to help you. She sounds special."

"She is," I concur. "If only the timing were better."

Lisa shrugs her shoulders, confused. "What do you mean?"

"Well, first of all, that God-awful relationship and break-up with Edie; and now this stuff I'm finding out about my father. I don't feel on steady feet these days. I think Jacqueline may be special, and I don't want to fuck it up."

"So, be friends."

I nod. "Yeah. That's probably best right now." I sip my tea. "Poor girl. She'll be so disappointed," I add sarcastically.

"You heartbreaker, you. Sometimes I wonder how I've managed to resist the Matteo charm all these years." Lisa takes a bite of toast and fixes her eyes on me. "Seriously, Anna. I've always wondered.... Did you ever have a thing for me?"

I nearly spit out my tea. "Are you kidding?"

Lisa places the half-eaten piece of toast back on the plate. "So, what are you saying? I'm not good enough for you? I always thought you loved me." Lisa's expression is dead serious and I can see the hurt in her eyes.

I take her hand in both of mine. "Oh, God, Lisa. I..." I'm at a loss for words. I never knew she felt this way. "Of course I love you. You're my best friend," I stammer. Tears well in my eyes. "I didn't mean anything bad by that. You know I think the world of you. I *adore* you."

Lisa hangs her head; that's when I notice she is fighting back laughter. "You shit!" I slap at her arm. "You really had me going!" I get up from the table and pour the rest of my tea down the sink's drain. "That really sucked, Lisa," I say with anger. "The thought that I had hurt you in some way all these years was tearing at me."

Lisa comes over to me. "I'm sorry, Anna. I was just joking around." She tries to wrap her arms around me, but I step back.

"Christ! And after the day I just had?" I huff in irritation.

148

"I'm sorry, Anna. Really. I was just trying to make you laugh." She reaches out again to hug me, but I push her away. "You're absolutely right. That was insensitive of me."

I turn my back to her. "You got that right." I sniffle and rub at my eyes with the palm of my hand. And just as I sense Lisa is standing behind me, I whip around and sassily shake my hips and wag my finger in her face. "And I got you back, babe!"

Lisa grabs the *mopine* from the counter and snaps it at me. I run away, but she comes after me. "You little shit, you!" she says whipping the *mopine* in my direction.

We play dodge around the table, all the while I taunt her. "You can't get me! You can't get me!" We end up in each other's arms sharing a good and hearty laugh.

"I'm gonna heat up more water. You want another cup of tea?" I ask.

"Yeah." Lisa cups my chin in her hand. "I do love you, Matteo."

"I know. And I adore you, Paradides."

"Give this thing with Jacqueline proper attention. I've a good feeling about this. It's serendipitous."

I smile at my dear friend as I study her face. Her gray-blue eyes still resonate with compassion and understanding, deepened by the passing of years and heightened by the responsibilities of motherhood. "I couldn't have gotten through those days after my father's death without you, Lisa. Mom was utterly devastated. She loved that man so deeply, despite all the shit he put her through over the years. And Tony, my God! Tony was acting crazed."

Lisa nods vigorously. "I remember that night I found out. I was waitressing at Escargot."

"I use to love that restaurant! And they did have the best escargot Florentine!"

"I remember I was standing at the bar waiting for a drink order," Lisa says. "The television behind the bar was blaring as usual. You know how that is, after awhile it becomes ambient sound." I nod. "Suddenly the word 'Matteo' jumped out at me.

"Holy Mother of God!" Lisa exclaims, suddenly back in that moment

149

in time. "I remember saying to Lew: That's my best friend's father they're talking about. I need to leave. And you know what that shit said to me? He said: You can leave when your shift ends at ten."

Lisa shakes her head. "So I beg him: Lew, I say, I've never asked you for a favor before. But I've got to go now. And he still refuses!" Lisa's ire is right at the surface now. "You've got three other girls on tonight, I tell him. We've handled it with three before."

"That's not the point," Lisa imitates his gruff voice.

"So I say: What *is* the point, Lew?"

Suddenly she is Lew again. "The point is: you leave when I tell you to leave. Am I clear?"

Lisa mimes tearing off an apron, balling it up, and throwing it on the bar top. "Well, let me be clear, Lew. You can shove your point up your ass!"

"You walked out?" I ask, astonished.

"He left me no choice."

"I never knew you quit your job that night." I reach across the table and squeeze Lisa's hand.

"When I got to your mother's house I remember your aunts and uncles were surrounding your mother, comforting her. And your brother was in the kitchen sitting at the table surrounded by his friends."

I chuckle. "I remember that scene. Pete Fafaro, Johnny-D, Frankie Riccio, my cousin Vito—all sitting around that table tossing out theories about who did it and why, and who should 'whack' who. The only thing missing from that scene was some fat Clemenza-type standing at the stove making a big pot of sauce."

Lisa and I laugh. "But what I remember most vividly," Lisa says, "was you. Sitting all alone with a sadness etched so deep onto your face it seemed to reach down to your soul."

I start to tear from the memory. "You didn't leave my side for days. I remember begging you to go home, to get some sleep. And even when you did finally go home, you were back in less than an hour." I look deep into the eyes of my oldest and dearest friend. "Did I ever tell you that when we were first becoming friends, your mother said: What you and my Lisa have

150

is very special. You two will know each other all your lives."

Lisa smiles. "I guess once in awhile she did make some sense."

"I always envied you. Remember that night I had dinner at your house?"

Lisa's expression is serious. "You mean the one and only time I lied to you?"

"What are you talking about?"

"When you asked me to tell you the God's honest truth about the hors d'oeuvres, the drinks, the dinner in the dining room, and did we do that every night." Lisa looks embarrassed. "I lied to you when I said yes. That whole scene was one big show that night."

I am genuinely shocked. "But, why did you lie about it?"

"You were so impressed, and I wanted you to think I had a great life. But truth be told? My parents fought like cats and dogs. You know how my mother gets. She knows everything. She knows your every thought, every mood, every breath you take better than you do. She was intolerable and impossible to live with; especially after she got a few drinks in her, which was most nights. My father?" Lisa places her hand over her heart. "My father was a saint. And I always hated her for the way she treated him.

"But that night, you had this naïve perspective that that's how it was for everyone but you. And I lied to you because I wanted you to believe that people could be happy."

I'm touched that she felt so protective of me. But that was then, and this is now. "Are you and Matthew happy?"

Lisa nods almost imperceptibly. "We are. But that doesn't mean we don't fight, and that there aren't times I'd like to stick his head in the toilet and flush. That's part and parcel of married life. But if I learned anything from watching my parents, it's that you have to talk to one another, listen to each other, and respect each other's points of view. And do your darnedest to not assume what the other thinks or means."

I take Lisa's hand and press a gentle kiss onto her fingers. "I guess no one's family was like the Cleavers."

151

"Thank God!" She clutches her heart. "What a beige existence that would be!"

"And I think to myself," I serenade Lisa with my best Louie Armstrong impersonation, "what a Wonder Bread world!"

Chapter Twelve

The next morning I'm awakened by the sound of Lisa's voice. "Anna," she says softly, "sorry to wake you. I just wanted to let you know I'm going to the Playhouse for a few hours. I fed Jazz, and Katie took her for a walk, so sleep in. I'll be back around eleven." She kisses my forehead and leaves quietly.

I try to fall back asleep, but once I'm awake that's usually it. I wait until I hear Lisa's car pull out of the garage before getting up. Downstairs in the living room I find Jazz splay-legged on her back, napping in the rays of the sun streaming in through the picture window. She doesn't hear me as I walk past her on my way to the kitchen.

An assortment of teas is displayed on the kitchen table along with the remaining loaf of cinnamon-raisin bread from last night. I pick up the note propped against the bread and read the familiar cursive script.

> *Good morning, Anna. Help yourself to anything you'd like. Matt prepared a pot of coffee, Starbucks, of course. Just plug in the pot and turn it on. See you around eleven. L*

While the coffee is brewing, I take a quick shower and dress. I grab the manila envelope with the news articles and head back downstairs. This time as I pass by Jazz, she opens her eyes. Her tail swishes to and fro along the rug. "Morning, angel. How's my little love?" I lay alongside her and massage her hips and legs, a morning ritual since arthritis has set into her old bones. I finish off with a kiss on her head. "Want some coffee?"

Jazz gets to her feet and shakes, vigorously, head-to-toe; liberating her body of all the negative energy released by the deep massage. She follows me into the kitchen and stands by my side, eagerly awaiting her caffeine fix.

I pour a little coffee into her food bowl, swish in some Half N' Half, and blow on it several times. After testing the now lukewarm liquid with my forefinger, I place the bowl on the floor and Jazz laps it clean before my coffee mug is even filled.

I settle at the kitchen table with Jazz at my feet and take a deep breath. "Round two," I say. As I extract the articles from the envelope, the top headline fills me with disgust. And I know that any remaining shreds of my dwindling belief in the Catholic religion are about to disintegrate.

FRIDAY NOV. 17, 1978
Nun Provides Alibi

Defense counsel Gregory Haynes called a Catholic nun to provide alibi testimony for Angelo Capraro. Sister Alicia Mullen told the jury she called the Capraro home on the night of Dec. 20, 1976, the night prosecutor Patrick O'Connell contends Capraro gunned down Cranston produce dealer Paul Matteo.

The nun was one of five witnesses who testified that Capraro was home on the night of the murder. Her testimony is crucial to the defense since the other witnesses are related to Capraro.

Her testimony is connected with that of Capraro's wife, Mrs. Concetta Capraro. Mrs. Capraro said that she and Angelo's mother, Mrs. Vincenzo Capraro, were with Capraro "the entire night of Dec. 20, 1976. Ang was sick and was home watching television. Angie was the only man in the house that night."

Sister Alicia testified that she called "at about 8:30 to 8:45 p.m. Angie answered the telephone. I said either 'Angie, is Connie there' or 'Connie, was that Angie?'"

A nun! They get a friggin' nun to testify. Like anyone's gonna question the veracity of her statements? But I knew differently. I knew nuns lied.

"We found her in the lavatory pitching coins. Seems your daughter was running her own little gambling den."

I knew from my mother's tight-lipped facial expression I was in deep doo-doo. "Where's the money you took from those kids, Anna?"

But before I can answer Sister Patrice interjected. "We had her give all the money back to the kids."

I glared at her. It was a bald face lie. But I knew better than to say anything because when it came to the church and those "sainted nuns," my mother would choose to believe them, not me.

As soon as we were in the car, Ma slapped my face. "You're acting just like your father. And that's the last thing I ever expected from you."

The next morning when Dad came to pick me up Ma walked out to his car with me and told my father what had happened at school. "It's enough Anthony is turning out like you, but I won't have my daughter acting like a *cafone*!"

We drove three blocks before he spoke to me. As we waited at the traffic light, Dad turned to me. "How much did you score?"

"Nine bucks."

"Nine bucks?" I saw the look of pride he was trying hard to squelch. "You won nine bucks pitchin' pennies and nickels?"

"Some of it I won, but I figured I got dibs on the game. You know, 'cause I kinda organized it. So everybody who won had to give me ten percent of their take."

My father laughed in spite of himself. I could see he was proud, but he was also trying to be all parental-like. "Your mother's right, Anna. You shouldn't be doin' that. It's not," he thought for a moment, "lady-like."

"It's got nothin' to do with being a lady, Dad. It's business."

"Still, I don't want you doin' it any more. *Capisco?*"

"*Capisco.*" I turned my back to my father and stared out the window for the next few blocks. "She lied, you know," I said, still watching the rows of houses fly by.

"Who? Your mother? She lied? About what?"

I turned to look at my father. "Not, Ma. Sister Patrice. She told Ma I

155

gave the money back to the kids, but the truth is she took it from me and kept it. And I know that for a fact because I asked Nick and Ricky if they got their money back, and they said no. So, I'm supposed to be bad for runnin' a pitch, but the nun can lie and keep money that's not hers and get away with it? Where's the justice?"

W here's the justice? Forty years later, and I'm still asking that same question. And still no answer. I refill my coffee mug before starting the next article.

THURSDAY NOV. 23, 1978
Hung Jury in Capraro Trial
Judge Declares Mistrial

Providence County Judge Lewis Bell declared a mistrial Wednesday in the murder case against Angelo Capraro after jurors reported a deadlock. The vote was eight to four in favor of acquittal. "I don't think anybody can quarrel with your decision," Judge Bell told the jurors who had deliberated about 14 hours over two days.

Patrick O'Connell, an Organized Crime Task Force prosecutor, said Capraro would "certainly" be tried again on the murder charges. "A hung jury," he lamented, "is like a kiss from your sister."

As he was escorted down the hall, Capraro seemed pleased with the verdict, but displeased with the continued prosecution. "How much money they gonna spend on Jimmy Hedrick before they realize he's a bum?" Capraro asked reporters.

The prosecution tried to introduce a Providence connection to show Capraro may have killed Matteo "at someone else's bidding and with someone else's help." The Organized Crime Task Force suggested a debt Matteo owed to Providence attorney Joseph Casella may have provided the motive for Matteo's killing.

Casella reportedly is to go on trial December 4 in Providence on perjury charges leveled by an Organized Crime Task Force grand jury. The attorney is accused of intentionally convincing Providence car dealer Alfonso Pennachia to swear falsely that he (Pennachia) was in a certain car on Dec. 9, 1976. A Cranston policeman testified at the Capraro trial that he stopped a vehicle that had been waiting outside Matteo's apartment building on that date. The car was allegedly driven by a Providence man who OCTF investigators theorize participated in the Matteo killing, but who has never been indicted.

Defense counsel Gregory Haynes, who defended Capraro on the murder and the arson charges, said he was pleased with the jury's finding. "I just wish it was unanimous. The proof wasn't there; it will never be there," he said.

Jurors later confided that Haynes' analysis of their decision was correct. They talked of a general feeling—shared even by those who voted for innocence—that Capraro was guilty and did kill Matteo. But, they added, the prosecution did not prove the case beyond a reasonable doubt.

Haynes said he felt "frustrated" after the mistrial was declared. "I certainly would like to end this once and for all with an acquittal," said Haynes. "I can't say I'm satisfied. If we have to go (to trial) again, we'll go."

They did go to trial again, and on December 7, 1979; a State Supreme Court jury acquitted Angelo Capraro of all charges.

I decided to stay with Lisa for another night. Matt, bless his heart, gave Lisa and I a lot of time and space. He took Katie to Chuck E. Cheese's for dinner and on the way home he stopped at the video store and rented *Finding Nemo* for them to watch together when they got home. It is an unusually warm November evening. Wrapped in shawls that once belonged to Lisa's grandmother, we are sitting in the wicker rocking chairs on the front porch enjoying the brisk night air when Matthew comes to say goodnight.

"You're a love, Matt," I say as I throw my arms around him. "I really needed this time with Lisa. Thank you for being so understanding."

Matt kisses my forehead. "I admire you, Anna, for what you're doing. It's hard enough living with the ghosts of our past, but to confront them head on? That takes courage."

"I don't know about that, Matt, but thank you."

"Katie's all tucked in," Matt says to Lisa. "Oh, and by the way," Matt turns to me. "If you're looking for Jazzy, you'll find her on the bed next to Katie."

"I think it's time to get your daughter a dog," I say smiling.

"Convince her," Matt says pointing to his wife. Lisa plays deaf to our exchange. "I'm turning in as well. You girls stay up and have fun."

Lisa gets up and gathers our empty mugs. "It's getting a little too brisk. Maybe we should go inside," Lisa suggests.

"I'll be in in a minute," I say.

Lisa follows Matt inside to say goodnight to Katie and to spend a few private moments with her husband.

As I rock back and forth, I think about Matt's comment. Courage? Truth is, I never felt so cowardly in all my life. It would have been courageous to have stayed in Cranston during the years of the murder trials and support my mother. Instead, I ran away. Ma was courageous. In spite of the anguish she must have felt and the humiliation she must have endured having our family secrets splashed across the newspapers and television stations day after day, she stayed the course with her head held high.

"Ready for another cup of tea?" Lisa says through the screen door.

"Actually, I went out this morning and picked up a jug of Chianti. Whattaya say I come inside and we get drunk?"

"I'll get two glasses."

We settle in her cozy living room drinking the Chianti Italian-style—from tumblers instead of wineglasses. "You could have been an interior decorator," I say admiring the room. The eggshell walls, a light beige sofa, and white oak floors form a monochromatic background. A pomegranate side table and bright throw pillows in orange and yellow add splashes of color to the room's canvas. "Still shopping at Pier One, I see."

"Absolutely! I'm in love with that store. Remember when we went shopping for India prints and pillows for our dorm rooms?"

"Yeah. I think of those days whenever I step foot in Pier One." I look at my dear friend. "I have so many great memories with you, Lisa."

"And me of you."

We're halfway through the jug when, out of the blue, Lisa asks, "Did you and Tony ever talk about your father's murder?"

I nod. "Once. But let's not go there now. Enough about me, and my family. Tell me about the Playhouse..."

As I lay in bed later that night, I think about Lisa's question. Tony had called me only a handful of times in my life: when Virginia was pregnant for the third time, when Elvis Presley died, and when the Mets won the World Series in 1986. "I'd like to break Buckner's fucking bowed legs," he said. Tony was upset the Red Sox blew the game, not because of any New England loyalty and pride, but because he had big money riding on a win. Tony also called me when the date was set for Angelo Capraro's second trial for the murder of our father.

"Tony, do you think this jury will be hung too? Or worse, do you think they'll acquit that fuck?" I now had no problem saying the F-word.

"I don't know, Anna. There's a different prosecutor on this trial. He's had almost another year to come up with more evidence and make a stronger case. Everyone knows Ang did it. I know he did it," he said with conviction.

I found it surprising that Tony still called that fucker 'Ang'. Like he was still his best buddy or something. I could barely get Capraro past my lips. "What do you know that you haven't told me?"

Tony laughed. "There's a lot I haven't told you, Sis, and never will. But trust me, the evidence is there. We gotta hope this new guy, Kelley, can prove it is all. But I got to hand it to Ang, he got himself one fuckin' good attorney in Haynes. I'd love to know how he's payin' him. Somebody's gotta be bankrollin' his defense."

"I think they'll get Capraro this time. I know they will." If only I could have backed that statement with a feeling in my gut, but there was none.

Tony reached back to one of his favorite childhood sayings. "Anna, all I can tell you is: Never calculate the number of juvenile poultry until the process of incubation has been completed."

I laughed heartily, as did Tony, and in the sound of our momentary joy I noticed our laughs resonated with the same timbre and beat. It was the most connected I ever felt to my big brother. But my laughter was short-lived. "Hey, Tone? I gotta ask you something." And then my mouth went dry. I was glad we were on the telephone so Tony couldn't see the tears welling in my eyes. "Was Dad mad at me? I was home for three days and he never returned my calls." My voice wavered as the tears crashed through. "Did Daddy die angry with me?"

Tony spoke with a gentleness I had never heard in him before. "Anna, no. Dad loved you. He was so proud of you, going to Smith and all. He wasn't mad at you. Why would you even think that?"

"Because he didn't call me. And the last time I saw him over Thanksgiving break, we had this quick breakfast together. I remember it was weird. We met at this little hole-in-the-wall, motor lodge diner all the way out in West Warwick. He seemed agitated that morning. Like he was mad at me about something."

"What could he possibly have been mad at you about?"

I couldn't tell my brother, but I was certain Dad had found out I was gay. I didn't know how, but when you were a Matteo, everyone seemed to know everything about you. It was another reason I had chosen to not live in Rhode Island anymore.

"Anna, Dad was not mad at you. I think he knew something was coming down. I think he was protecting you, is all."

Chapter Thirteen

When I get home the next day there are two telephone messages. The first is from Sophie:

Hi Anna, Michelle gave me your message. You really had me going there about Thanksgiving. We're still in Belize, but I did talk with Pat O'Connell. He said for you to give him a call. Here's his cell. 401-555-3859. I'll call you when we get back. Good luck with Pat.

The second message makes me smile:

Hi, Anna, it's Jacqueline -- from the library. I hope you are doing a little better. Just wanted you to know you were in my thoughts. If you'd like to talk my number is 401-555-2123.

I decide to return her call now, figuring she's still at work and I'll get her answering machine. I need to "dance" a bit more. "Hi, Jacqueline, it's Anna Matteo." *Anna Matteo? What an idiot I am.* "I just got back and got your message. Thanks for the concern." *Thanks for the concern? Could I be any lamer?* "I'll try calling again over the weekend." *Could I be any more of a chicken shit?*

Although Jacqueline was by my side as I scoured the microfilm for articles about my father's murder, we didn't talk about it at all. And as wonderful as it was to hear her voice, I needed time before we spoke again. Time to figure out how I was going to address the giraffe in the room. I didn't want to operate from a set of ground rules: I'd like us to get to know one another more, Jacqueline, but don't ask about my father; don't ask about the effect his way of life had on my childhood; and don't ask how I

161

feel about him now that I've uncovered all this mobster-related crap about his death. Oh yeah…a great way to start a friendship, and a helluva way to start a relationship.

Later that evening when the telephone rings I check Caller I.D. Cornejoulois, J. 401-555-2123. I let it go to voice mail. I wait a few minutes before retrieving my messages. "You have no new messages." Guess I'm not the only chicken in the hen house.

In keeping with my newly found status as Queen of the Clucks, I manage to put off calling Pat O'Connell until Wednesday. As I wait for him to answer the call, I break out in a cold sweat.

"This is Pat O'Connell."

I introduce myself and we exchange a few pleasantries. "Sophia told me you were looking into your father's murder trial," Pat says.

"Yes. I tried getting the trial transcripts, but they're sealed because of the acquittal. She thought you may have some information I can see."

"We've looked, but the case is so old. After the hung jury, the one I tried, most of the records went to Jim Kelley. He re-tried the case."

"Sophie mentioned, too, that you would be willing to talk with me about the case. I'm not interested in roiling the waters, Pat. What's done is done." I tell him about the articles from the 1990s, particularly about Capraro's taped conversation where he bragged about getting away with murder. "I just want some answers for myself. Could I make an appointment and talk with you? I'm more than happy to compensate you for your time, Pat."

"Of course we can meet. And thank you, but it's not necessary to pay me. I'm happy to talk with you." I hear the flipping of pages in the background. "How's your schedule look for the week after Thanksgiving? We could meet at Franklin and Peabody, my law firm in Providence, on that Tuesday. Say, two o'clock?"

"That would be great." I take down his address. His office is four blocks away from the library.

"Is there anything in particular you want to know?"

"I'm just trying to learn what I can. I was in college when my father was murdered and so I never went to any of the trials. And I've only recently read the news reports from back then. Reading Capraro's comments made me realize there was a lot about my father I didn't know in fact, but had surmised." I pause before asking the vital question. "Pat, do you think Capraro was guilty?"

"I have no doubt. I thought we had a strong case against him. That damned Greg!" He laughs, as Greg is his good friend as well as his former adversary.

Now Pat takes a measured pause. "There is one person who knows the truth."

"But I read Capraro died a few years ago," I say, somewhat confused.

"I'm not talking about Angie."

"Who, then?"

"There was this big wheel, Providence lawyer--"

"--Joey Casella?" I interrupt.

"You know him?" Pat seems surprised.

"Since I was a little girl. Is he still practicing law?"

"He's retired. Now he owns this hoity-toity restaurant on Block Island. Casella's."

I jot down Casella's, Block Island on the notepad next to the telephone. "Have you been there?" I ask.

Pat huffs. "I wouldn't waste my time or money. But I understand he's there all the time, doing the meet and greet." The thought makes Pat chuckle. "Anna," he pauses, "Just so you know, your father wasn't a bad man. I mean, he wasn't killed because he did something bad."

"Thank you for saying that, Pat. But I've been reading the old news clippings. I know my father wasn't a saint."

Pat laughs.

"I'm looking forward to meeting with you, Pat. Here's my telephone number in case anything comes up and you need to reschedule."

After we hang up I go on-line and Google Casella's Block Island. I'm not surprised to find a web site for the restaurant. I click on the hyperlink. The home page features three pictures of the restaurant, two inside views— one of the dining room and one of the bar—and an exterior shot highlighting the name, Casella's. I can feel the *agita* rise. The interior décor has an Italian-theme, naturally, with high ceilings and arched windows. The bar and cabinetry are well crafted in dark wood suggesting cherry or mahogany. Above the cash register behind the bar is an etched-glass pane featuring the Casella name and logo.

I click on About Us. As the page scrolls into view, I see the familiar blue eyes and that smile. His thick and wavy brown-black hair is now gray. I look closer at the photo and laugh. "It's a fucking toupee! And a cheap one at that!" I write the address on my notepad and bookmark the web site.

I wait until after dinnertime and call Jacqueline again. I had left a message over the weekend, but my call wasn't returned. Maybe she got to thinking about those news articles and decided I was bad news too. After five rings, the system goes over to voice mail. What the hell. What's one more message? If I don't hear back, then I'll know for sure that she's not interested in getting to know me.

Chapter Fourteen

On the Tuesday after Thanksgiving I drive, yet again, to Providence–this time to meet with Patrick O'Connell. I had spent more time in Rhode Island in the last few weeks than I had in years. As I approach the exit for Washington Street, I notice I have forty-five minutes to spare. Not wanting to be late, I had left well in advance of my two o'clock appointment. I park in a garage halfway between Pat's office and the library. I decide to kill time over a caramel macchiato at Starbucks.

Ten feet from the entrance, I see Jacqueline emerge carrying the familiar white paper cup with the green and black sun-goddess logo. "Hey there," I say with a writer's eloquence.

"Anna!" Her surprise immediately transforms into happiness to see me. "I've been meaning to call you. I've been out of town. Just got back two days ago."

"Someplace fabulous, I see," noting her golden and glowing skin.

"Yes," she says and offers nothing more. "What are you doing in town?"

"I have an appointment. I'm early so I thought I'd grab a coffee. Can you join me?"

Jacqueline looks at her wristwatch. "My lunch break is just about over. But would you like to meet later for an early dinner? There's a great little bistro nearby."

I weigh this quickly. What could Patrick O'Connell tell me that would be anymore shocking than the newspaper account of my father's last ride? What is the chance I'll leave the meeting with him a basket case? I really don't want to inflict my emotional turmoil on this woman a second time.

She misreads my pondering. "Maybe another time, then."

"No. No, Jacqueline, that would be great. I was just…" now I'm flustered "you know…thinking about my appointment. What time are you done?"

"Five."

"Good. Great. I'll meet you at the front desk."

And then I see the smile I'd been daydreaming about for the past several days. "See you at five, Anna."

I watch her walk down the street, her stride is confident, self-assured. Just as she reaches the corner she turns and looks back in my direction. I smile broadly, and top it off with the Matteo nod.

While I am enjoying my coffee I make several mental notes about dinner tonight: *Keep the conversation tonight focused on Jacqueline. Don't talk about your father unless she brings him up, and only if she really, really seems interested. Find out if she's dating anyone. Most important— confirm that she's a sister.* I check my wristwatch. 1:50 P.M. I better get going.

I'm surprisingly at ease when I arrive at Franklin and Peabody. I take a seat in the reception area and skim through *The Providence Journal* while I wait for Pat. A few minutes later I hear my name. I look up and see a cherub-faced gentleman with curly gray hair. His suit jacket is off; his easy smile is on. He extends his hand. His grip is firm, trustworthy. "Good to meet you, Anna. Let's go into the conference room. Can I get you something to drink? Soda? Water? Coffee?"

"No thank you, Pat. I'm fine." I take a seat and look across the conference table at him. Suddenly, I don't know where to begin.

Pat helps me along. "I was thinking, there's Michael Reiser. He was the Assistant State Attorney General. He's retired now, but still lives in Providence. He may have some information for you. I think Crawford, the FBI agent in charge, may have passed away, but one of the sheriff's deputies on the case, Peter Reed, teaches at John Jay in New York. I did make a few calls on your behalf. I talked with Jim Kelley, but unfortunately, his office doesn't have the files anymore either. Too bad. Those tapes had some good stuff. Have you talked with anyone else?"

"All that I've managed to learn, so far, is from old news articles at the library. There were quite a few stories filed."

166

Pat laughs. "Yeah, there was that one reporter, Jim Testa or maybe it was John Testa…"

"George Testa"

"Right. George Testa. He followed every move of that case. I used to tease Greg about it. Told him he had an admirer!"

"I know what you mean," I chime in. "It was like he had his own column. Every story had the same banner, The Capraro Trial." Pat smiles knowingly. "So all I know of the testimony is what was reported."

"I wish you could have heard those tapes. I thought we had him dead-to-rights with that taped evidence. Especially when Angie talked about how Paulie was begging for his life, offering him all sorts of stuff…money, an apartment…" he stops himself.

"My God! I'm sorry, Anna. That's your father I'm talking about. I didn't mean to be cavalier. After a while, when you're involved in these cases, you forget that they extend beyond the courtroom."

I take a measured breath and reach deep inside and find my mother's grace. "I understand. Luckily, I read the news accounts of those tapes where Capraro bragged about 'the last ride.' Otherwise…"

"I'm truly sorry, Anna."

"It's all right, Pat. Let's move on." My calm state surprises even me.

"Not to harp on those tapes, but if you could have heard them, the way those guys talked. Some of it was kinda funny, the language they used. We used to listen to these tapes and laugh at these characters. Ang thought this thing with your father was going to make him."

I'm surprised how, like my brother, O'Connell so easily refers to Capraro as 'Ang' or 'Angie.' Maybe that's how people in his line of work do their job. Get to know the guy. Talk with him on his level. Get him relaxed in hopes he'll trip himself up.

"At one point Angie says on the tape: They're gonna respect me now. I'm gonna be wearing hundred-dollar suits and everybody's gonna be calling me Mr. Capraro." Pat laughs and I pretend to find it funny and join in.

"Why did you think Joey Casella was behind my father's murder?" I ask.

"Casella was into a lot. His name surfaced in a number of investigations over the years. He represented the bottom-feeders— pornographers, arsonists, murderers. Several years after your father's murder, one of Casella's associates was tied up and shot to death, right in the law offices." Pat's brow furrows. "Do the names Massimo Pandozzi and Carmine Nastri ring familiar?"

I thought for a moment. "I do remember meeting Carmine a few times, when I was a kid. My father would bring me around these guys all the time." I snigger. Did my father even consider keeping me away from these characters? "I never met Pandozzi. I know the name, though. They call him 'the Panda.' I remember he was arrested one time along with my father, Capraro, and a couple other guys."

"When was that?" Pat asks.

"1968. I remember because it happened on my thirteen birthday." I shake my head in disgust. "I read that Pandozzi may have been with Capraro that night in the car. If that was the case, Pat, why wasn't he indicted?"

"He was in the car. But we couldn't touch him. We only knew of it because Angie told that to Jimmy Hedrick, so it was considered hearsay. We couldn't get any direct evidence placing Pandozzi in the car that night. And Angie wasn't going to give him up. He knew Carmine would kill him. That Nastri was one bad seed. Ended up getting killed in a standoff with the FBI."

"Do you know who pulled the trigger?"

"At one point on the tapes Capraro supposedly says he used a .38. That information wasn't released, so it was something only the killer would know. But Bell, the judge for that trial, wouldn't allow that portion of the tape to be admitted as evidence because the sound was fuzzy. The technology back then wasn't like what we have today. Back then, they used these miniature Nagra tape recorders. The FBI gave Jimmy a car with the recorder built into the dashboard, and it picked up engine sounds, everything. The quality was poor in spots. Hedrick went nuts when Bell disallowed it. I remember he yelled: I risked my life for this!

"So, to answer your question, honestly, it could have been either of

168

them. Your father was shot six times. For all we know they each pumped three." I take a deep breath. It doesn't go unnoticed. "Are you okay?"

"I am," I lie.

"When I was with the OCTF, Pandozzi was on our radar as an enforcer for Casella. Actually, your brother testified that Pandozzi worked for Casella as a collector." Pat leaned across the table. "I was sorry to hear about your brother. I liked Tony."

I nod my appreciation and thanks.

"I never knew your father, but he certainly was mixed up in this big, tangled web." Pat stops to think a moment. "There was another murder case I was involved with. A guy named Vito Cerbone."

"Cerbone. That's familiar."

"It was after your father's murder. Cerbone had testified at a couple of trials that led to the convictions of three Warwick guys for the murder of his wife. Carmella, I think her name was."

"Carmella Cerbone? I remember reading about that. She was a friend of a friend of a friend. You know what I mean? Someone whose name you know, but you don't really *know* the person."

Pat nods. "Casella defended one of the guys. Vito told a grand jury that after the trial he met up with Casella at a restaurant and they had a fight. He claimed Joey followed him to his car and shot at him. Casella was indicted. Now, keep in mind here, something very similar happened with your father. Seems your father and Joey got into it one night at a restaurant and your father punched him.

"So anyway, Casella is acquitted of the charges, and a few weeks later Cerbone is killed while sitting at a bar having a drink. A masked gunman walks in and shoots him in the head and body at close range. We believed Nastri was the gunman."

"Was Casella investigated?"

"Absolutely. But the guy's a master bricklayer. Builds enough layers and walls around himself and manages to skate every time."

"And that's why you think the Capraro-Casella connection was there? Because of the similar circumstances, the fights?"

"The circumstances were very similar. Jim Kelley can tell you more

169

since he prosecuted the case."

"But I read, too, that my father owed Joey money."

"He did. Something like eight grand. But your father owed a lot of people money. And some a helluva lot more than eight grand. But add to it that Old World, Italian-thing those kinda guys have. Your father not only owed him money, he punched him, disrespected him." Pat takes a sip of his Coke. "Have you talked with Greg? Gotten his perspective?"

"Not yet. But I will." Pat seems surprised by my answer.

"Greg and I don't see eye to eye on the Casella connection. But Casella was indicted on several counts of perjury and conspiracy in connection with your father's murder. He allegedly got this Providence hood, Alphonso Pennachia, to lie to the grand jury about Pandozzi's whereabouts several days before your father was murdered. That night, the Cranston police responded to a call about a suspicious car with two men inside parked outside your father's apartment building. The patrolman who responded didn't ask the two men for identification at the time, but later identified— from police photographs—the driver as Pandozzi. He couldn't make a positive I.D. on Capraro, although he thought it might be him. Turns out, too, that the car was registered to Pandozzi."

I sigh, a bit overwhelmed by all he is telling me.

"So, supposedly, Casella gets Pennachia to say he himself was the driver and the passenger was another friend of his."

"Excuse me, Pat, but if the car was registered to Pandozzi, why was this other guy, Pennachia, supposedly driving it?"

Pat laughs. "This is what I mean about the layers. Pennachia said he was test-driving it because he was thinking of buying it as a gift for his girlfriend. And to add some validity to the story, Pennachia actually buys the car a couple days later."

I shake my head in disbelief.

"And, it gets better—the car is stolen and eventually turns up torched."

"Unbelievable."

"Casella covers his tracks. Did you know that he filed a judgment against your father for the money he owed him the same day as the murder? That was Casella's big defense: If I was going to kill somebody, I wouldn't

170

have put a judgment on the record for everybody to see it."

"Ah! The intended alibi," I snicker. "Like Catherine Tramell in *Basic Instinct*. 'I'd have to be pretty stupid to write about killing and then kill somebody the way I described in my book.'"

Pat laughs. "That's right."

I glance at my watch. It is a few minutes before three. I gather my purse and stand up. "Thank you, Pat, for your time and honesty." I reach across the table and shake his hand.

"I hope this helped you. Call me if you have any other questions. And I'll let you know if we track down those tapes." Pat escorts me back to the reception area. He shakes my hand again. "I'm sorry, Anna. I wish I could have put them both away."

I decide to go back to Starbucks. Jacqueline won't be off work for another two hours, which is perfect. I need time to digest all that Pat told me. What if Casella was behind it? My father's long dead and Joey's still living the good life—now under the guise of a Block Island restaurateur. Mr. Respectable. What a fucking joke!

Two teenage boys pass by and I whiff a familiar odor. It's been decades since I got high on weed—thirty years to be exact—but I'll never forget that fragrant scent. The memory makes me chuckle, since I owe the end of my pot smoking days to Joey Casella.

Final exam time my sophomore year was particularly grueling. Maybe it was because I had skipped one too many classes, or maybe it was because I had fallen way behind in my reading assignments. Whichever reason was correct, it was the home stretch of the semester and I needed to pull some serious all-nighters.

White cross was everyone's drug of choice and easy to score on campus. The amphetamine got its nickname because each small tablet was scored with the sign of the cross. The perfect "upper" for a good Catholic

171

girl. After two-and-a-half weeks of virtually no sleep—and the little sleep I did manage to get was on the floor under the table in the study library—I was exhausted beyond belief and wired beyond comprehension. I needed to seriously come down.

Before heading home for Christmas break I stopped to see my supplier, Christine Wright. Christine's family had more money than God, but that didn't stop her from running the most lucrative drug business on campus. And she was untouchable—a descendent of a Founding Father, great-great-grand-daughter of a former United States president, and the granddaughter of a well-known senator. My plan was to score a couple of joints.

"Why not get an ounce?" Christine suggested. "We're out of school for the next four weeks."

"How much?"

"Twenty. And it's clean. No seeds, no stems. What you see is what you smoke."

I counted off four of her great-granddaddy. "Wait here," she said as she exited her room.

I sat on her bed while she fetched the goods. Christine took great pains to keep the location of her supply a secret. Sometimes you waited in your room, sometimes she arranged for you to meet her elsewhere on campus. This was the first time I had ever waited in her dorm room. I figured the stash was nearby, ready to be transported home over winter break. Christine was back in less than five minutes. "Wrap the bag in tin foil and hide it in the spare tire well of your car when you're on the road."

"Thanks for the good advice," I said.

Back in my dorm room I pulled my hardbound copy of *The Complete Sherlock Holmes* from the bookshelf above my desk. I had bought the book at Aberdeen's Bargain Basement when I was ten years old. I got the idea after seeing a *Batman* episode. Take a thick, hardcover book, cut out a recess, and voilà! a secret compartment. I opened the latter third of the book and lifted out my joint roller and packet of papers. I slid in a Zig Zag—the rolling paper of choice—sprinkled in some Green Goddess and turned the knob. A perfect joint every time! I lit two incense sticks before lighting up. I smoked half the joint while I rolled two more for later.

Three hours later I pulled into the snow-covered gravel driveway of my childhood home, parked behind Ma's green Buick and took a deep breath. It was good to be home. I got out of the car and opened the trunk. After a quick check up and down the street, I lifted the spare tire out, grabbed Mary Jane, and shoved her in my pea coat pocket.

Ma's walkway was layered with a good four inches of snow. I trudged through to the front door. No sooner did I step foot into the hallway I heard the butchered strains of *Fleur de Lis* coming from Ma's basement studio. "Watch your fingering!" I heard her say with a touch of exasperation. "Four, three, one not three, two, one. Use your fourth finger. Then your fifth will be where you need it to be, on the A sharp!" God bless her! Even I knew the correct fingering for *Fleur de Lis*, and I never even played the song. Growing up, I'd heard her say that over and over and over again.

I ran upstairs to my bedroom and put Mary Jane to bed between the mattresses before heading down to say a quick hello to Ma. As I descended the steps to her studio, I breathed in deeply the scent of *Interlude*. It was Ma's signature fragrance. Last month when I was home for Thanksgiving break, I was waiting for Ma at Tony and Ginny's house. I was upstairs in Tess's room reading to her from her favorite Dr. Seuss book, when suddenly, Tess bolted from my lap.

"Nana's here!"

I listened a moment. I couldn't hear Ma's normally booming voice.

"I don't think so, Tess. I don't hear her downstairs."

"I don't hear Nana; I smell her!"

The memory made me smile; I inhaled deeply again.

"No, no, no! Look at the staff! How many sharps are there, Justin?"

"Hi, Ma. Don't mean to interrupt." Justin, however, looked thrilled to have Ma's attention off him at this moment. "Just wanted to let you know I'm home." I kissed her cheek.

"Justin, this is my daughter, Anna. This is Justin Bucci. Remember Patty Connelly? This is her son."

"Hi, Justin." I reached into Ma's ever-present candy jar and took out a butterscotch candy. "How late are you teaching?" I asked her as I peeled the wrapper off.

"I'll be done at eight. There're cold cuts in the icebox, but don't eat too much. We'll go to the Broadway afterwards. Did you call your father?"

"Ma, I just got home."

"Well, he called here looking for you already."

"Okay. I'll call him now. Nice to meet you, Justin. Say 'hi' to your mom for me. You remember my name?"

He nods. "Anna."

I kissed Ma's cheek again before heading back upstairs. I opened the refrigerator and took out the stack of cold cuts wrapped in white wax paper. Cappicola, Genoa salami, sharp provolone. I took a slice of each and rolled them together like a tight joint. I downed the taste of *Italia* in three bites. The telephone rang as I was putting the food back in the refrigerator.

"Anna! It's your father!" Ma yelled up to me.

I grabbed the wall phone in the kitchen. "I got it, Ma!"

"Hi, Daddy. I was just gonna call you. I just got home a few minutes ago."

"How's my baby?"

"Grown up, Dad."

"Wanna have dinner with me tonight?"

"I already told Ma I'd have dinner with her."

"That's okay, baby. Do that with your mother tonight. How about keeping tomorrow night open for me? I'm meeting an old friend for dinner, but I know he'd love to see you again."

"Who?"

"You'll find out tomorrow. Why don't you meet us at Dante's around seven."

"Sounds great."

"You need any money?"

I chuckled to myself. The conversation never changes. "No, Dad. I'm fine."

The following night I walked into Dante's Ristorante and found my father at the bar in heavy conversation with another man whose back was to me. I hung back, not wanting to interrupt him.

"*Madonn'*! I can't-a believe-a my eyes. Anna Matteo! *Bella, bella*!"

174

I turned around to see who had called out to me. At first I didn't recognize him; he seemed to have shrunk a good six inches. And I never remembered being so much taller than he. He was still reed thin, but long hours and hard, physical work had taken its toll. "Signore Palermo! *Come siete stati?*"

"*Bene, bene*, Anna. You home-a for *Natale?*"

"*Si, si.*"

"You come-a by for espresso. You still like-a *pasticiotti?*"

"*Si, si.* And I haven't had a *pasticiotii delizioso* since I left Cranston."

"There's my baby!" My father exclaimed as he wrapped me in a bear hug.

"Paolo, your Anna," he put his aged fingertips to his withered lips and blew a kiss into the air. "*Una ragazza molta bella.*"

"*Grazie*, Gino. *Ha occhi bei della sua madre, si?*"

"And I have my father's smile!" I piped in.

Mr. Palermo kissed me Italian-style, on both cheeks. "You have-a nice-a dinner with-a you father. You come for espresso. *Si?*"

"*Si. Grazie*, Signore Palermo. *Buon Natale!*"

"God, he's gotten old," I said to my father as I watched Mr. Palermo hobble out the door.

"You know, he just turned eighty-five? And he still goes to that bakery every morning at four-thirty and makes all the pastry."

"Well, he looks it."

"Anna!"

"I don't mean to be rude, Dad, but c'mon…the guy looks like he's held together with a flour and water paste."

Dad burst out laughing, then kissed my cheek again. "Let's go eat, baby."

He took my hand and led me to his table in the far-back corner. "Is that Joey Casella?" I said as we approached.

"Sure is. And he couldn't wait to see you tonight."

Joey jumped up from the table. "Annabella!" He kissed me Italian-style.

"Joey! What a wonderful surprise!" I had to admit I felt giddy. Joey looked dapper as ever in his custom-made gray silk suit. I swear he and my father had the same tailor. His pocket square and tie matched perfectly, and were he to open his jacket, I was certain they would match the lining as well. "My, my, Anna. From my little Annabella to a beautiful young woman!" He kissed my cheeks again.

I drew in a long and deep breath. At that precise moment I personified the word *swoon.* "Thank you, Joey. And you might want to say that 'young woman' part again—to my father. He still calls me his baby."

"You'll always be my baby," Dad said. And then he did the ultimate act in keeping me his little girl. He pulled his black plastic comb from his rear pants pocket and combed my bangs, which I now wore off my forehead.

"Dad! I don't wear bangs anymore! Now I look like Cousin It!" I pushed my long bangs back where they belonged.

Daddy had a good laugh and wriggled his eyebrows. "Do your Groucho for Joey."

It was a great dinner with Dad and Joey. We talked and laughed and drank a lot of wine and ate a lot of Mrs. Dante's fabulous cooking— escarole soup, braccioli, and carbonara. I was mesmerized by Joey. I drank in his every move. The way his hands danced as he spoke; the way he swallowed quickly rather than speak with a mouth full of food; the way he wiped the corners of his lips with his napkin. So genteel, not *cafone.* And in spite of my penchant for the girls, I found I still had a crush on Joey after all these years.

F ive nights later, Ma and I were awakened in the middle of the night by the persistent ringing of the doorbell and pounding on the front door. I looked at the illuminated dial on my clock radio. "Jesus," I muttered. "It's two in the morning!" I stumbled out of bed and into the hallway.

Ma, wrapped in a lilac polar fleece bathrobe, was making her way down the stairs to answer the door. I hung back—out of sight, but not out of hearing range. "Who's there?" she called out.

"FBI, Mrs. Matteo. Open the door."

176

Shit! I ran into the bedroom and grabbed Mary Jane from under the mattress and stuffed her inside my underpants. I stopped at the top of the stairs and tried to get a peek as to what was going on. From my lookout I saw two men at the foot of the staircase. Their overcoats were covered in snow; one man held a briefcase.

"Is your husband at home?" the taller man asked.

"He doesn't live here," Ma said. "We've been separated for years."

"Who's that upstairs?"

I dashed into the bathroom and closed the door. I grabbed the water glass from the sink, placed it on the door, and pressed my ear to it. Suddenly, I was ten again.

"That's my daughter. She's home from college."

"Mind if we have a talk with her?"

"Why do you want to talk with Anna?" I heard Ma ask.

Fuck! Fuck! I wasn't taking any chances. I grabbed my stash out of my undies and tossed it, baggie and all, into the toilet and flushed. I washed my hand thoroughly with soap and water, flushed the toilet again, and then headed, as nonchalantly as possible, down the stairs.

"Everything okay, Ma?"

"Are you Anna Matteo?" the taller man asked.

I gave him the Matteo nod. "Yes. May I ask who you are?"

"I'm Agent Freed and this is Agent Tomlin. Do you know a Joseph Casella?"

"Before I answer any questions, may I see some identification, please?" I was cool, calm, and collected. I was Paulie Matteo's daughter.

The two men unbuttoned their overcoats, reached into the liner pockets, and retrieved leather billfolds. I checked both I.D.s carefully.

"Would you gentlemen like some coffee?" Ma asked.

I glared at her. "I can't imagine they'll be staying that long, Ma."

"As I was saying, Miss Matteo, do you know a Joseph Casella?"

"I might."

Holding the briefcase to his chest, Agent Tomlin clicked open the locks, reached in and extracted a file folder with the words *Federal Bureau of Investigation* embossed on the front along with the familiar blue and gold emblem. He opened the folder and pulled out several black-and-white photographs of Dad, Joey, and me having dinner at Dante's last week.

"What the…?" I said.

"Now that we've conclusively established that you know Joseph Casella, would you like to tell us why you were dining with him last week?"

"Maybe we should call your father," Ma interjected.

"No, Ma. That's what they want us to do." I faced the agents squarely. "I'm home for winter break. I met my father for dinner. Mr. Casella, a longtime family friend, joined us. We talked about school, my plans after I graduate, and a lot of nothin' in particular. Now, before you get my mother any more upset, do you mind telling me what this is about?"

"We don't have to tell you anything," Agent Freed answered brusquely.

"Do I need a lawyer?" I asked.

"You tell us," said Freed.

"Well, I believe I don't. So I suggest, then, that you leave."

My mother elbowed my ribs. "Anna!" she said in her motherly don't-be- rude way.

"What, Ma? I've done nothing wrong and the only reason they're here at two o'clock in the morning is to intimidate us." I turned back to the two agents. "Am I right, gentlemen?"

Agent Tomlin snickered. "Just remember, we have these." He patted the folder with the photos, then placed the file folder back in his briefcase and snapped it shut. "Sorry to have disturbed you, Mrs. Matteo. Have a Merry Christmas," he said snidely.

The agents left, and Ma was a mix of emotions: anger, worry, annoyance. "It never ends with that father of yours. And now he's dragged you into his mess."

"He didn't drag me into anything, Ma. We had dinner, that's all." I walked into the living room and turned on the light. "How about a little anisette? It'll help you get back to sleep." I wished I had a little joint to help me get back to sleep. Instead, the entire ounce was making its way through the Cranston sewerage system.

She nodded. "What do you suppose that was all about?" Ma asked as I filled two burgundy and gold Murano aperitif glasses with the sweet liquor.

The licorice-like aroma wafted tantalizingly. I carried both glasses and the bottle into the living room and sat on the sofa next to my mother.

"I don't know, Ma. They're too smart to have not known Dad doesn't live here. I'm thinking they pulled this little stunt so that I would tell Dad what happened. Maybe they want him to know they're on his trail about something, but they don't want to approach him directly. And, I'm thinking, they're more interested in Joey than they are in Dad."

Thinking back to that night in 1975, I now wonder if the Feds knew Dad was in harm's way. I stopped by the produce company the next morning to tell my father what happened. I wanted to talk in person. I didn't trust that the phones weren't tapped. It wouldn't have been the first time. Dad laughed it off, like he did most things.

"Keep your nose clean," he kidded me. "You got a file now!"

I took his halfhearted advice. I never bought an illegal drug again. I also never saw Joey again. Unfortunately, I was to be hassled again.

A few weeks after I returned to college that winter, I was called out of class. "The Dean needs to see you in her office," said Sheila Tucker, Assistant to the Dean of Students.

My first thought was something had happened to my mother. "Do you know why?" Sheila avoided my eyes. Her look was more one of embarrassment than sorrow.

Dean Ross met me in the outer office. Her manner was direct and to the point. "Anna, I consulted with our legal counsel and they said for you to cooperate for now and to discuss the situation afterwards with your family attorney."

"Cooperate with what? What's going on?"

"Perhaps I should come into the office with you. Would that be all right with you?"

"I don't even know what you're talking about." I was genuinely confused and starting to feel a little frightened.

"It might be better if I'm in there with you," Dean Ross said, making up my mind for me.

As we entered her office I noticed a tall, lanky man standing by her desk. "Are you Anna Matteo?" he asked without introduction.

"Yes," I answered warily.

"I'm Agent Coleman of the Internal Revenue Service. I'm here to issue you a summons." He handed the papers to me. "You are required to appear before a panel of the Internal Revenue Service regarding an investigation of Paul Matteo. If you fail to appear, you will be arrested for contempt of court. Do you understand what I've told you?"

I felt my body temperature plummet. "Whoa. Wait a minute. Is this some sort of joke?" I could not for the life of me comprehend what was happening.

Dean Ross spoke first. "No, Anna. As I told you, I talked with the college counsel. They advise that you accept the summons."

"Why?"

"Because it's in your best interest, Miss Matteo," Agent Coleman answered.

"How do you figure that?" I remarked snidely.

"Again, let me reiterate. If you fail to appear you will be arrested for contempt of court. Do you understand what I've told you?"

"Yes," I answered. And with that Agent Coleman left.

Dean Ross placed her hand on my shoulder. "Anna, come sit down." I allowed her to direct me to a chair. She poured a glass of water and brought it to me. "Would you like to use my phone and call your father?" I nodded. "I'll give you privacy. Take as long as you need."

It took a few tries before I was finally able to track my father down at the club. "Son-of-a-fucking-bitch!" was my father's response. "I'm sorry, baby. I'm sorry this is happening to you. Francis warned me this might happen. You remember Francis Paglia, the attorney?"

"I can't testify against you, Dad."

"Baby, don't you worry. I'm gonna set something up for you and Francis. He'll get you through this. Anna, don't tell your mother for now.

Let me handle this."

But he couldn't "handle" it. One month later, I spent five grueling hours being interrogated by Agents Coleman and Thayer. They seemed to take great pleasure in reminding me every ten minutes that the penalty for perjury was a five-thousand dollar fine and three-to-five years in jail.

Their strategy didn't work. I lied through my teeth.

I've always wondered if that day would have come back to haunt me if Dad had not been murdered. Five days after the funeral, Agent Coleman had the audacity to show up at Ma's house. I wouldn't let him in. Made him talk to me while he stood on the stoop in the snow.

"I wanted to let you know in person that with your father's passing the investigation is closed. I'm sorry for your loss, Anna," he said.

"The fuck you are," I answered as I closed the door in his face.

Noting the clock behind the barista's station, I see there are still ninety minutes until Jacqueline's shift ends. I decide to go to the library and use the Internet. I log on to my account at Projo.com and go to the archives. I type J-o-s-e-p-h C-a-s-e-l-l-a. Click and Search.

Results **1 of 7** of about **48** for **Joseph Casella**.

"Pay dirt," I mutter. I skim through the first set of headlines.

> March 2, 1983 – EXTORTION TRIAL NEARS END
> February 11, 1984 – PROVIDENCE MURDER MAY BE LINKED TO NEW YORK PROBE
> June 26, 1984 – CASELLA INDICTED IN SHOOTING
> August 22, 1984 – JURY ACQUITS CASELLA
> September 19, 1986 – EXECUTION-STYLE KILLING FOCUS OF MOB PROBE
> May 7, 1987 – DEFENSE LAWYER FACES ALLEGATIONS
> April 30, 1992 - LAWYER SNARLED IN MURDER PLOT

"Joey, Joey, Joey," I say under my breath. "Un-fucking-believable." I click on the last item.

THURSDAY APRIL 30, 1992
Lawyer Snarled In Murder Plot

Providence defense attorney **Joseph Casella** was part of a conspiracy to kill a Providence man six years ago, federal prosecutors alleged Thursday. **Casella** was named as an unindicted co-conspirator in the attempted murder of Albert Pannicone, Assistant U.S. Attorney Michael Munch said in legal papers.

Casella's name came up frequently in the 1978 and 1979 trials of a man charged with gangland-style slaying of Paul Matteo, a Cranston gambler and produce dealer. Angelo Capraro, a man who prosecutors described as a debt collector for **Casella,** was accused at the trial of killing Matteo because Matteo owed **Casella** $8,000. Capraro's first murder trial ended in a hung jury and his second trial ended with his acquittal.

I decide to bring up the two 1984 articles, figuring they refer to the Cerbone case Pat O'Connell mentioned.

TUESDAY, JUNE 26, 1984
Casella Indicted In Shooting

Providence lawyer **Joseph Casella** pleaded innocent today to two counts of first-degree reckless endangerment and one count of unlawful use of a weapon. **Casella** is accused of shooting at Vito Cerbone during a dispute April 29 at Mario's Restaurant.

Casella was charged in a sealed indictment filed by the Providence County grand jury. If found guilty of first-degree reckless endangerment, a Class D felony, **Casella** could face a maximum sentence of three-and-a-half to seven years in jail.

Cerbone was married to Carmella Cerbone, whose decomposed body was found January 1982 in an abandoned lot in the Kent

County town of East Natick. Last year **Casella** defended one of the three men convicted of killing the 28-year old woman.

According to police reports, Casella's run-in with Cerbone began shortly after 2 A.M. on April 29. Sheriff Roy Cowan said **Casella** fired several shots from a .38 semi-automatic pistol at Cerbone during an argument in front of Mario's Restaurant in Providence. One of the shots shattered the restaurant's front window. No one was injured.

Cerbone was charged with third-degree assault in connection with the incident. The charge was dropped in Providence City Court in exchange for Cerbone's testimony before the grand jury. **Casella's** case was adjourned to July 9, when motions will be filed in Providence County Court.

Casella, a noted Providence attorney with reported ties to the Patriarca Crime Family could not be reached for comment.

WEDNESDAY, AUGUST 15, 1984
JURY ACQUITS CASELLA

Well-known lawyer **Joseph Casella** was acquitted by a Providence County jury of charges filed in connection with a June shooting incident outside Mario's Restaurant in Providence. The innocent verdict came just before 4 P.M. yesterday, five-and-a-half hours after the jury began its deliberations.

Law enforcement officials have tried on several occasions to link **Casella** with organized crime investigations involving murder, arson, perjury and pornography. In a few cases, **Casella** may have been the victim of criminal activity.

In February, Casella's law associate, Peter Agnelli, was found brutally murdered in their law offices. Two buildings owned by **Casella** were burned to the ground in 1979 and 1981. Investigations revealed the fires were the work of arsonists.

"Anna Matteo?" The male voice startles me. I look up and see the familiar blue eyes. Eyes that had not set upon me since my childhood days.

"You are Anna Matteo, aren't you?" My eyes travel from his blue eyes down to his mouth. His lips are open and curved. It is a smile I've seen many times in my youth. He's not a tall man, but his body is strong. "Don't you remember me?" His blue suit is well-made, tailored with matching pocket square and bow tie. "It's me…" and before he pronounces his name I recognize the distinctive voice.

"Peter. Peter Veneziano," I say as I stand up and extend my hand. He takes my hand and nestles it in his two large, yet delicate ones.

"I know, the bow tie was a dead giveaway," he says, adding that sweet smile I remember. "You look wonderful, Anna. And you haven't changed a bit."

"That's kind of you to say." I pat my girth. "Although, I'm looking more and more like my mother these days, I'm afraid!"

"Ah, your mother!" Peter's hands flitter like two dragonflies and come to rest one over the other above his heart. "I was so sorry to hear she passed away. I was on sabbatical; otherwise I would have attended her funeral. She was a great woman, your mother."

"That she was, and you're kind to say so, Peter." And then his words come back at me. "Did you say you were on sabbatical? Are you a teacher?"

I study his face as he speaks. Peter still has the same gentle eyes. His jaw is strong, masculine; his voice is baritone rich, although a slight lisp is still evident. "I teach music at Providence College," he says.

"Music? Really."

He nods, and I see a little of the old insecurity come out through. "You seemed surprised."

I reach out and touch his arm. "No…well yes…I mean…" here comes that writer's eloquence again "…I mean, I knew you were talented. Ma always said that about you. But I guess I was expecting you to say English literature. You were such a voracious reader." *I handed him a worn copy of* Compulsion *I'd found. "Ever read this?"* Images of that day at Aberdeen's flood my mind. I try to push it away. *"Anna…What are you thinking of doing?…Are you thinking of harming Ricky?* I can't. Instead, I mask my thoughts and fake the Matteo smile. "My Ma would be proud."

Peter's broad smile is genuine. "I think she was. She came to my senior recital at the Conservatory. Even wrote a stellar reference for me when I applied for the Providence College position."

"Now that you mention it, I remember her telling me about your recital. She was very proud of you, Peter." *I don't know. But if I did want to…I paused for effect…harm him, would you do it with me?*

"Did you know your mother would meet me every Thursday morning at seven-thirty in the basement at St. Stephen's church and give me a piano lesson?"

I shook my head for two reasons: One, I didn't know that; and two, I was hoping to shake the ghosts from my mind. *Well, think about it. Because if something does happen to Ricky…*

It was going to take a lot more than a shake or two.

He smiles and nods. "Every week, until I graduated from high school, she taught me on that rickety piano in the church basement. When she realized I quit because my parents couldn't afford my lessons, she offered to teach me for free. But my parents were too proud to accept her generosity. So, unbeknownst to them, we met in the church basement every Thursday until I graduated. I guess it truly was our little secret."

I smile. Ma had her own little secrets, too.

"I read somewhere you're a writer, published a novel," he continued. "I'm not surprised. You were always a prolific reader."

Remember that day you saw me here? The day you asked me to be your reading buddy? You asked me what I was reading. I never told you…But I'm gonna tell you now. I was reading the Encyclopedia of Murder. *And I bought the book that day.*

"Calling me a writer might be stretching it these days. I basically do commercial writing, creative copy for businesses. It pays the bills. I was working on another novel," I shrug my shoulders. "I may get back to it one day."

And I read it every night. I study the cases. Study how they did it and why they got caught. I study their mistakes….I won't make a mistake."

I can't stop the flood of memories and I can't stop the tears filling my eyes. "Peter, could you ever forgive me for what I did to you? For those

185

cruel things I said to you that day at Aberdeen's." I try to swallow the lump that has formed in my throat, but it won't go down. Tears roll down my face. "You were always so sweet and kind. I don't know why I did it. But I hope you can find it in your heart to forgive me one day."

Peter pulls me into his arms and hugs me warmly. "I forgave you a long time ago, Anna." He breaks the embrace and takes my hands in his. "Actually, I remember the exact day. It was December 24, 1976. I was home for Christmas vacation. I was attending Boston Conservatory of Music at that time. I saw your father's funeral on the news. I remember thinking that it couldn't have been easy for you, growing up Paulie Matteo's daughter. And suddenly, what had happened at Aberdeen's made some sort of sense to me. I went to St. Stephen's later that day and lit three candles— one for your mother, one for your father, and one for you."

I touch his cheek with my fingertips. "Oh, Peter. You are the kindest of men."

Peter is a touch embarrassed. "In some ways, Anna, what you did that day changed me for the better. I knew I would always be victimized because I was" he wiggles his fingers effeminately, poking fun at himself, "different. So, I began to look for ways to make myself stronger, more confident, and less ashamed. I used to think I felt shame because my parents were immigrants, because they were elderly and didn't speak English very well. But, then, I realized the shame I felt had to do with me, with my being gay. And I knew Petey Pantywaist had to die, and Peter had to accept who he is. And I have."

I look at him. "So, what you're saying is: You're here, you're queer, get used to it?"

Peter bursts into laughter and I join it. I touch his cheek again. "Me, too, by the way."

"I knew it! I always suspected you, Anna."

"Oh?" I say feigning surprise. "What was the tip off? The gun and shoulder holster?"

"Actually, it was the brown shoes," Peter quips.

We share a good laugh again for several moments. Peter looks at his watch. "I have to get going. I have class tonight. But it was sure great to see you again. Let's keep in touch. I really mean that."

"I'd like that, Peter." I reach into my purse for my wallet. "Let me give you my card. It has my home telephone number and e-mail address." I extract a business card from my wallet and hand it to him. We hug each other tightly, and in that embrace I feel a massive weight fall from my soul.

I take a few bites of the *osso buco*. "This veal is incredible, Jacqueline. I know it's not a politically correct food, but I love it. If I lived in Providence, I'd eat here every night."

Jacqueline looks pleased. "This is my favorite restaurant. I'm glad you are enjoying your dinner."

"Absolutely! The meal is exquisite." I take another mouthful and follow it with a sip of Chianti Classico-Riserva. "So, where did you go over the holiday? Were you visiting family or taking a vacation?" We had done the ice-breaker conversation over appetizers. Now it was time for some 'meat-and-potatoes' talk.

"A vacation, of sorts. My partner and I..." she stops herself. "Let me clarify here. My ex-partner and I ended our relationship four months ago, but we had made nonrefundable reservations for a trip to Key West last March. So we agreed to be adults and take separate vacations together. In other words, we traveled down together, shared a room that, thankfully, had two beds, and traveled back together. Otherwise, we were on our own. It was awkward, to say the least, and re-affirming, to say the most, in that I knew I had made the right decision to leave her."

"How long were you together?"

"Twenty-two years."

"Really!" I could not stop the shock from registering on my face. "That's a long time. Why the break up? If you don't mind my asking."

"The usual...infidelity. Hers, not mine. Now, I know you may not believe this, but when I read your novel and the soul-searching your character went through, it was like the waters parted. I believed I could leave her and be all right." She shakes her head in wonderment. "And here I

187

am, having dinner with the author who gave me strength through her words. Small world, huh?"

I titter. "I'll say." And she was right. I wasn't sure I believed her. But, I've come to recognize that trust is not my strong suit. So, I decide to take her at her word.

"And speaking of small worlds, I mentioned to my cousin Renee that I met you. Renee is married to Frank Guardino. And it turns out that Frank's sister, Rosie, dated your brother Anthony."

"I remember Rosie." I smile at the memory and keep it to myself. Rosie "Dirty Tosies" Guardino—got the nickname because she always wore open-toed sandals and never washed her feet, or so it seemed. Her toenails were black and you could grow a small garden in the dirt packed between her toes. Tony, God only knows why, dated her for about two weeks the summer after he graduated from high school. He and Ginny were in the midst of one of their infamous break-ups. But after his stint with Dirty Tosies, he proposed to Ginny.

"Does your brother still live in Rhode Island?"

My smile vanishes and tears spring into my eyes. "Tony's dead."

Jacqueline takes my hand. I dab my eyes with the white linen napkin leaving a mascara stain I attempt to hide by folding it. "I always seem to be crying when I'm with you. I'm sorry. I've been on this emotional journey through my life the last few months. If it's true that your life flashes before you when you're about to die, then I'm meetin' my Maker any time now."

"Don't say that! Don't even joke about it!"

The waiter brings the check and I insist on paying the tab. "Thank you, Anna. But, you have to promise me that I get the next one."

"So, there'll be a next one?" I give her my best Matteo smile.

Jacqueline leans across the table. "I'm hoping there will be many."

Chapter Fifteen

In January of 1980, two months after he was acquitted of my father's murder, Angelo Capraro was re-tried on the arson indictment and found guilty. He was sentenced to nine years at the Maximum Security Facility in Cranston. At last, some measure of justice had been meted out.

July 14, 1989 was a steamy summer night. Stripped down to my bra and shorts, I was sitting in front of the fan downing my umpteenth glass of ice tea when someone began pounding on the side-entrance door of my house. I looked out the kitchen window and saw a Buick Le Sabre in the driveway. "Anna, it's Tony. Open up."

I quickly grabbed a T-shirt from the bedroom and pulled it on as I scurried to the kitchen door. "Hang on," I yelled. "I'm coming." I opened the door and Tony's alcohol-laced breath preceded him into the kitchen by about five feet.

"Got a beer?"

"No," I lied. I was surprised he could walk, never mind drive the fifty-some-odd miles from Cranston to my house. I was also surprised he even knew where I lived. Tony had never been to my home in all the years I lived in Massachusetts. I didn't know what to make of this visit. And I wasn't sure how to handle it. I knew Tony, like Dad, could be a mean drunk.

"The fuck is out," he slurred.

I proceeded with as much caution as possible. "Tony, sit down. I'm gonna put on some coffee."

"I don't want any fuckin' coffee!" he screamed. "I want that fuck and I'm gonna get him." And with those words, he reached into his pocket and laid a .22 on the table.

I felt my face blanch. "*Mannagge*, Tony! What the fuck are you doin' with that gun?"

189

"I just told you. I'm gonna whack that fucker."

Tony may have been a pain-in-the-ass big brother when we were younger, but at this moment he truly frightened me. The look in his eyes was cold-blooded.

"Whack what fucker?" I asked cautiously.

"Capraro," he slurred. "He's outta jail. And now I'm gonna get him for killin' Dad."

I fell back in my chair. "What are you, *oobatz?"*

"No. I'm no *oobatz.*" Tony was now having difficulty controlling his movements. His arms were flailing and he kept slumping and sliding in his seat. "Ang is finally gonna get what's comin' to him, that's all."

I realized that Tony was drunker than I first thought. I could use this to my advantage. I kept my eye on the gun as I spoke. "Tony," I said softly. "Listen to me. I wanted to see Capraro get his. I wanted him to rot in jail the rest of his life for killing Dad. But what's done is done. You gotta think of your kids now, Tony. Think of Tess and Little Paulie and the baby. Especially the baby."

"I don't give a fuck."

"I don't believe that. What if you kill him and you go to jail? Or worse, what if he shoots you? You want your kids to grow up without a father?" I let that sink in a moment. "Angelo Capraro took our father from us. Don't give him the chance to take your kids' father away from them."

Tony began to cry, hard and deep. "It was my fault, Anna. Dad's dead and it's all my fault."

I put my arm around his shoulder. "Ssh, Tone. It's not your fault. You didn't do anything."

He choked out his words through his sobs. "No, it's my fault. I never told you what happened. I always followed Dad home from the club. But I didn't do it that night." He paused, and in that pause I could see the disgust he felt with himself. "Had I followed him like I was supposed to, I coulda stopped it. But I wasn't there. I was screwin' my *gomatta* when Dad died. I coulda stopped it, Anna. I coulda. Dad would still be alive if I did was I was

190

supposed to do."

Tony was wailing from deep within his gut. I held him and comforted him for the first time in our lives. "Let it out, Tony. It's okay. It's okay." Tony buried his head into my shoulder as he cried. I took advantage of the moment and slowly reached for the gun with my left hand. I tucked the pistol into the waistband of my shorts. I could feel the cold steel pressing on my back and I prayed it had some sort of safety lock.

After a few minutes he began to settle down. "You hungry, Tone? Let me make you something to eat." He nodded. "Go wash your face and I'll put on a pot of coffee and make us something to eat." While Tony was in the bathroom I raided the refrigerator. Garlic, scallions, red bell pepper, sausage, Gorgonzola, Pecorino Romano cheese, fresh basil, and eggs—perfect ingredients for a savory *frittata*. I had picked up a fresh loaf of Italian bread earlier in the day. I pulled it from the cupboard for toast. I also hid the gun in the freezer, burying it behind the stack of frozen dinners and under the bag of frozen peas.

The evening turned into one of the nicest times I had ever spent with my brother. He drank a few quick cups of Italian roast and slowly sobered up. As we ate the *frittata* we shared fond memories of Ma and Dad, laughing until tears of joy washed over us. Tony surprised me, too, when he cleared the table and rinsed our dishes.

"Wow, Tony. I wouldn't have believed this if I hadn't seen it with my own eyes! You standing at a sink!" He responded by flicking my ass with the *mopine*. He reached into his pants pocket and pulled out a thick wad of bills. "You need any money?"

I laughed. "No, Dad, I'm fine."

"Here," he peeled off three one hundred dollar bills. "Treat yourself to something. And I mean it. Spend it on you. No bill paying with this. *Capisco?"*

"Tony, I don't need it."

He slapped the money on the kitchen table. "Don't argue with me. Buy yourself somethin' nice." And then Tony opened the freezer, studied it a moment. And with a slight snigger, he reached behind the stack of Lean

Cuisine's and retrieved his gun from under the bag of frozen peas. My surprised expression made him laugh. "It's the first place a burglar's gonna look."

I walked over to him and extended my hand, palm up. "Tony, leave the gun with me."

He shook his head and reached for the doorknob. And then he stopped, turned around and looked endearingly at me. "I love you, Anna."

My eyes filled. It was the first time he had ever spoken those words to me. "I love you too, Tony."

It was the last time I saw my brother alive. A few months later he used that gun on himself.

Chapter Sixteen

True to her word, Sophie calls soon after returning from Belize. In her inimitable fashion she gets right to the point. "Did you talk with Pat yet?"

"Did you have a nice vacation?"

"What?" she pauses, and then gets my drift. Sophia titters. "Yes. It was wonderful. You'll have to come with us some time."

Right, I think. *Me and Greg Haynes stuck together on an island.*

"So did you talk with Pat?"

"I did. Actually, I met with him last week. What a very nice man he is. I learned a lot."

"You know, Greg still wants to talk with you too. He remembers a lot about that case."

"I know."

"What are you doing for Christmas? Why don't you come for Christmas, stay a few days. It'll be fun. Like when we were kids," she bombards me. If I could bottle her energy and sell it, I'd be richer than Sam Walton.

"It would be fun, Sophie. But…" I stumble for words. "It's strange. For the first time in nearly thirty years I'm looking forward to Christmas. I even bought a tree. I can't remember the last time I had a Christmas tree."

"You don't put up a tree? I can't believe you don't put up a tree!" Sophie is truly surprised. "Especially the way Aunt Theresa use to decorate every inch of the house." It was true. Ma decorated our home with Christmas village scenes and mangers featuring a menagerie of animals. Every room looked like one of Macy's windows. "I was so touched when you gave me some of her ornaments."

I smile. "I have some too. Tony's kids have the rest. I guess what I'm trying to say, Sophie, is that this year feels different. Maybe it's because

193

I've been learning more about my father and putting life with him in perspective. Maybe I'm starting to let the sadness go. Whatever the reason, I feel joyous about the season for the first time in a long time."

"So, what are you planning to do?"

"Well, I'm planning on decorating my Christmas tree tonight. And on Christmas Eve I'm gonna prepare Ma's Christmas Eve dinner—pasta *alia e olio* and sautéed jumbo shrimp. And I gonna set the table with her "good dishes" and "good silver," and after dinner, Jazz and I are gonna open presents and watch *A Christmas Story*—the last movie I watched with Ma."

"But you're going to be alone?"

"Not really. I feel Ma and Dad and Tony are here with me now, all together in my heart for the first time. It's gonna be a real family Christmas."

"Why don't you come after the holidays? We spend most of January in Belize. You could come there. Spend time with me; talk with Greg. I'll buy your plane ticket and once we're there it's nothing. We have a house."

"You have a house in Belize? I didn't know that. I'm so proud of you, Sophia! You've worked very hard and deserve your success."

"Thanks, Anna. That means a lot coming from you."

"And thank you for the generous offer, Sophia. Maybe another time." I could feel her disappointment over the telephone wires. "Sophie, I will come to Providence after you get back home. I promise." I try to read her silence. I know what she wants to say, but she is holding her tongue. So, I answer her unspoken question.

"I don't dislike Greg, Sophie. I know he's a good man. You wouldn't love him if he wasn't. It's just that I don't know how to be with him. But, I give you my word; I'll figure it out. Just give me a little more time."

After we hang up, I call for my beloved dog. "Jazzy! C'mon girl! Let's go for a walk." Walking clears my mind and I needed to think about Greg and my future relationship with him. Once Jazz and I are off the road and on a well-trodden path in the woods, I let her off her lead. I smile watching her bum bounce up and down as she gallops in her arthritic way. She doesn't seem to care that running now means limping later. Like Jazz, I too ignore the fact my body isn't as young as my mind.

194

Jazz stops suddenly. Her nose is buried in the tall grass and her tail is wagging to and fro. I catch up with her and try to spy what has her interest. She lets out a pathetic woof! and there is sudden movement as a wood frog takes a tentative hop. The wood frog has a black, bandit-like stripe around its eyes and its brown-green skin provides camouflage from predators. Camouflage. I chuckle softly. During our dinner that night at the Charles Hotel a few months ago, Sophia told me the story of the first time Greg met the family.

"We were having a birthday party for my father," she said. "You know how my mother loves to throw theme parties." It was true. Aunt Jeannie's parties were legendary for their creativity. "Since my father is a military buff, my mother decided the theme would be World War II. Now, at this point, I knew Greg and I were deeply in love and would most likely be getting married. But, I also knew that I had to have Aunt Theresa's blessing, otherwise I couldn't marry him. So I decided to spring him on the family on the night of the party."

"No! Are you saying no one knew he was coming?"

"Yup! Not even my mother."

"Oh God! So Uncle Peter, my Ma, your parents don't know? No one knows Greg Haynes is coming to the party?"

"Yup!" Sophia laughed. "Now, my dad is dressed in his old Air Force uniform, my mother and Aunt Theresa go as the Andrews Sisters, and Greg," she started laughing, "shows up in camouflage!"

I guffawed so loudly the other dining patrons looked my way.

"Wait! It gets better! So Greg comes with me and immediately goes downstairs to the basement rec room."

"To hide," I added.

"Yup! Now, I don't know what I was thinking." She was laughing so hard she had to stop talking.

"Oh, how naïve you were back then! You were probably thinking no one would make a scene. Wrong! In our family?" Neither of us could

195

control our hysterical laughter.

"My mother's shooting daggers at me, my father's wishing that he were the Invisible Man, then all of a sudden Uncle Peter comes running up from the basement bellowing: Do you know who's downstairs? Greg Haynes is downstairs!" Sophie was in full animation, waving her arms in the air. "And do you know who invited him? Sophia invited him!"

I was practically falling off my chair from laughter. Diners seated nearby our table were eavesdropping and laughing in spite of themselves.

"Oh my God, Anna, I wanted to die right then and there. And then it was like the whole world turned into slow motion. I see Aunt Theresa's head slo-o-ow-ly turn in my direction: Is that true? she says to me. I just nodded. And she looked at me for what seemed like *forever!* And I'm thinking: Oh boy, Aunt Theresa's gonna have my head on a pike. And she looks me right in the eye and says: Then tell him to come upstairs and join the party." Sophia clutched her heart. "Oh! That Aunt Theresa! There never has been, and never will be, a more gracious soul!"

Now it was my turn to be a gracious soul. I know I have to talk with Greg. I need to talk with him. And not because of the information he can tell me, but because it's time I heal my relationship with him.

Chapter Seventeen

In my attempt to paint the portrait of my Invisible Man, I realize that I will, at best, end up with a representation that is a semblance of my father. What led him ultimately down that path to hell I will never know. But what I have painted thus far—from memory, from talks with those who knew his life only through his death—was a portrait of a man whose heart was good, but whose soul was tainted.

What I did not realize, however, was that two other portraits would emerge. The first was a picture of a man I had drawn in my youth, only to discover now that I had not painted him with true colors. And I knew I couldn't retouch this canvas from memory. I needed to see the subject again.

But how? With every new piece of information I learned about Joey Casella, every childhood fear arose in me from the abyss of my being. But I had to see him. I decide to call Lisa and talk it over with her.

"Are you crazy?" Lisa says with vehemence. "Why would you want to see him? What possible good would it do you? From all you told me, this man redefines dangerous!"

"I just want to walk into his restaurant and look him in the eyes. The last time I looked into Joey Casella's eyes I felt love for him."

"What you *felt* was a schoolgirl crush," Lisa corrects me.

"Okay, you're right," I concede the difference in point. "But a young girl's first love, when she begins to feel love for a man other than her father, is significant. My first love was Joey. I felt it when I was ten; I felt it when I was nineteen. The feeling of love was always there. I need to look into those eyes again and feel hate."

"What if he recognizes you?"

"He hasn't seen me in thirty years. He won't recognize me."

"Oh, right. You're your father through and through. You've got the Paulie Matteo smile. He'll recognize you, Anna. He'll recognize you. I'm begging you. Don't go there." Her last words are precise and firm. "Promise me," she begs.

"I can't promise you, Lisa. I have to do this."

One benefit of being a freelance writer is that you meet people from a variety of businesses. Keith Lanier owned One-Stop Auto, a used car and auto leasing dealership in Worcester. I knew his business was in a lull, and I also knew he could benefit from some good press coverage. I offered him a deal: rent a car to me for one day—off the books and with absolutely no record of the transaction—and I'll write a press release no charge. I also needed him to deliver the car to a location to be determined.

"You're not gonna do anything illegal are you?" he asked half jokingly.

"Damn!" I responded. "That Italian last name gives it away every time!" Then I turned on the Matteo charm. "I have a friend who's going through a rough patch. We kinda want to check a few things out."

"Aahh! Husband's gotta girlfriend—and you two wanna spy on him," he said knowingly.

I didn't want to lie to him again. Instead, I said nothing and let him draw his own conclusions. Still, I felt bad. Lies of omission were the worst kind of lies.

But I couldn't lie to Lisa in any way, shape, or form. So when I called and asked if I could borrow a blonde wig and a pair of blue, nonprescription contact lenses from the costume department of the Providence Playhouse, I had to let her in on my plan. I tried to make light of it.

"You know, I spent my youth pretending I was a secret agent and doing stake outs. Little did I know then, it was preparing me for now."

"Tell me your plan again?" she asks reluctantly.

"I'm taking an untraceable rental car to Port Judith where I'll catch the ferry to Block Island. And I'm going in disguise. That's why I need the wig."

"You know, Matteo, you watch far too much television."

"That's what my mother used to tell me." I sigh. "I know it sounds crazy, but it's the only way I can do it and feel safe."

"You'd *be* safe if you just don't do it at all," Lisa counters. "When are you planning on doing this?"

"Weather permitting, between Christmas and New Years."

"How do you know he'll even be there? It's brutal on the island during the winter and he must be, what, in his seventies now? He could be in Florida, for all you know."

"Oh, he'll be there. I saw on-line that the restaurant hosts a huge holiday party for the islanders. Lots of local press coverage. Trust me, his ego wouldn't allow him to be anywhere else."

The day before Operation Joey, Lisa and I meet for lunch at the Macaroni Grill in Manchester, Connecticut. Before she even sits down, she hands me a brown paper bag containing the wig and contact lenses. "I'm doing this because I love you, Matteo. And because I know you love me, I'm hoping you'll change your mind."

I manage to keep Lisa off the Operation Joey topic throughout the rest of our lunch. Later, as we say goodbye in the parking lot, Lisa gives it one more try. "Please reconsider. I'm going to be worried sick about you all day tomorrow."

"I promise I'll call you the minute I'm off the island, and again when I get home. It's gonna be okay. I know what I'm doing."

And then I do my best to convince myself of this all the way home.

Later that night in preparation for the trip, I fill a plastic deli container with potting soil and stir in a little water until it is viscous mud. I snap on the lid, grab an old pair of latex gloves, and pack the gloves and container in a plastic grocery bag. I leave the bag in the hallway next to my faux leather overnight tote.

The following morning I dress in the navy blue wool pants suit and gray pumps I bought at Sal's Thrift Shop earlier in the week. I had also picked up a vintage fur coat for fifty bucks. The blonde wig Lisa chose is tasteful and natural looking—not too yellow in tone, more golden. I check myself out in the mirror. "You really weren't meant to be a blonde,

Matteo," I say aloud. I study my reflection. The change in hair color and style does not look false. It just isn't me. It makes me look surprisingly ordinary. "I guess this blonde won't be having more fun."

After a few tries, I pop the blue contact lenses in place. "Now these look awesome!" I look at my reflection again, inhale deeply, and then slowly and steadily expel the breath and anxiousness building inside of me.

The weather this morning is perfect—forty-one degrees under clear skies. The hour- long ferry ride shouldn't be too bad. I kiss my beloved Jazz on her head and muzzle. "Mama will be home in a few hours." I grab the grocery bag and my faux leather travel tote and head out.

Forty minutes later I'm in Auburn circling row D-3 of the parking lot of Home Depot, looking for a green Ford Taurus with a Support Our Troops magnetic ribbon on the lip of the trunk. "Thank you, Keith," I say as soon as I spy the car. I park my car two spaces down and retrieve the extra set of car keys Keith had given me yesterday when I stopped by to finalize arrangements and pay him cash. We have a handshake agreement that if anything happens to his car, I will pay for it. I grab the tote from the trunk of my car and place it in the backseat of the Ford. While I wait for the car to warm up I pray aloud. "If you're up there, Daddy, watch over me today."

Several miles down Route 395 is a rest area. I drive up to the picnic area which is somewhat obscured from the highway. It's too chilly a day so no one is there. I park the car and retrieve the grocery bag from the backseat. I slip on the gloves, open the tub, and smear the mud onto the front and back license plates, making the tag number virtually unreadable. I throw the tub, gloves, and bag into the trash bin provided for picnickers.

An hour-and-a-half later I journey through Jerusalem into Galilee, two small fishing villages just outside Port Judith. As I enter Galilee, I see the fishing boats of its residents and I think about my abandoned novel. Set in Provincetown, *Newmanuscript.doc* is the story of Carmen, a young girl battling her self-identity in a family steeped in Portuguese traditions and Catholicism. Her father and brothers are fishermen—a profession that belongs only to the men in her family. And though Carmen shares their love of the sea, she is shut out from their line of work, their way of life, by virtue of her gender.

PAINTING THE INVISIBLE MAN

Had I been born a boy, a son of Paulie Matteo, I have no doubt that I would have charted a far different course...there was no place for a girl in my father's world other than that of mother, wife, daughter, comare.

As Carmen comes of age a young lesbian, she is forced to bury her true self so deeply a hatred emerges that exacts revenge on the residents and visitors of Provincetown who dare to live their lives so open and free.

Exact revenge. Is that what I had hoped I could do today? Walk up to Joey Casella and say, "This is for Paulie" and *bang!* No. I may be Paulie Matteo's daughter, but I'm Theresa Franconi's daughter, too. Yet, as I travel this road through Galilee to my private Jericho, I hope there is enough Paulie in me to feel the sin of hatred. I want to look into his eyes— eyes that I once thought to be charming and charismatic, and see now that they are really cunning and cruel.

I pull into the parking area for the Port Judith ferry dock. Even though the ferry offers automobile transportation, I leave the car and purchase a round trip passenger ticket. Once we are on our way I go to the upper deck. The air is very brisk, but the fur coat keeps me quite warm as we cross the Atlantic. Between the blonde wig, the blue eyes, and the politically incorrect clothing, I feel like a different person altogether. I notice that my gait is different too—precise, short, quick steps, rather than my usual stride.

Before long the island comes into view. Block Island is a popular and accessible vacation resort. Old Harbor is vintage New England with its white clapboard Victorian buildings that line the waterfront street. I see the Mohegan Bluffs, which rise high above the shore offering breathtaking views of the Rhode Island coast. I read up on the island in preparation for today's excursion. Block Island is home to Southeast Light, a restored lighthouse originally built in the 1870s. There are numerous biking and hiking trails and the island offers refuge to several rare and endangered wildlife species. I had never been to Block Island before, and sadly, I knew I would never return.

Casella's is easy enough to find. Located on Water Street, the restaurant has a commanding view of Old Harbor and the Atlantic Ocean. Around the corner from Joey's hideaway I find what I'm looking for—a pub that serves lunch and dinner, and has Happy Hour from 4:00 P.M. –

6:00 P.M.

I take off my coat upon entering and drape it over my tote. "Sit anywhere you'd like," the bartender says. I take a small table near the back. I place the tote on the seat to my left and cover it with my bulky fur.

"What is the soup today?" I ask the young waitress who spies my coat and wrinkles her nose in distaste.

"Seafood chowder."

"I'd like a bowl of the chowder please and a cup of hot tea."

She walks away without a word, which is fine with me. I want to stay under the radar. Since it is well-past lunch hour and it is off-season, the pub has very few customers. While I am waiting for my soup I take my tote, unnoticed, from the chair and head into the Ladies Room. It is clean and tidy with a vanity sink and a utility closet. I open the doors to the vanity. Inside I find extra toilet paper and cleaning supplies. The utility closet does not have a lock. I peer inside and find a broom, a mop and commercial-grade pail, plunger, towels, stacks of paper towel packages, trash bags, and more toilet paper. Perfect. I take my small handbag out of the tote before tucking it inside the utility closet. I push the mop and the large aluminum pail against my tote, hiding it from sight.

A steaming bowl of chowder is waiting for me when I get back to my table. I try to enjoy the soup, which is absolutely luscious, but my mind is focused on the task at hand—seeing Joey Casella one last time. I have a second cup of tea and ask for my check. Before I leave I make one last trip to the Ladies Room. I open the utility closet. Good. The bag is hidden from view. The floor looks like it has been mopped today. As long as no one plugs up the toilet and causes a flood, no one should be using the mop and pail until closing.

As I leave the pub I notice the corner boutique a few doors down has a side entrance as well as a main entrance on Water Street. I check my watch: 3:42. Casella's doesn't open until four and the ferry back to the mainland leaves at four-forty-five, so my timing must be exact. I browse the boutique to kill some time, but my heart begins pounding in my chest and my hands have turned to ice. Despite the fur coat I begin to shiver. I leave the store hoping the fresh air will help. I walk slowly towards the restaurant, but my heart will not settle down. And then I get that sick feeling in my gut. "Shit!" I mutter. I feel myself turning green and grab onto the windowsill of Casella's.

"Are you all right, Miss?"

I turn and see a gentleman in a black cashmere coat and white cashmere scarf. His face is tanned; his eyes are a brilliant sky blue. His smile is gentle and engaging...and familiar. And in that instant, my vision collapses to a pinpoint and I sway backwards.

His gloved hand reaches out to steady me. He takes hold of my elbow. "Come with me inside and sit a moment. You don't look well."

Joey leads me into his den and I am helpless. He ushers me to a small table in the bar area. "Tino, bring the lady a brandy." He holds the chair for me. "Here. Sit down." From his position behind me, he reaches around me and slowly starts to glide my coat off my shoulders.

"No...that's okay." I stammer as I pull the coat back on. "I'm chilled."

"Tino," he calls out again. "Hurry up with that brandy!" He sits in the chair beside me and studies my face. I try to ascertain what he is trying to read in my demeanor. "Is there someone I can call for you?"

Even though everything in me is screaming, "Run!" I sip the brandy Tino places before me. "That's all right. I'm feeling a little better," I lie. I start to peel off my gloves, then stop abruptly. I was wearing my father's ring. I had meant to take it off and slip my mother's wedding ring onto the appropriate finger.

The movement does not go unnoticed. He looks deep into my now-blue eyes and smiles. "The brandy is not doing its job. Would you prefer a cup of tea? An espresso, perhaps?"

"Buon compleanno, Anna! Espresso o café americano?"

"Espresso, please, Mr. Palermo. I'm ten now," I boasted.

His manner is gentle and kind. He is the Joey I remember. I force myself to look away, to remind myself who this man is at his core. I think of Pat's words: *Casella was into a lot.... He represented the bottom-feeders—pornographers, arsonists, murderers.*

"You're not an islander," he says. "What brings you here in the dead of winter?"

I take another sip of brandy and try to recall the script I had prepared just for this moment. "It's my wedding anniversary," I recite. "Twenty years."

His smile is still charming and engaging. "Congratulations! I hope you're planning to have your anniversary dinner with us."

I feel myself getting my bearings. "Actually, that's why I stopped at your window. I was reading the menu."

"And then you felt ill? That's not good!" he quips.

I laugh and I am momentarily again under Joey's spell. "I think I'm still a little queasy from the ferry ride."

"The brandy will settle your stomach."

"So, would you be able to accommodate four people tomorrow night?"

"Ah! You are here with friends?"

I nod.

"How very nice. It would be a shame to celebrate such a special occasion with strangers."

"Open your present," the stranger said.

"I'm not suppose to take things from strangers," I said.

"I'm not a stranger. I'm a friend of your father. Really, it's okay."

"Yes, it is. Our friends' anniversary is on the thirtieth."

"Tino! Bring me the reservation book." Tino brings the leather-bound reservation book and places it on the table in front of Joey. "This is my grandson, Tino. His father, my son Emilio, is the chef."

"Such a beautiful girl you are, Anna. I hope to have a daughter just as beautiful as you someday."

"Nice to meet you, Tino."

Tino merely nods and hurries back to the bar area to tend to his daily opening tasks.

Joey reaches inside his jacket and pulls out a red and black marbled Waterman pen. I notice that his aged hands are still immaculately manicured as he twists the pen revealing its ballpoint. "And you are?"

I'm Annabella. Remember? That's what you used to call me. Beautiful Anna. I'm the young girl who's had a crush on you since I was ten. I'm the young woman whose father you had murdered. I'm Anna Matteo, Paulie's

204

daughter.

"Amato," I say. "Gloria Amato."

"Amato," he says. "Gloria." And as the name escapes his lips, I realize what a dumb choice it was. And I wonder, too, if in spite of the blonde wig and the blue contact lenses and the rental car and the entire ruse I had plotted, had I really wanted Joey Casella to know that Paulie Matteo's daughter had come before him, to look him the eye once more?

Joey glances at me, his blue eyes squint slightly, his lips quiver as if fighting back a knowing smile, and for a moment I am certain he has seen through my disguise and into me. Annabella.

"Gloria." He extends his hand and I am loath to take it. "I'm Joseph Casella." His handshake is surprisingly limp; yet it is persistent in that he does not let go. He keeps my hand—and me—snared within his grip. "What time would you like to dine?"

"We were thinking about seven."

He let's go on my hand and writes "Amato" in the reservation book. "Where are you staying on the island?"

"At the Hotel Manisses." Thank God I did my homework.

He writes that down. "Very nice."

I look at my watch. The ferry will be leaving in twenty-five minutes. "I really should be going, Mr. Casella," I say as I stand up. "My husband is probably wondering where I've wandered off to."

"Joey, call me Joey. Everybody does."

"Even the judge?"

"How much do I owe you for the brandy, Mr. Casella?" I can't bring myself to say "Joey." I reach into my purse, but he waves me off. "It's on the house. And it's Joey." He smiles. "It was my pleasure to assist you." And with that he kisses me on both cheeks. "Forgive me for being forward. I'm Italian!"

I smile. But as soon as the Matteo smile alights my face, I regret it.

Joey looks at me intently. "You have a beautiful smile, Mrs.," he pauses, "Amato. Or may I call you Gloria?"

"Yes, but what will my husband think?" Joey laughs. And I notice that it is still hearty and full of life.

205

"Thank you, again," I say.

"Are you sure you are feeling up to walking back to the hotel? Maybe I should give you a ride."

Maybe he had an accomplice waiting outside ready to snatch me. They'd push me into the backseat of a car and screech and squeal down the street and out of sight before my father even knew I was missing.

I shake the ghosts of my past from my mind. "Thank you, but that's not necessary. Besides, I want to make a quick stop in that boutique I spied on the corner," I say as I start towards the door.

Joey follows me outside and lights up a cigarette. "I look forward to seeing you tomorrow night," he says.

"Yes. Seven o'clock."

From the corner of my eye I see him watching me as I head into the boutique. I take a minute to browse quickly through a few racks before exiting the side door. With a brisk pace I head back to Finian's Pub. Happy Hour has begun and several locals are at the bar and filling a few tables. I take the same back table I occupied before and the same bored waitress comes over. "May I have a Cosmopolitan, please?"

I take off my coat and leave it draped over the back of my chair. I grab a ten-dollar bill from my purse and place it discreetly under the salt and pepper shakers. As soon as the waitress is out of sight, I head into the bathroom and lock the door. I open the utility closet and get my tote, which looks undisturbed. Like an actress changing costumes between scenes, I quickly change out of the pants suit and into the black wool skirt and green sweater I had packed in the tote. I change from shoes to knee-high boots, and throw on my leather Bomber's jacket. I whip the wig off and pop out the contact lenses. I brush out my hair until it is full and flowing.

I pull the thirteen-gallon size trash bag I had packed, too, from the tote and load in the shoes and pants suit. I bury it in the restroom trash bin under a pile of paper hand towels. The tote holds one last item—a medium-sized handbag. I pack the wig, contact lenses, and my small handbag into it. I place the empty tote on the coat hook of the "Handicap Only" stall door.

Exiting the bathroom, I see my Cosmo waiting on the table. I hurry past and out the door as the next group of Happy Hour customers make their way in. As I reach the corner I glance up Water Street in the direction of Joey's restaurant. He is still outside smoking. I cross to the opposite side of the street. As I walk past him from across the street he looks in my direction, flicks his butt into the road, and heads back inside. I get to the ferry with only minutes to spare. As the island fades into the distance, I call Lisa. "I'm on my way home."

During the car ride back to Massachusetts I try to make sense of my encounter with Joey Casella, but my mind can't yet get a grasp on it. I let it go for now.

A light snow begins to fall as I reach the Home Depot parking lot in Auburn. The lot has several dozen cars and trucks parked in it; amazingly, the parking space alongside my car is vacant. I place the keys under the front mat and leave an envelope on the passenger seat. Inside is a set of instructions for Keith.

Hi Keith,

One last favor. Please use the phone booth outside Home Depot and call this number: 1-401-555-7938. Use the enclosed calling card. Cancel the dinner reservation for the Amato party of four for tomorrow evening at 7:00. Say your wife has taken ill. Here's a little something extra for all your help. I'll call you next week and talk with you about the press release.

Secret Agent Girl

Forty minutes later I am back home, safe and sound. True to my word I call Lisa.

"Thank God!" she says in her dramatic way. "Did you see him?"

"I did. And he was kind and gentle and sweet. He was the man I remember." I shake my head. "I really wanted to walk out of there with an eternal flame of hate burning in my heart. And no matter how much I replayed in my mind all that I had heard and read about him, I couldn't summon up the hatred."

"Do you think he recognized you?"

"For a split second there, Lisa, I thought maybe he did. And if he had said to me: You're Anna. You're Paulie's daughter. I'm sorry for what happened to your father. I think I would have forgiven him." I shake my head again. "How do you like them apples?"

"I guess the apple doesn't fall far from the tree," Lisa says. "After all, you are Theresa's daughter, and she was one forgiving soul."

I smile. "Yes, I am." And in acknowledging Lisa's words, I knew I was ready to make peace with Greg Haynes.

Chapter Eighteen

The second portrait that emerged was that of Greg Haynes. His true image began to undergo exposure the night Sophia told me the camouflage story. The story was a glimpse into his personality, a study of his character. What I began to see was that his camouflage was not a disguise, but a protective appearance.

After the holidays and after Sophia and Greg returned from their winter retreat in Belize, I agreed to go to Providence and talk with Greg Haynes. While waiting at the stoplight five blocks from Sophia and Greg's home, I notice the woman in the car next to me has a smudge on her forehead. And so does the child in the backseat. "Ash Wednesday," I mutter.

On this day, priests mark the foreheads of the faithful with black ashes in the sign of a cross. "Remember man that thou art dust and to dust thou shalt return." The words come back to me with ease. Ash Wednesday marks the beginning of Lent, when all good Christians practice self-renunciation for forty days. No eating meat on Fridays—sacrifice! But, like with most kids that translated to giving up chocolate until the Easter bunny arrived with enough candy to more than compensate for all my sacrifice.

Yet, somewhere in my Catholic schooling I learned the true meaning of the Lenten season. It is a time of reflection, repentance, resurrection. In bringing my father's memory to life I've reflected on my own life, faced my fears, and recognized my limitations. I felt renewed. And now it was time for repentance. It was time to right a wrong.

I pull into Sophia and Greg's driveway and turn off the engine. Their Italianate home on Benefit Street stands proudly among the pre-Revolutionary War-era homes on the Mile of History on Providence's East Side. I've been here only one other time and stayed the length of five breaths. Sophie runs out to meet me, snaring me in a bear hug. "How was the drive? Did you eat lunch? Are you hungry? I'll make coffee."

I laugh, thankful that some things never change.

Beyond the foyer is a curved staircase. On the wall leading upstairs is a four-foot high, lifelike portrait of Greg standing alongside the defendant's table in court. He is tall, self-assured—the master of his domain. The detail of the courtroom is so realistic I can smell the mahogany of the walls and the judge's bench. The irony is not lost on me.

Like good Italian girls, we settle in the kitchen. Sophia is talking her usual mile a minute as she makes coffee and fills a small platter with Italian pastries from Gino's on Federal Hill.

"What time does Greg get home?" I ask. Even though my mission today was clear, I still felt uneasy. I wanted to control as much as possible. No surprises. Be prepared.

Sophie looks up at the clock on the wall. "Any minute." Her words are still hanging in the air when the side door opens. Within seconds, Greg comes into the kitchen. He smiles first at his wife and then looks in my direction. I am not prepared. My hands turn ice cold. *Just breathe*, I tell myself.

"Hey, Greg," I say. I walk over and give him a quick hug.

"When did you get in?" he asks.

"About ten minutes ago," I answer.

We stand looking at one another in silence. Thick silence. A silence so heavy even Sophia can't break it. I turn and go back to my station at the island.

Sophie gets up from her stool and goes to her husband and kisses his cheek.

"Ready to go to dinner?" Greg asks.

"It's only four-thirty," Sophie notes.

"Oh." Greg turns to me. "What type of food do you like to eat?"

"Anything, really."

And then the thick silence returns.

Sophia breaks the tension. "Greg, tell Anna she's not treating us to dinner tonight."

"I insist," I say.

"Absolutely not," answers Greg. "You're our guest. When we come to visit you, then you can treat us."

When we come to visit you.... My hands begin to warm. A small smile crosses my lips. "It's a deal."

Greg comes over to where we are standing and grabs a mini-cannoli. "Did you ever talk with Pat O'Connell?" he asks. The small talk portion of this session has ended.

I nod. "A few months ago. I came into town and met him at his office."

"How'd that go?"

"Good."

Again silence.

"Is there anything I can tell you? Anything you want to ask me?"

"Well," I sigh. So much for easing in to this. "I learned a lot from Pat, and from news articles I found on microfilm at the library." From the corner of my eye I notice that Sophia has quietly left the room. I take a deep breath and decide to hit it head on.

"Greg, I really didn't come here today to talk about the trial. Although, I certainly appreciate anything you are willing to share with me. This visit isn't about that." Greg nods imperceptibly. I take a step closer to him. "It's about healing. It's about forgiveness." I try to read his face. He is poker faced. "I need you to forgive me, Greg, for being so distant. I need you to forgive me for not coming to your wedding. I need to apologize to you for turning down every invitation you and Sophia have extended to me over the years. And I need to tell you how very sorry I am that I let so many years go by without giving you a chance. "

Greg looks at me and then averts his eyes. "I never knew you hated me." His tone is sorrowful.

Tears gush into my eyes. I take another step closer to him. "Oh my God, Greg. I don't hate you. I never hated you. I just..." the tears are falling so hard Greg tears a paper towel from the roll and hands it to me. I dry my cheeks, turning my head momentarily to blow my nose. I take a deep breath and move to within twelve inches of him.

"Greg, I never hated you. I just didn't know how to *be* with you," I tap my chest with my fingertips, "within myself. It's like you were suddenly

211

there in my life, and yet there was this chasm that separated us. And I was standing on the precipice, staring into this abyss that was so deep and so dark, and I had no clue how to bridge it. And every time I'd talk with Sophia, I'd think to myself: I've got to find a way. And then the terror would set in. Would I find a hellhole? A bottomless pit? Would it be my road to perdition? And so I'd back away from the edge, again and again.

"Then I found those articles on-line last October. And just as I'm thinking I need to talk with Sophia about it, she calls. Says she'll be in Boston that night and can we have dinner. And after talking with her that night, I knew with certainty that I could not begin to build our bridge unless I dove headlong into that abyss." I take a step closer and smile. "Greg, that leap has freed me in more ways than I ever dreamed."

Greg closes the gap. He wraps me in his bear-like arms. "I want us to be a family too. It's important to Sophia, but I want you to know that it is important to me too."

Later that night over dinner with Greg, Sophia and I talk and laugh and share stories of our childhood days together. Greg is a listening man; but when he speaks, his words are meaningful and sincere. And I see why Sophia fell in love with him.

Greg has to leave town early the next morning and so we say goodbye that night. "We'll see you soon?" he asks.

"Absolutely. I promise." I watch him walk up the stairs. As he passes by his portrait, I smile. The painting has captured his likeness, his power and dominion. But in my mind's eye, I see the image that lays underneath: A man who lives his life with moral certainty, benevolence, and devotion.

The next morning after Greg leaves for his office, I have one more Act of Contrition to make. I find Sophia downstairs in the kitchen. "How'd did you sleep?" she asks.

"I slept great. It's the first time since my father died that I've been able to sleep through the night when I'm in Rhode Island."

"Really?" Sophia is amazed.

"Yeah, really." I pour myself a mug of coffee and join Sophia at the island.

"Greg was sorry he had to leave so early this morning. He really likes you. Must have told me that ten times."

"I really like him too. And I'm looking forward to spending more time with him, getting to really know him." Sophia beams. I put down my mug and take her hand. "Sophie, I'm sorry I turned you down when you asked me to be in your wedding."

Sophia begins to tear. "I was thinking about that last night. God, Anna, that was so insensitive of me. I didn't think—"

"—You didn't know," I interrupt her. "You couldn't know the pain I was still feeling all those years later. It's like childbirth. You can't know the pain of childbirth unless you've experienced it. It's the same with losing someone you love to a murder: You can't know it unless you've experienced it. But unlike childbirth, that pain is never-ending. Sure, at the time it happens, everyone is shocked and horrified. But when the funeral is over and the trials are eventually over and life goes on, those who are on the periphery are able to move on, while those close inside wallow in the miasma."

"But I should have realized what you were going through."

"How could you? You were young when Paulie died; I was finishing college. And then I left Rhode Island. I never wanted to come back to Cranston. I hate that damn city. And yet, that city—this area—is filled with people I love. People I don't see anymore because of all the anguish I carried inside me all these years."

"Still, it was insensitive."

"Sweetie, no. You were not insensitive. By the time you met Greg and got married, my father's murder was a decade-old memory. But for me, it was raw. I don't have my mother's peerless grace."

"No one does," Sophia says.

"Did you know that when Dad died, Ma called Gloria and welcomed her to come to the wake and funeral? I couldn't have done that."

"I think you would have."

"No. I wouldn't have. Not then." I take a sip of coffee. "I finished my

213

senior thesis the week before my father died. It was on the dialectical method. I got to thinking about that a few months ago when this whole thing started. My parents were the base of the triad; related, yet oppositional in nature, conflicting in terms. As their child I've had to pass through each of them, in my own way and in varying degrees."

Sophia looks at me totally nonplussed. "I've no idea what you are talking about."

I laugh. "It's Philosophy 101, the dialectical method: thesis, antithesis, and synthesis. Hegel termed it Being, Nothingness, and Becoming. I guess what I'm saying is: I've synthesized." I hold out my hands, palm up like the Scales of Justice. "I've found the balance between Paulie and Theresa. I've become."

As I drive home, I think about the last aspect of the Lenten season: the Resurrection. Paul wrote "...there shall be a resurrection of the dead, both of the just and unjust." Christianity teaches that it is only as a result of atonement that we are spared eternal punishment as judgment for our sins. The Resurrection of Jesus symbolized hope—hope that we will transcend our limitations and triumph over our fears.

I'll never know if my father, in those last moments of his life, prayed for forgiveness, atoned for his past mistakes. I do know that in resurrecting his memory—and my memories—I have found forgiveness and have been forgiven.

Chapter Nineteen

A few weeks after my trip to Providence, the Museum of Fine Arts in Boston hosted the opening of the Picasso exhibition. Jacqueline and I arranged to meet at the museum, see the exhibit, and have dinner together in the North End. Over the past few months we had talked on the telephone almost nightly, sharing our histories and our future hopes. I felt an easiness with her that was refreshing. And when the demons would come knocking, I'd make a conscious effort to cast them away. My journey through my life the last six months had given me a greater understanding of my issues regarding trust, and I began to develop a more reliable barometer by which to measure the actions of others. That night, we acknowledged that our friendship had undergone a metamorphosis.

"Here you go, Jazzy! Fetch!" I toss the stick far across the backyard. Jazz is scampering after it top speed, when she stops suddenly in her tracks. We both turn in the direction of tires on gravel. As Jacqueline emerges from her car, Jazz hies it to the driveway. "Don't jump," I yell.

"Who you talking to? Me or her?" Jacqueline says with a smile.

We share a good laugh and hug each other warmly. She kneels down and graciously accepts Jazzy's kisses. "She's sweet, and so beautiful! What a beautiful face you have Jazzy!"

"Okay, Jazz. Let's give our guest a break," I say, grabbing for her collar.

Jacqueline opens the car door and reaches into her backseat. "Here, Happy Easter." The green and yellow basket is filled with pink "grass" nesting several hand-painted Easter eggs, a chocolate bunny, a colorful assortment of jelly beans, and a half-dozen Reese's Peanut Butter Easter Eggs. I laugh knowingly, since a similar basket, sans the hand-painted, hard-boiled eggs, awaits her inside.

Jacqueline tours my house with Jazz at her heels. "It's lovely, " she says much too kindly.

"It's okay. It needs work. New flooring, new rugs --"

"Ssh!" She places her fingertips on my lips. "It's lovely."

"Here's my office." I step into the cluttered room and immediately regret it, as she remains in the hallway just outside the doorway.

"This is where you write?" A look of disbelief crosses her face.

"This is where I work. Client stuff. When I write, or more correct, when I use to write, I preferred to write in the dining room."

"Hmm," is all she says.

Later that evening Jacqueline insists on cooking "I hope you like garlic."

"Please! I'm Italian!" And I'm thrilled. Edie hated garlic.

Her mastery of knife skills impresses me as she minces a head of elephant garlic. "I love elephant garlic. It's mild and sweeter."

I nod. "Actually, I read that it's not a true garlic. From the leek family, I believe."

"That would explain why it's less pungent."

I set the dining room table while Jacqueline puts the finishing touches on our dinner. "The world's best shrimp scampi," she says as she sets the overflowing pasta bowl on the table. And it is: Plump, succulent shrimp sautéed with white wine and brandy, herbs, lemon butter, and all that garlic. After dinner we sit on the porch enjoying the warm spring air, talking until the moon, full and bright, is high above bathing us in its rays.

Mythologists and astrologers differ as to the gender of the moon and the sun. To me, the moon is decidedly male. My father was the moon, waxing and waning and disappearing for a time each month. And Ma was the sun; an eternal light, a life-giving force. And when he would absorb her rays, in those moments when he was visible, I saw the best in him.

Jacqueline and I go to bed and make love through the night. As the rays of Mother Sun reach out and touch the earth, we fall asleep safe in each other's arms.

The bonfires blazing just above the surface of the three rivers seem to dance in rhythm to the eclectic strains of music filling the night air. The cobblestone and brick walkways that weave along the water's edge are bustling with pedestrians. A black-clad figure tending to its gondola stops along the river's bank.

"It's time." The Gondolier's voice surprises me. It is female—lilting and with a distinct Asian accent.

Jacqueline's voice resounds from behind me. "Yes. It is time."

The Gondolier extends her hand and helps us onto the long, narrow, flat-bottomed boat. Within moments, we are floating down the river weaving 'round the crackling flames. As we reach the Venetian-style arched footbridge aglow in the flickering firelight, the Gondolier stops her craft. The scent of burning cedar and pine wafts under my nostrils. I breathe in the fragrant night air.

The Gondolier leans over and peers into the water below. "Ah! There!" She nudges Jacqueline. "There!" Using her oar, the Gondolier skims the water just below the surface, back and forth, until she snags a line. "You help me," she says to Jacqueline.

Together, they pull hand over hand on a thick rope. A fishing net emerges from the river below. The Gondolier grasps it gingerly and hands it carefully to Jacqueline. They work together, unfolding the netting as if peeling an onion, revealing a hand-painted, egg-shaped vase. The Gondolier hands the elaborately painted vase to me.

I look inside and see a thick, black liquid. Jacqueline sidles next to me and peers into the vase. She looks at the Gondolier and smiles. Jacqueline sticks her finger deep into the belly of the vase, and when she pulls it out it is dripping with a syrupy black liquid.

"It's time." They tell me in unison.

217

The dream melds into my conscious mind. I open my eyes and see a familiar face staring at me. *Time to write!* I close my eyes and drift back to sleep. *Time to write! Write for you!* I open my eyes again. The face is gone.

I turn onto my side and watch Jacqueline sleep. It feels voyeuristic, only in that it is new. She sleeps soundly, curled on her side, hands tucked prayer-like under her chin, her bum in the air. I kiss her forehead and quietly get out of bed.

Once a pot of Caffé Verona is brewing, I hop into the shower. As the warm water streams across my chest, I notice a small mark on my breast. I stroke the purple-hued blotch with my fingertips and smile at the memory of how it came to be. I wash my hair, turn off the spigot, and towel off. As I come out of the bathroom wrapped in a white terrycloth robe, I find Jacqueline standing in the doorway perusing my office. Her over-sized T-shirt falls to mid-thigh; her lustrous chestnut hair is tousled from lovemaking and sleep.

I kiss her cheek. "Morning. How'd you sleep?"

"Amazingly well." She returns the kiss. "Can I ask you something? Why don't you write in here?"

Here it starts. I take a moment to towel-dry my hair, to buy a little time and hopefully prevent the annoyance I feel from coming out in my voice. "I don't know. I've never been able to. Maybe it's because my office is where I do client work. I can't write for me in there." This conversation was all too familiar. I feel embarrassed as she steps into my office and looks around. "I know it's cluttered."

"It's not the clutter, Anna, it's the energy. I can feel her in here."

"Feel who? Edie?"

Jacqueline nods.

"I don't see how. She never used this room. I mean that, literally. She rarely stepped foot in here."

Jacqueline shrugs her shoulders.

"I'm not lying to you. It's always been my office, my space. So, if the energy in there sucks, it's because of me." So much for trying to control my annoyance. I've resorted to testy, too.

"Oh, honey, I'm not criticizing you. But," she looks sheepish, "you were talking in your sleep. You kept saying, 'Time to write! Time to write!' And it is time that you start writing again. You're a good writer, Anna. Your words touch people."

"Yeah, right."

"They do. " Her tone is firm. "I told you that the first time we had dinner together."

"That's true. But you were trying to, you know, have your way with me." I try making light of this uncomfortable conversation, but Jacqueline isn't biting.

"I'm serious! I saw myself in that story. And I began to believe that I, too, had the strength to walk away and own my life. Your words changed me."

I hang my head. "Thank you."

Jacqueline places her fingertips under my chin and lifts my head. She kisses my lips lightly, tenderly. "You have to start writing again. Okay?"

I smile sheepishly. "Okay."

"Now, let's get serious here. Your office needs considerable feng shui-ing!" Jacqueline ventures further in. She looks about the room like a builder surveying raw land. "That's east?" she points to the window.

I nod.

Three more steps puts her in the eye of the storm. She points to my old, solid oak desk buried under stacks of folders, magazines, and junk mail. "Why do you need that big desk when you use a table for your computer?"

"I love that desk. I bought it at a garage sale for ten bucks; refinished it myself. Look," I lift the brass handle centered on the lip of the desktop. "It has a built-in typewriter table. And look at these drawers." I pull open one of six long, deep drawers, stacked three on each side. "This drawer has wooden slats for stationery. And look at these adjustable wooden partitions. And the pocket shelves." I slide one out to show her. "The entire desk is comprised of three sections set tongue-and-groove." Which was a great and valuable feature since I had been hauling this desk around with me for thirty years. Jacqueline smiles, appreciative of my enthusiasm and love for this

219

relic. "Anyway, to answer your question, the table's longer. I can't fit the computer and the printer on the desk and still have room to spread out papers or whatever it is I'm working on."

Jacqueline lifts a massive pile of bills, circulars, and magazines from the desktop and runs her hand over its smooth surface. "It is a beautiful desk. You should use it."

"I do. I write my bills here."

"Hmm!" Jacqueline looks at my computer table kitty-corner from the desk with furrowed brow. "Aha! That's the problem. There's no flow between the money coming in and the money going out. The energies are opposing, fighting one another."

Even in finances I have opposing forces, I muse to myself. "Guess that explains why I'm always broke."

She offers me that gorgeous smile. "Move things around in here. Establish a flow. You'll see. It'll make a difference." Jacqueline takes my hands and kisses them. "I don't know what you were dreaming about, but it is time for you to write. Promise me you will."

Later that evening after Jacqueline leaves for Providence, I go into my office and try to see it through her eyes. *Move things around. Establish a flow.* Suddenly, it all makes sense. I move the small desk that had belonged to Ma from the guestroom into my office and place it linear with my computer table. The small desk has cubbyholes ideal for sorting bills. I throw out the old magazines and circulars, and give my beloved desk a polish and shine. Jacqueline was right. The shift in energy was immediate.

Before going to bed, I take my laptop out of its case and place it squarely on the desk. I open the bottom drawer and free Amy from her prison. While cleaning through the closet this evening I found an acrylic file holder. I place Amy into it and position her along the back of the desk. I open the laptop to check positioning. Her eyes watch directly over me from her new home.

"Okay Amy. I'm ready. See you in the morning."

Chapter Twenty

The voice enters my dreams. *Time to write! Time to write! Write for you!* "All right already!" I say as I roll reluctantly out of bed. I wanted nothing more than to turn over and go back to sleep, but I had promised Jacqueline and Amy that I would start writing again. I shuffle into the kitchen, open the cupboard and reach for the Caffé Verona.

"No. Let's do the Dragon instead," I say aloud. I carefully measure ten heaping teaspoons of Komodo Dragon into the filter and fill the reservoir with cold water.

While the coffee is brewing, I open my laptop and boot up. I retrieve my writing talismans from their dormancy, placing Webster and Roget on the desk to my left. I scroll through the hard drive in search of *Newmanuscript.doc.*

"Thank you, Lisa, for insisting I save this." I glance over the top of my screen. Amy's intense eyes and big smile look back at me proudly.

"Oh, jeez, the Thermos!" Back in the kitchen, I fill the Thermos with hot water preparing it for the coffee. I pull the Half 'N' Half from the 'fridge so it won't be too cold. I check the coffeemaker. It has a ways to go.

Back in my office I sit at the desk and move the pointer onto the file. Click. The text appears on the screen, exactly as I had left it. It has been so long since I worked on the story that I need to read it through from the beginning.

I suppose there are people who envy me for growing up in this beautiful seafaring village embraced by the sea. I am third generation Portuguese. My father and brothers, and his father and brothers before him, toiled these seas—casting nets, sinking lobster traps and marking the lines with white-and-green floats. No matter where you are on Cape

Cod you can smell the sea, and for fishermen that smell becomes the taste of their brown, weathered skin. Yes, people envy me for growing up in "God's Country," as it's called.

As I scroll through page after page, stopping along the way to read a paragraph or two, I feel Amy's eyes boring into my soul. I look up at her. "You know, Amy, the writing's not bad."

Not bad, but not right.

The voice is so real I peek over the screen to see if her mouth is moving. Her full smile looks innocent enough, though it casts a touch of mischievousness.

"Oh, not again. You got something you want to say to me, Amy? Then just say it, for chrissakes. "

Her stare is penetrating, almost fierce. If I were writing a movie script, this would be the part where the book levitates and slowly and eerily floats towards me, dropping with a THUD onto my laptop.

Good writing, yes. But disingenuous no?

I jump up from the desk. "Disingenuous? I put my heart into my writing!"

Ah, but not your soul. Write. Write for you. Write for you.

"I *am* writing for me," I protest. "Christ, Amy, what more do you want from me?" I wait for her response. Ten seconds…thirty seconds…sixty seconds…ninety seconds. The only sound I hear is the slowing gurgle of the coffeemaker. "So, I guess you've nothing else to say, huh?" I stare at her face, at her brilliant dark eyes.

I've been saying; you don't listen.

"Don't listen? I'm up at friggin' O-dark-hundred! I'm committed to writing, just like I was before! What do you want from me?"

I want you to write for you.

Her words are followed by a silence so deep I can hear my heart beating. I lower the screen and look at Amy full in the face. I stare intently into her eyes until she and I are one. Her smile broadens, and I begin to chuckle until I am laughing to the point of tears. "Write…for…you," I say through my laughter. "Write for me. Write for *me*!" I take Amy from the

222

stand and kiss her face. "Write for me." I inhale deeply, taking in a cleansing breath and the ambrosial aroma of full-bodied roasted beans. The brewing has stopped.

I set Amy back in her place of honor and head into the kitchen. I dump the water from the Thermos and fill it with Komodo Dragon. While searching through the cupboard for my *Sex and the City* cappuccino cup, I spy the mug Sophia gave me last October. I take it out. *I Write, Therefore I Am.*

I pour a small amount of Half 'N' Half into the mug and fill it with coffee. I take a soothing sip. With cup and Thermos in tow, I head back to my office. I settle at my desk, save and close *Newmanuscript.doc* and drag it onto the hard drive. Sliding my finger across the track pad, I move the pointer to File. Click. Drag down to New...Click. I drag down to Save As...Click. I move the pointer to Save Current Document As and type in *Newmanuscript.doc.* A message screen comes up.

*Word cannot give a document the same name as
an existing document. Type a different name for
the document you want to save.*

I look over the top of my screen. Amy's smile broadens. I smile and nod my thanks, click Okay, and type, *PaintingtheInvisibleMan.doc.* Save. The blank page comes up. And I begin to write for me.

It's said fate leads the willing, and drags along the reluctant. I don't know about that. I've never been one to bandy about pithy nuggets of wisdom. Life's experiences are far too complex to be whittled down to nine words. I want to think that what happened on the morning of October 20, 2004 was a keying error, a simple mistake; and that the telephone call was synchronal, rather than some sort of causal determinism.

That morning I was energized, focused, and ready to work...

About The Author

Rita wanted to be a writer ever since Santa Claus gave her a Tom Thumb typewriter when she was six years old. Her first story, "My Mom is Love a Bull," was an instant hit with the family.

Years later, at the ripe old age of eleven, Rita began writing *Girl From U.N.C.L.E.* episodes after her then favorite television show was cancelled. Her homeroom teacher, Sr. Mary Andrews, set aside thirty minutes each week for Rita to read the latest adventures of April Dancer and Mark Slade to her classmates.

After college, Rita followed in her mother's footsteps and moved to New York City to pursue a career in music. She spent seven years performing at various clubs including the Red Parrot, Trax, Inner Circle, Studio 54, to name just a few.

Fast forward to 1989…pursuing yet another dream, Rita opened an Italian-Japanese restaurant in Sturbridge, Massachusetts. She cooked, baked, and operated The Casual Café for eleven years with her longtime friend and business partner, Karen.

During that time, Rita began writing late at night "to relax" after the long hours a restaurant demands. She went on to write a novel, *Sweet Bitter Love*, published in 1997 by Rising Tide Press, (New York), contributed several short stories to magazines, as well as stories in two anthologies, *Early Embraces* and *New Beginnings,* published by Alyson Publications.

Rita is also a published songwriter and member of ASCAP. She co-wrote two children's songs for KidsTerrain, Inc.—*The Magic in Me* and *Tiny Acts of Kindness*, the latter a tribute to the goodwill of children who found ways to reach out to the firefighters, police officers, and friends and family members of the victims of the September 11 attacks.

Upon selling her restaurant in July 2000, Rita went back to her first love: writing. In 2003, Rita bought back the rights to her novel, *Sweet Bitter Love*, and wrote the screenplay. Later that year, a mutual friend introduced Rita to Paul Gemme. Both sensed they were kindred spirits, and thus began writing as a team. *T.I.M.E. Share, Inc.* and *G.E.O.P.S.*, a full-length movie screenplay, are two of Rita and Paul's projects. A third screenplay, *The Legend of Johnny Lantern,* is in process.

Never one to give up on her dreams, Rita is determined to write for television and the movies.

Other Works By Rita Schiano

*Sweet Bitter Love** published by Rising Tide Press (1997)

*Available through The Reed Edwards Company www.ReedEdwards.com

What People Are Saying About *Sweet Bitter Love*...

"The reader sees the relationship from Jenny's point of view, from her beginning fascination with Susan, through to the end. It is an interesting look into the highs and lows of life with an alcoholic...This is not an easy subject ...It is, however, a situation
common to many. Schiano has opened the door to an important subject that few want to discuss."
— R. Lynne Watson, *Mega Scene,* Palm Springs, Vol. #14

"Schiano serves up passion, courage, and clear-eyed honesty in this dramatic debut novel. A roller-coaster romance which vividly captures the rhythm and feel of love's sometimes rocky ride."
— Womankind Books, New York

"Sexy, passionate, and humorous, the book is a great 'fast read.'"
— Linda Wong, *Sojourner*

"...Schiano captures the passion, pain and fragility of modern day romantic relationships...Readers will cycle through feelings of joy, bitterness, excitement and anger as they learn how and why the relationship unfolds as it does...Schiano presents this dramatic tale of love, pain and soul-searching in clear, easy-to-read prose with an energizing style that dares the reader to set the book down. Highly recommended!"
— Susan Phelps, author *A Lady Without a Latitude*

Schiano, Rita. "Brown Shoes." *Early Embraces*. Ed. Lindsey Elder. Alyson Publications. Los Angeles. 1996. 136-139.

Schiano, Rita. " The SurfMaid's Promise." *Beginnings*. Ed. Lindsey Elder. Alyson Publications. Los Angeles. 1998. 8-12.